**"You, Ellie O'Brien,
are afraid to take off the blinders
that keep you from seeing yourself
as everyone else sees you—as a kind,
beautiful, spontaneous woman."**

Ellie stared at Lawson in awe. He thought she
was beautiful? Hadn't he always thought of her as
one of the boys? Hadn't he always seen her as a
surrogate little sister? Apparently somehow that
had changed. He now saw her as beautiful—a
woman. She swallowed. Why did that send her
heart galloping in her chest?

He carefully guided her chin up until she was
forced to meet the knowing smile in his eyes.
"You're the kind of woman who wouldn't have any
trouble finding herself a husband, if she didn't try
so hard to cross every suitable man off her list or
give him away to her friends."

She didn't have anything to say because she'd
suddenly realized why those relatively suitable men
had seemed so unsuitable. She realized it because
she was staring the reason right in the face. She,
Ellie O'Brien, had a crush on Lawson Williams.

Books by Noelle Marchand

Love Inspired Historical

Unlawfully Wedded Bride
The Runaway Bride
A Texas-Made Match

NOELLE MARCHAND

Her love of literature began as a child when she would spend hours reading beneath the covers long after she was supposed to be asleep. Over the years, God began prompting her to write. Eventually those stories became like "fire shut up in her bones," leading her to complete her first novel at fifteen. Now, at the age of twenty-four, that fire of inspiration continues to burn.

Noelle is a Houston native who graduated from Houston Baptist University in May 2012. She received a bachelor's degree in Mass Communication with a focus in journalism and Speech Communication.

A Texas-Made Match

NOELLE MARCHAND

HARLEQUIN® LOVE INSPIRED® HISTORICAL

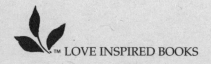

™ LOVE INSPIRED BOOKS

ISBN-13: 978-0-373-82957-6

A TEXAS-MADE MATCH

Copyright © 2013 by Noelle Marchand

www.LoveInspiredBooks.com

Printed in U.S.A.

Brothers and sisters, I do not consider myself yet to have taken hold of it. But one thing I do: forgetting what is behind and straining toward what is ahead, I press on toward the goal to win the prize for which God has called me heavenward in Christ Jesus.

—*Philippians* 3:13,14

Dedicated with love to my father and brother.

Special thanks to Elizabeth Mazer
for allowing me to share all three of
the O'Brien's stories! Also, thanks to Karen Ball
of Steve Laube Agency for all her hard work.

Chapter One

Peppin, Texas
September 1888

Ellie O'Brien was not the type of girl to chase after men.

That might have to change.

After all, today was her twenty-first birthday. While that hadn't stopped her from revisiting her mischievous youth by climbing to her favorite place in the whole world—the top of the waterfall that pooled into her family's creek—it was pushing marriageable age. This wouldn't have been a problem in most Western towns, where the scarcity of women allowed them to take their time picking husbands. The town of Peppin didn't have that problem, though. Women were plentiful, and the competition between them, while friendly, was still fierce. Ellie had never attempted to jump into the fray before. Now, though it might be too late, she wanted to at least try.

But first, one more moment of being a child.

Her fingers teased the hairpins from her hair with

a familiarity born of desperation, then tossed them to the dry ground below like the nuisances they were. She shook out her curly golden tresses, reveling in her newfound freedom as the wind made her hair bounce in disarray. Warm mud oozed between her bare toes as she stepped closer to the precipice. The water rushed past her feet, urging her to join its free fall away from the side of the waterfall and into the creek seven feet below. If she took that final step forward, there would be no going back.

Literally and figuratively. She bit her bottom lip as she peered over through the treetops at the rolling green hills that stretched beyond their property. Perhaps it was too romantic to hope that courtship would be as exhilarating as a sheer fall or as refreshing as the cool shock of cold water that followed—but a gal could hope.

It wasn't as if she were only interested in the romance part of getting a husband. Oh, no. Ellie also wanted the adventure that would come with it. After all, her sister Kate had quite the adventure when she fell in love with Nathan Rutledge. Their courtship commenced with a shoot-out, continued with Kate's abduction and was clinched with an arson fire. And then there was Lorelei, Ellie's sister-in-law of nearly one year. She found love through a run-in with a con artist, a secret engagement and a bank robbery.

Ellie blew out a frustrated sigh then whispered to a God she knew was listening. "It isn't as if I want to be abducted or almost killed or anything. I just know what a girl needs to do to get a little excitement around here—find love."

And it worked both ways. There was nothing like a little excitement and danger to make people look at each other in new ways, see things about each other that they hadn't noticed before. In that respect, she could use all the help she could get, living in a town where every eligible man saw her as a little sister.

She couldn't exactly blame them. She'd been a consummate tomboy growing up. She didn't regret one moment she'd spent climbing trees, riding horses, swimming in the creek—they'd all held far more appeal than giggling and flirting with boys like the girls too afraid of mussing their dresses to have any fun. At some point those giggling, flirting girls had started getting beaus who turned into suitors and then into husbands. But not Ellie. Even though she'd abandoned her hoydenish ways years ago, she hadn't been able to shake the label of "tomboy" the town had given her or change the way the young men saw her—yet.

She was ready for the most important adventures of her life, like love, marriage, motherhood. She just needed someone to share them with. And if it took a little danger or excitement to make that happen…well, she was up for it.

"I'm ready to do my part, Lord. Is a little help too much to ask?"

She didn't wait for an answer. She knew only God could join two hearts together—but that didn't mean He couldn't have help. When it came to her siblings, Ellie had helped Him along as much as possible. There was a reason she'd been dubbed the best matchmaker in Peppin. She was the best in town at spotting a match and pulling it off.

But who would help the matchmaker find a match?

No one. That's who. She was going to have to do it on her own, and she was starting today. First things first: she had to figure out a way to climb down from the waterfall without messing up her day dress. *Being adventurous was easier when I wore bloomers.*

There was a simpler way to get down. She peered over the waterfall's tabletop once more, knowing that if she didn't have plans for the afternoon she would have taken that route. Suddenly, Kate's voice shot through the air with startling volume. "Ellie, *don't!*"

She jerked toward the sound, knocking herself off balance and sending her arms churning like a tilted windmill. She fell into the creek with a loud splash. The cool water enveloped her and swept her skirts up around her ears before Ellie pushed off the muddy bottom. She surfaced and searched for her cinnamon-haired sister. Kate's sensible blue dress stood out against the riot of red, orange and yellow wildflowers that painted the banks of the creek.

Ellie swam toward the shore. "I wasn't going to jump. You startled me!"

"Oh, no!" Kate placed one hand over her mouth and another on her hip as she shook her head. "I'm so sorry. What were you doing up there in the first place?"

Ellie shivered in the slight breeze as she stepped onto dry grass. "Reliving my youth."

"You'd better not—after all you put me through." Kate grabbed the picnic blanket from the ground to wrap it around Ellie's shoulders.

"I don't know what you're talking about. I was perfect." She lifted her nose, ignoring a laugh from her sister as she gathered the blanket closer. "What are you doing here so early, anyway? I thought you said I had two hours to myself."

"It's been longer than two hours. We are supposed to

meet Ms. Lettie and Lorelei at the café for your birth-day lunch in thirty minutes."

"I'm sorry. I must have lost track of time."

"That's all right. So did I." Kate grabbed the picnic basket from the ground and began to lead the way to the farmhouse. "It can't be helped now. You'll have to change clothes and redo your hair."

Ellie paused. "I hadn't thought of that. Do you think it would make a difference?"

Kate tossed a confused look over her shoulder. "Of course it would. You can't go into town drenched."

She laughed. "I forgot you can't read my mind. I meant do you think it would make a difference with men if I changed my hair or clothes?"

"What men? Why should it make a difference? Why would you want to…?" Kate shook her head. "What *are* you talking about?"

"I'm twenty-one. Isn't it time I tried to catch a hus-band?" It was a little difficult to force the words out through her chattering teeth. "Do you think I even could?"

Kate rubbed her back to try to warm her. "You're more likely to catch a cold if you don't get changed. As for a husband, there's no need to rush. Why? Are you interested in someone?"

"No."

They caught sight of the two-story farmhouse and Kate ushered her toward it. "Then don't worry about it. Go change and try to be quick."

Ellie nodded then hurried into the house and up the stairs to her room. She quickly changed into dry clothes. A distant peal of laughter drew her attention to the large window facing the barn. She grabbed a hand towel from the vanity and dried her hair as she watched her brother-in-law tease her sister about something. Her nieces and nephew danced around their legs in anticipation of the promised ride that would keep them occupied while Kate and Ellie went into town. The couple stole a quick kiss before the whole family walked toward the barn.

The smile that slipped across Ellie's lips preempted a wistful sigh. She combed her fingers through her hair. *It must make a girl feel awfully special to be loved. If a man loved me the way Nathan loves Kate and Sean loves Lorelei, well, it might make up for certain other things.*

On the heels of that thought rode a familiar yet vague feeling of guilt. She pushed it away stubbornly. Today was for celebrating the future, not belaboring distant memories of the past that probably meant nothing. A glimpse of Kate walking toward the house served as a welcome reminder of the need to hurry and sent her rushing to make up for the time she'd spent lollygagging.

Thirty minutes later, Ellie glanced at the three women who'd taken time out of their busy day to help her celebrate her birthday. Kate sat across from her. Their dearly departed mother's best friend, Mrs. Lettie Williams, sat to her right. Lorelei, her sister-in-law, sat on her left. They were all beautiful. They were all strong. They were all married. And Ellie? Well, she wasn't sure she could lay a legitimate claim to any of those things.

Either I'm being obsessive or I'm detecting a theme. She narrowed her eyes as Maddie settled their drinks on the table. "Maddie, would you happen to have a pencil and piece of paper I could use?"

"Certainly." Maddie pulled the pencil from behind her ear and tore a sheet of paper from the small tablet she carried in her pocket.

"Thanks." Ellie tilted her head, then wrote down on one side of the paper a list of the local bachelors who attended church. Then she started going down the list and writing in initials of certain young women in town alongside a few of the men's names.

Lettie's curious voice broke through her thoughts. "Ellie, what *are* you doing?"

Her hand paused in its feverish pace. She glanced up to find all three women watching her. Her gaze dropped to the paper in her hands before she offered them an innocent smile. "I'm finding myself a husband."

Kate nearly choked on the sip of water she'd taken. Lorelei stared at her, mouth agape. Lettie started chuckling and couldn't seem to stop. "The world would be a dull place without you, Ellie."

Ellie grinned. "Wouldn't it?"

Lettie leaned forward. "How exactly is that piece of paper going to help you find a husband?"

Ellie shrugged. "By process of elimination. I'll match the eligible young men with the women they are interested in and go from there."

"Oh, Ellie." Lorelei laughed then leaned across the table for a better view. "Let me help."

Kate had always tried to put a damper on Ellie's escapades. Nathan was content to sit on the sidelines and enjoy whatever scene she'd caused. As a child, her brother, Sean, had always been in the thick of things with her, but eventually he became too sensible to be involved in any excitement she might cause. Then he'd married Lorelei. Ellie's world had not been the same since. She finally had a partner in crime.

Lorelei scooted her chair closer. Ellie glanced up at Kate's exasperated sigh. She didn't buy that for a moment. Kate's eyes were filled with just as much laughter as Lettie's. Ellie picked up the pencil and got back to work. Kate covered her grin by taking another sip of water. "Ellie does seem to have a sixth sense when it comes to detecting romance."

Ellie glanced at Lettie. The woman was responsible for Ellie's "sixth sense" and didn't even know it. Lettie told her at a young age that it didn't always matter so much what a person said as what a person didn't say. For that reason, Ellie had spent her life picking up on the little clues no one else noticed. Like the way Maddie's tone of voice changed when she asked for Jeff Bridger's order, and the way his nervous fingers straightened his collar while he gave it.

She added Maddie's initials to Jeff's name before handing it to Lorelei. "Now, tell me who is left without initials by his name. I'm going to ask you to mark off the men I could not possibly see myself with. Hopefully, we'll find a winner."

"Christian Johansen."

Ellie shook her head. The young man had been her good friend for years, but she couldn't imagine him as anything more.

"Rhett Granger." Lorelei glanced up. "He's handsome."

"I thought I marked him off. He's taken."

Lorelei leaned toward her. "Taken by whom?"

"Never mind that." She leaned back to give the women a knowing glance. "Just mark my words."

"Donovan Turner."

Ellie froze. Her gaze shot to Lorelei's mirth-filled eyes and she frowned. "Lorelei O'Brien, that man was not allowed on my list. He gives me the willies. Who's left?"

Lorelei exchanged a glance with Kate. "No one."

"What? How is that possible?"

Kate leaned over to look at the list. "Everyone else has initials. Some have question marks by them, though. What do those mean?"

Ellie frowned. "It means I'm sure of what the man thinks, or the woman, but not both. I suppose those are still possibilities—until I find out for sure if they're really taken. But there's really no one else without initials?"

Kate shook her head. "You paired off every decent man on the list."

Ellie sat in stunned silence. "I'm going to be a spinster."

"Don't say that." Lorelei sounded horrified.

She buried her face in her hands. "Why not? It's true."

"What's true, Ellie?" Maddie sidled up to the table with their plates.

Ellie spread her fingers to peer up at Maddie. "I'm going to die a decrepit old maid."

Maddie laughed. "Don't be silly."

Ellie straightened abruptly and nearly managed to bump her head on the plate Maddie was setting in front of her. She met the woman's dark brown eyes adamantly. "It isn't silly. It isn't silly at all. I went through every bachelor in town and I'm pretty sure that none of them work."

"You did what?" The woman backed away as if afraid to find out the answer.

"I think you should try again," Lettie said as Kate handed her the list. "Something as serious as this should not be taken lightly or composed hastily. Give yourself time to think about it."

"Ms. Lettie is right," Kate said, though Ellie had a feeling her sister was just trying to make her feel better about not finding a match. "Maybe you made a mistake."

"You left someone off."

Ellie frowned at Lettie. "I did? I thought I listed every decent, God-fearing man in town."

"That's why." The woman nodded as if the mysteries of the world had been explained to her, while eyeing her thoughtfully. "I don't know why I never thought of it before."

"Thought of what?" Lorelei asked as everyone seemed to lean forward in anticipation.

Lettie exchanged a meaningful look with Kate. At first, Kate's brow furrowed, then slowly the illuminating light of intuition seemed to fill her eyes. "You mean…?"

Lettie nodded.

Kate's eyes widened, then she stared at Ellie before sitting back in her chair. "Hmm."

Ellie exchanged a confused glance with Lorelei. "Who is it?"

A slow smile lifted Kate's lips. "This could be good. This could be very good."

It was always good to get letters from home. Lawson glanced at Nathan Rutledge's letter then turned to the one from the woman he called Mother. Reaching his room in the boarding house, he tugged off his dirty boots, threw his Stetson on his desk and fell back onto his bed, allowing himself to give in to exhaustion for just a moment before opening his mail.

It had been a long, hard year filled with dangerous work and too many secrets. As a Texas Ranger, he'd rounded up more than his fair share of outlaws, and he tried to find some satisfaction in that. But this near-vagabond existence was too much like the life he'd left behind when he'd stumbled into Peppin, Texas, abandoned and alone with nowhere to go until the O'Brien family took him in. A few months later, when he was fourteen, Doc and Lettie Williams adopted him. They'd been the parents he'd always dreamed of. His life in Peppin had been so good that he'd nearly forgotten about the past. Here…he seemed to run across it every day in the smell of liquor, the haunted eyes of the saloon girls, the solitude and the need to be on constant alert.

His commanding officer in the Rangers constantly told him not to lose the chip on his shoulder. "That's what makes you stand out from the other Rangers. That's what makes you tough. That's what enables you to get your man. Never lose that chip."

Lawson wasn't stupid enough to believe him. God was the one enabling him to catch those criminals. As for the chip on his shoulder—well, he reckoned he'd picked it up sometime between being abandoned and wandering into Peppin. Unfortunately, it didn't keep the harshness of this life from wearing away at him, day by day.

Time for a distraction. He tore open the letter from his parents first. It was a thick one so it ought to be good. He lifted the letter above his head just high enough for it to catch the sunlight shining through the window behind him. The room was so silent that he decided to read it out loud: "'Dear Lawson, You really should come home.'"

He sat up in concern and pulled the letter closer. "'Now, don't get all excited. Everyone here is fine. Your pa and I just miss you like crazy. We haven't seen you in more than a year. You haven't come home for any of the holidays. I know you work hard and what you do is important. This isn't to make you feel guilty. This is just to tell you that we love you and we want to see you. Surely you can apply for a leave of absence. Just a few weeks of your company—that's all I ask. Now, I've said my piece so I won't mention it again.'"

She kept her promise and went on to talk about some of the things Lawson had mentioned in his last letter, but he kept going back to that first paragraph. She was right. He hadn't been home since he'd left a few weeks after his almost wedding to Lorelei.

Pretty Lorelei Wilkins had been his sweetheart for years. Asking her to marry him had seemed like the next logical step. He had cared for her, had been determined to be a good husband to her—but before that could happen, she'd run out on their wedding, leaving him literally at the altar. When he'd chased after her, she'd told him the truth: that she didn't think she loved him in the right way to be his wife…and that she didn't think he loved her the right way, either.

She was right. He'd been so hungry to have a family of his own, to make a life for himself that was completely different from the childhood he left behind, that he'd rushed into a wedding that came more from his head than his heart. He'd realized that she deserved more and maybe he did, too, so he did the honorable thing. He let her go. Then he did what his pride demanded, and left. He wasn't there to see her marry Sean O'Brien, Lawson's best friend and the man Lorelei had always secretly loved, though he was happy for her—happy for both of them—that they'd found the love they deserved.

He knew that calling off the wedding had been the right decision, but it had still hurt. The wedding was supposed to prove that he'd overcome his past, that he was starting a new life and a new family. Instead, it seemed to prove the opposite and reminded him of all the rejection he'd experienced before. In truth, it was no wonder she'd walked away so easily. The people who mattered most often did.

He read the letter from Sean's brother-in-law, Nathan Rutledge, then let it fall to his chest as he stared at the ceiling. There must be some conspiracy to make him come home. Nathan wrote that his horse ranch had been doing so well that he'd decided to expand. He was offering Lawson the job of foreman just in case he'd grown tired of being a Ranger.

"Lord, is this from You?"

It was possible that God was bringing his time as a Ranger to a close. If so, Lawson planned to listen. God had been getting Lawson out of danger since he'd been a scraggly ten-year-old fending for himself on the streets, even if he hadn't known Whom to thank for it right away. God had helped him find a fresh start once. Maybe it was time for another new beginning.

Lawson Williams still had something to prove—that he was nothing like the parents who'd given him life then done their best to ruin it. He'd keep proving it to himself over and over again until he could finally believe it. He'd thought being a lawman would provide the opportunity to do that but perhaps the best way to prove it was by going home.

Ellie was trying her best to ignore the young man who'd been trailing after her for the past ten minutes. It wasn't working. She turned and planted her hands on her hips as she eyed the dashing young blacksmith. "Rhett, if you insist on following me then you might as well make yourself useful."

She pointed to the signs for the booths resting on the church stairs. The Founder's Day activities had already started but the signs needed extra time to dry. Rhett really must have been desperate because he picked them up and began helping her hand them out to the booth workers. "Ellie, I'm sure I'm on your list. You've got to tell me. Jeff Bridger says you told him about Maddie and they are already engaged."

She smiled as she handed Mrs. Redding the sign for her lemonade stand then moved on. "I know they're engaged. I invited you to the party I'm having for them at the ranch. Don't tell me you forgot about it already."

"I didn't forget and you aren't going to distract me." His muscles bulged as he shifted the remaining signs to his shoulder, which somehow made his pleading look seem all the more pitiful. "I've just *got* to know who you think my match is."

She rolled her eyes. It had been two weeks since the fateful day she'd created the "Bachelor List." The whole thing had turned into a disaster. Everyone in town knew about it. She'd had plenty of available men seeking her out after word got around. Unfortunately, they weren't looking for her. They'd just wanted to know whose initials were next to their names on the list.

She could understand them wanting an answer. She'd wanted one, too, but Lettie and Kate never told her who the mystery suitor for her was. Try as she might to extricate the information from them, she'd gained little more for her efforts than a headache.

She sighed. "Well, Rhett, who do you want it to be?"

She followed his gaze as it trailed to where Amy Bradley stood with her sisters. He watched Amy for a full minute before Ellie shook her head and smiled. "Yep, that's what I thought."

His gaze jumped back to hers, and then he grinned. "Thank you."

"I didn't say anything."

He nodded then set off toward Amy. She grabbed his massive arm and dug her heels into the ground to stop him. "Oh, no you don't. You're going to help me deliver all these signs because you're *so* grateful. Isn't that right?"

"Yeah, that's right. I shouldn't get ahead of myself." He patted her hand in brotherly affection and began trailing her again but remained decidedly distracted. He seemed to grow less confident as they continued and when she finally set him free, he went in the opposite direction from where his thoughts had been taking him.

Now, what's wrong with him? She pulled the new list from her pocket and crossed out the question mark beside Amy's initials by his name. He was the only one besides Deputy Jeff Bridger who she'd officially paired a girl with so far. There were plenty of others still with question marks—for now.

She felt someone's eyes on her and turned to find Donovan Turner watching her from near the gazebo. She tucked the list out of sight before barely managing to hide her grimace behind a polite smile and a nod. The man pulled the piece of hay from his mouth and tossed it to the ground before pacing toward her. Now, there was one man who made no effort to hide his opinion of her, which was definitely *not* brotherly. He always seemed to pop up at the most inopportune times—like when she was alone. If he caught her, he'd spend the next thirty minutes bending her ear about that pig farm of his. *If* he caught her; but she wasn't going to let him.

She slipped into a group of people, dashed behind a booth and surfaced behind a tree. She thought she'd lost him, but to make sure, she scanned the crowd as she continued walking backward. She spotted the man scratching his head, glancing about. She was about to turn around when she backed right into someone. She gasped. "Oh, I'm so sorry!"

She tried to step away from the man but strong arms slipped around her waist and pulled her against a solid chest. She froze, then caught her breath as a warm, masculine voice filled her ear. "Hey there, beautiful."

Her eyes narrowed. Slowly, she glanced over her shoulder to look at him. The way his lips curved made her cheeks warm but she forgot all about that when her gaze tangled with those unforgettable hazel eyes. Her breath caught in her throat then her lips blossomed into a smile. "Lawson Williams, as I live and breathe!"

He loosened his arms enough for her to turn around and throw herself back into them. He hugged her back just as tightly as she hugged him. She pushed away to look at his face. "I almost didn't recognize you."

He grinned that slow, steady grin of his that set every female heart in a fifty-mile radius beating wildly. He stepped back to survey her. "Look who's talking. You sure have changed in the last few months."

She laughed. "Last few months? Are you crazy? It's been a year and no less! Of course I've changed. Did you get my letters?"

"I did."

"You only wrote back twice."

"I'm sorry." He shrugged. "I was on assignment most of the time so it wasn't easy to keep up with mail."

She lifted her chin. "Well, how is a person to know whether you fell off your saddle and broke your head or got laid up sick for a week if you don't write?"

He dipped his head to send her a suspicious look. "Were you worrying about me, Ellie?"

"Not me. Just…certain other people."

"I see." His eyes continued to tease her.

She pushed away from his arms, only belatedly remembering the reason she'd run into him in the first place. She glanced over her shoulder to look for Donovan Turner. He'd stopped to speak to someone and they pointed in the direction she'd dashed. She winced. It would only be a matter of time before he found her. Lawson's voice drew her attention.

"I just got into town. I came here first since I figured everyone would be at the celebration. I wanted to surprise my parents, but I wasn't counting on not being able to find them in this crowd." He scanned the flurry of activity around the churchyard. "Have you seen them recently?"

"No." She glanced over her shoulder and saw that Donovan had gotten closer but still hadn't spotted her.

She tugged Lawson's arm in the opposite direction. "Let's try this way and hurry up. I'm on the run."

"From the law?"

"No, silly, a man."

His gaze sharply honed in on hers. "What did you do—hit him with a mud pie?"

"No. I'm twenty-one, not twelve."

He snorted. She jostled him lightly with her shoulder and he jostled her right back then caught her around the waist to keep her from stumbling. She rolled her eyes. *Well, that was mature.* Sometimes with Lawson, she couldn't help reverting back to the mischievous ten-year-old she'd been when he'd come into her life.

Lawson glanced around at the crowded churchyard. "This event has gotten larger since I left."

"More people have started coming from outside of Peppin to celebrate with us. Not much else has changed." Satisfied they'd completely lost Donovan, she turned her attention to finding Lawson's parents— or her family since they were probably close together. "Oh, actually, Sean started a new tradition last year when he got up on the podium and proposed to Lorelei in front of everyone. We've all been wondering who'll continue it."

"Naturally, it should be you."

She stopped to stare at him. *"Me?"*

"Well, sure." He tipped his hat up to stare right back at her. "You should try to keep it in the family. Besides, you have men chasing you all the time. That isn't good. You need to pick one and settle down."

"I do *not* have men chasing me. There is *one* man and I don't want him. Everyone else thinks I'm their little sister."

His hazel eyes sparkled with laughter as he stepped a bit closer and lowered his voice. "I bet all those men are just waiting for you to pick one of them so they can declare their feelings."

She tilted her head. "Don't you have that backward?"

"They just need a little encouragement." At her scoff, he narrowed his eyes. "Oh, come on. Show me a little of that charm."

"No."

"I know you have it in you."

"I do not."

"Sure, you do."

She narrowed her eyes at him. He gave her an encouraging little nod then took a step back as though giving her room to work. Her hand went to her hip. A quick glance around told her no one was watching. She stepped close to him and placed a hand on his chest before throwing her head back to stare at him. She batted her eyelashes as fast as she could. "Lawson, honey, it's been you all this time. Tell me how you really feel."

"Well, there's something I've been meaning to ask you for a long time, Ellie O'Brien." His gaze traveled solemnly over her features. Without warning, he sank to one knee and stared up at her. "Will you marry me?"

Chapter Two

Ellie stared at Lawson, speechless. Her brain seemed to stop working. She had to repeat his words in her mind to make sure she'd understood them correctly. Finally, she gasped and punched him in the shoulder. "Get up before someone sees you!"

Her punch knocked him off balance and he put a hand on the ground to stabilize himself. He was laughing too hard to stand. She shook her head even as her lips curved. "You think you're so funny. I can't believe you did that!"

He staggered to his feet but continued laughing. "You should have seen your face."

"I hope it looked as appalled as I felt." She glanced around noting a few curious stares, including a few she recognized. "Don't you know this town is match happy right now? You can't pull a stunt like that. It's dangerous. What if someone thought you were serious?"

That ought to put some real fear into him. Not that it was all that likely since everyone in town knew his taste in women tended to run toward beautiful, sophisticated women like Lorelei. Ellie was more likely to catch a fish than an eligible bachelor like Lawson. He didn't seem concerned as he tried to hide a grin. "Isn't that the pot calling the kettle black? I thought you were Peppin's matchmaking queen."

She pierced him with a glare. "I refuse to discuss it. In fact, I think I'd better walk away from you now."

"Aw, don't leave." He easily kept time with her faster steps. "You promised to help me find my parents. Besides, it was funny. That's why you're trying so hard not to smile."

She rolled her eyes. Of course Lawson would know she was trying not to smile. He'd practically grown up with her and Sean so he had her pegged. That didn't mean she had to like it. "Oh, all right. I'll help you find your parents."

He'd almost forgotten how easy it was to read Ellie's face. Her every thought was written right there for him to see…and what a beautiful face it was. Had he ever taken the time to appreciate the way her full lips were almost always lifted into a smile? Had he ever noticed the faint freckles that danced across her pert nose? Or the way her large green eyes sparkled as if she was laughing at some private joke?

No, he hadn't and he sure as shooting shouldn't be doing it now. Ellie was and always had been his surrogate little sister. Nothing more and nothing less would do. That's the way it would stay. He wasn't about to jeopardize his close relationship with her or the O'Briens by changing things now. No matter how appealing her willowy figure appeared in that green dress. He shook away his odd thoughts to search the crowd for some glimpse of his family.

Ellie stopped and waved a sweeping hand toward the left. He followed her gesture to find his ma standing nearby. He cleared away the emotion in his throat, prompting Ellie to send him a knowing look. As they neared, Lettie turned away to signal to someone. He followed her signal to see Doc wave back. Neither of them had seen him yet.

"Ms. Lettie," Ellie's soft voice called.

The woman turned toward the sound. Her gaze rested on Ellie for an instant before it traveled to him. Lettie's eyes filled with tears even as a smile wreathed her face. He pulled her into a hug. "Hello, Ma."

"You came."

"Of course I did. I always do what you tell me, don't I?" He stepped away and looked down to see her smile.

"You always were a good boy."

Ellie snorted. "Let's not get carried away."

He shot her a glare over his mother's shoulder then glanced past her to see Doc standing quietly to the side with a grin on his face. Lawson stepped forward and met the man with a hearty handshake. "Hello, Pa."

"It's good to have you home, Son."

He stepped back and tried not to feel uncomfortable as everyone just stared at him like he might up and vanish on them. Ellie seemed to recover first. "I guess I'd better round up the rest of the O'Briens and Rutledges."

He sent her a grateful grin. "Thanks. I'd like to see them."

"Then turn around and look," a familiar voice called from behind him.

He turned to find Sean standing behind him, a wide grin on his face. Lawson reached out to one of the few men he'd let close enough to hug. They pounded each other on the back then quickly stepped apart.

Lawson couldn't stop smiling. "How are you, Sean?"

"Fine, just fine." Sean shook his hand for good measure. "It sure is good to see you in Peppin again."

"It's just good to see you period. Where's Lorelei? I heard you managed to get her down the aisle." Lorelei stepped up beside Sean and offered him a hopeful smile, looking just as beautiful as always. She looked so happy—just further proof of how right she'd been to stop her marriage to him just before saying "I do." Everything had turned out for the best, so there didn't need to be any awkwardness between them now. This was home. This was the only family he had and now she was a part of it.

He didn't question his instincts. He just pulled her into a quick brotherly hug then stepped away from her. "It looks like married life agrees with you."

She smiled and slipped her hand into Sean's. "It certainly does."

Nathan and Kate Rutledge appeared with their children. There was more hugging and more talking. Finally, they all settled into a rather familiar group with Kate and Nathan talking to his parents and him with Sean, Ellie and Lorelei. He glanced around at the festive celebration surrounding them and smiled in relief. Just like that he knew he was back where he belonged and everything else seemed to fade into the past.

Ellie glanced over her shoulder to give Lawson a parting smile as the caller had everyone switch partners. Sean spun her around as they danced across the grass together in time with the music. Her gaze traveled back to where it had rested many times since the dance started. Once again, Maddie and Jeff nearly ran into another couple because they couldn't keep their eyes off each other. Ellie frowned.

Sean followed her gaze then glanced down at her. "I would have thought you'd be proud."

"Proud of what? Proud that the tale of my desperate attempt to find a husband has been bandied across town like the joke of the century? Proud that not one of the men who approached me afterward wanted anything more than a point in the right direction? What am I supposed to be proud of, Sean? Tell me, because I'd sure like to know why everyone is patting me on the back. I am a joke, Sean, a household joke who can find love for everyone but herself."

Sean's arm tightened around her waist. "Stop saying that. You aren't a joke, Ellie. As for love, don't you know the Bible says 'do not stir or awaken love until the time is right'? Did you ever think that just maybe the time wasn't right?"

"No, I didn't."

"Well, maybe that's what it is. Maybe God knows you aren't ready for that. Or maybe you aren't the holdup at all. Maybe your future husband is the one who isn't ready."

She sighed. "I sure wish he'd hurry up. I'm tired of waiting."

He laughed. "What has you in such an all-fired hurry all of a sudden?"

"I don't know." She bit her lip. "Sometimes I think something must be wrong with me since I've never had anything close to a beau."

He stiffened. "There isn't a thing wrong with you."

She ignored his comment and narrowed her eyes. "You know what I think the problem is? All of the men in this town see me as a little sister."

"Stop acting like one and they'll stop treating you like one."

She pursed her lips to the side. Now, that was an interesting statement. She wasn't exactly sure how to do that but something had to change and it might need to be her behavior. She was plumb tired of being looked at merely as the town's source of amusement. She wanted to prove that she was more than that. She wanted to prove that she was worthy of being wanted.

Sean finished the dance with her before leading her to the table where their families sat. He pulled out the empty chair that had been left between Lawson and Kate for her, then went to sit beside Lorelei. As he did, Nathan cleared his throat. "Since we're all gathered here, I have an announcement to make. As you know, the horse ranch Kate and I started almost ten years ago has been doing very well lately. We've decided to expand."

This certainly wasn't news to Ellie, but she offered her congratulations, anyway. However, Nathan wasn't finished. "As part of that expansion, I decided to hire a new foreman. I'm pleased to announce that Lawson has agreed to take the position."

Happy gasps circled the table and Ellie's was among them. Her gaze flew to Lawson just as he gave a bashful shrug. "Surprise! I hope y'all don't mind that I'm going to stick around."

"Mind?" Sean's tone portrayed how completely ridiculous he found the question. "Why would we mind? This is great."

Ms. Lettie seemed to be glowing. "Does this mean no more traveling? You'll be settled in Peppin permanently?"

Lawson nodded. "The opportunity came at just the right time. I was ready to retire my badge."

Doc's approval shone in his eyes. "It will be good to have you home."

"It's perfect. Does this mean you'll live at the ranch again?" Ellie glanced at Kate for confirmation. "Perhaps in the cabin? Or will we build something new?"

Lawson shook his head. "The cabin will do just fine for me. I don't need anything fancy."

"We'll get that figured out soon," Nathan said just as Maddie and Jeff passed the table.

Jeff paused to speak to Ellie. "Thanks again, Ellie. If it wasn't for that list—"

"I know. You're welcome." She didn't mean to be abrupt, but really! Enough was enough.

The couple stepped away from the table. Lawson's voice drew her gaze as he regarded her. "What did Jeff say about a list?"

She leaned back in her chair as her family and closest friends launched into the story she was sick and tired of hearing. Sean caught her gaze and she returned his wry grin with a roll of her eyes. She took a sip of punch and managed to swallow her annoyance with a big gulp of the fruity concoction. Lawson sent her a measuring look once the story was through. "Looks like you've caused quite a stir."

She lifted her chin. "What else is new?"

Lawson chuckled. "Ellie, I'm just curious. Who did you match up with me?"

"I don't remember." Ellie's gaze swept toward Lettie

and Kate before she settled on Lorelei's face. Lorelei looked as baffled as she. Suddenly, Ellie's confusion fled and she turned back to him. "You weren't living here, so you weren't on the list."

"That's too bad. It would have been nice to—"

"Oh." She gasped the word as she realized what she'd just said. Her eyes widened. She stared into Lawson's hazel eyes for a drawn-out moment, vaguely aware his voice stumbled to a halt. She watched his gaze trail down to her lips—which had formed a perfect circle of incredulous indignation.

She dragged her gaze from his until she found Ms. Lettie's. The satisfaction on the woman's face told her everything she needed to know. A quick glance at her laughing sister confirmed it. Ellie shook her head at both of them even as she leaned back in her chair and pinned them with a look. "Ridiculous. You two are completely ridiculous."

Ellie heard Lorelei catch her breath but Ms. Lettie's knowing smile kept her from looking away. The woman lowered her chin and lifted one eyebrow as though to say "time will tell." Lawson's hand brushed her shoulder to gain her attention. She glanced up at him. He said something but all she could remember was earlier, ,the warmth of being in his arms and the sound of his voice in her ear. What had she felt the moment before she realized it was only Lawson? Attraction? Anticipation? She didn't want to label it.

Lawson—of all the silly ideas, to think that we might make a good couple. They were just friends—only friends. Besides, a man as attractive, interesting and worldly wise as he would never be interested in a simple girl like her, especially after all those years of courting

Lorelei, the most sophisticated girl in town. Why would he want Ellie? No one else ever had. Except Donovan, who she really didn't want to count.

She realized Lawson was still talking and shook the cloud from her thoughts. "What did you say?"

"I said, let me in on the joke. I want to laugh, too."

Her breath pulled from her lungs as if she'd been cut. Her gaze held his for a long moment then fell to her lap as she felt something within her snap. She slowly lifted her gaze to survey the faces of those around her. They were all waiting for her to say something. They wanted to laugh with her just like they'd done a thousand times before. But this time one thing was different.

She wasn't laughing.

She eyed her friends and family. "There is no joke, Lawson—not anymore."

Lawson eased his duffel bag from his shoulder to the floor of the cozy old cabin on the O'Brien property. This was the place where his life had truly begun nearly ten years ago when Kate and Nathan had taken him on as a farmhand and brought him into their family. In this cabin, he'd learned his first lesson about what it truly meant to belong somewhere. Only a few months after that, Doc and Lettie had become his legal guardians and his honorary parents.

It somehow felt right to begin again in this place—to once more forget the past that had been resurfacing in his thoughts so often. Glancing around the room, he took in a cleansing breath then quickly lost it when he spotted Ellie directly to his right. She stood on a stool she'd placed over a crate in an effort to reach a cobweb near the cabin's high ceiling. Every time she moved, the stool she perched on wobbled beneath her. Lawson strode over and plucked her from her perch.

"Hey," she protested as he set her on her feet. "I almost had it."

He nodded. "You certainly did…if *it* was a broken bone."

She wrinkled her nose at him then turned to gesture to the rest of the cabin. "Well, how do you like your new, old place?"

He surveyed the table with two chairs that had been placed by the window with a planter filled with cheery yellow flowers. A bed with a simple quilt, a large trunk and a small wardrobe stood on the opposite side of the room. A comfortable-looking chair sat next to the fireplace. He smiled. "It looks nice, clean, homey. Did you do all of this?"

"Guilty." She removed the stool from the crate and set it near the door.

"You didn't have to."

"I know. I wanted to." She tucked a loose tendril behind her ear. "I missed you, you know."

"What was there to miss?" He knew he was fishing for compliments but he didn't care. Mostly, he just wanted her to prove that her statement was true.

She kicked a large dark blue-and-green rag rug to unroll it over the middle of the wooden floor. "Oh, I don't know. It just hasn't been the same since you left and Sean got married. The three of us used to be as thick as thieves—you, Sean and I. Nothing felt right without you here."

He believed her. He'd wanted to, anyway. It was a nice feeling—being missed by someone.

She surveyed the room then must have been satisfied

because she allowed herself to collapse onto a kitchen chair. "I bet you didn't miss me."

"Of course I did." He sat across from her.

She shook her head. "You didn't but that's fine. You were busy bringing outlaws to justice. I wouldn't have missed me, either."

"It wasn't as exciting as you seem to think."

"What was it like, then?"

"It was like everything I've tried to forget."

That quieted her for a moment before she smiled sympathetically. "Well, you're home now. You can forget as much as you want."

Home. That one word sounded so sweet to his ear. He gave a solemn nod. "I was already planning on it."

"I've been wondering—" she fiddled with one of the flowers "—why do the Rangers call you Lawless?"

Lawson stared at Ellie, then frowned. "Now, where did you hear that?"

"Nathan sold a few horses to the Rangers. While he was in Austin, he asked about you. They told him you were one of the best Rangers on the force. They also told him you'd picked up the moniker *Lawless*. Why?"

He averted his gaze from her questioning eyes. "They assigned me the worst criminals, Ellie. Sometimes that meant I had to take risks, be ruthless and do things I wouldn't dream of in any other situation. I never broke protocol but I've certainly bent my fair share of rules."

She frowned. "They called you that because you bent a few rules?"

He gave a slow nod. She narrowed her eyes. It was clear she knew he wasn't letting her in on the whole truth. Well, that was too bad because he wasn't about to tell her that almost the entire Ranger force thought he'd make a better outlaw than a Ranger, and loved to tease him about it. He didn't find it particularly funny. Nor did he want his name to be associated with the term *outlaw,* especially if some of those foggy memories of his childhood were accurate. He figured it was time for a change of subject.

"Now it's my turn to ask a question. What was so important about me not being on that list of yours?" He asked the question before he could second-guess the wisdom of pursuing something that had upset her so much earlier.

Ellie was quiet for a long moment as if debating whether or not to tell him before she surprised him again by glancing up with teasing eyes. "Now that really *is* a dangerous question. You'll probably wish you hadn't asked, but since you want to know so badly, I'll tell you."

He gave her a nod. "I'll take my chances."

She leaned forward. "The whole point of the list was to find out who my match might be, right?"

"Right."

"Well, after I'd gone through the list without finding anyone, Ms. Lettie took the paper and looked it over. She told me I'd left someone off but she wouldn't tell me who it was."

He found himself leaning forward, as well. "That was me, right? I was the one you left off because I wasn't in town."

"Exactly." She sat back as if that settled everything.

Lawson stared at her. "You'll have to explain this to me, Ellie, because I still don't get it."

"You were *the one.*"

"*The one* what?"

Ellie laughed. "Lawson, really. Think about it. You were the only man left."

"So?"

"So—" her voice took on a bit of exasperation "—Ms. Lettie and Kate, they think that you and I…well, that we would be…what did Kate say? Oh, that we could be very good…*together.*"

Lawson stared at her for a long moment as understanding slowly dawned. "What?"

She smirked. "That's what I said."

He tried to wrap his mind around that thought. Honestly, it wasn't as hard as it should have been. He swallowed. His thoughts raced back to his recent interactions with Ellie—from his impulsive act of catching her in his arms at first sight to his pretend proposal. If he was honest with himself, he'd have to admit that he hadn't been treating Ellie like a sister. At least, not since he'd gotten back. In fact, if it were some other woman, he might have seen his behavior as flirtatious.

He ducked his head to keep her from reading his thoughts. He was crazy. He had to be. There was no way he could be attracted to little Ellie. Of course, she wasn't so little anymore. How old was she now? Twenty-one? She was pretty much a woman by now, wasn't she? His voice came out a little strained. "Ma and Kate really said that about us being good together?"

She sent him a curious glance. "It's funny but you don't seem nearly as shocked as I was. I thought they were completely ridiculous."

A wry grin lifted his lips. "I remember."

Her eyes widened. "Oh, that isn't to cast any sort of disparagement on you. I didn't mean that at all."

"I didn't think so."

"Good. I mean I'm sure some gal would be lucky to have you. I just can't imagine—" Her face twisted into a strange expression, as though she was desperately trying to conjure up some image of the two of them together.

He tried not to let that bother him…but why *was* it so hard for her to imagine? He shook his head. They were friends—nearly family. So Ellie had grown up. That didn't mean anything had to change between them or even that it should. He met her gaze with a grin. "It is pretty hard to imagine, isn't it?"

Her green eyes started dancing. "Well, since you won't have me, either, I guess I'd better start waiting at the train station for some handsome stranger to disembark. That looks to be my best bet."

He laughed along with her though he had to admit it was a bit forced. The thought of some stranger sweeping into town and carrying Ellie off didn't sit well with him. It was just his protective nature at work, he assured himself. That's all it was and nothing more. He was here to work. He was here to start over.

Most important, he was here to forget.

Chapter Three

Ellie thanked Mr. Johansen then tucked the small brown-paper-wrapped package under her arm. "Lawson and I will be back with the wagon to pick up the list of goods Kate ordered."

Lawson had moved out to the ranch less than a week ago and ever since then, Ellie hadn't been able to turn around without finding him nearby. She knew it was mostly due to the fact that they now lived on the same ranch. Still, a part of her wondered if a little tiny bit of it was through Kate's machinations. After all, Kate usually liked coming into town but today had sent Ellie in her stead. Nathan sent Lawson and so they had gone to town together with express directions to eat lunch there.

Guilt sprang onto her conscience. Of course, Nathan was busy, which was why he'd hired Lawson in the first place, and Kate had her hands full tending three children too young to go to school. Perhaps she really was imagining it. Mr. Johansen's voice pulled her from her short reverie. "I'll have the boys waiting by the loading dock in about thirty minutes."

Ellie nodded and managed to make it all the way

out the door and a few steps down the sidewalk before she tore open the brown package. The colorful cover of the dime novel looked even more intriguing than it had in the catalog. She opened the cover to reveal the first page and found herself in the midst of a stage-coach robbery. Her heart skipped a beat. She carefully read each word as she stepped onto Main Street's raised wooden sidewalk.

Suddenly, a hand caught her arm and firmly pulled her to a stop. Ellie glanced up from the page only to realize that if not for the restraining hand on her arm, her next step would have sent her tumbling off the side-walk. Her eyes widened then traveled to the man who stood slightly beside her with his hand still protectively on her arm. Lawson shook his head. "You really need to be more aware of your surroundings."

She wrinkled her nose at him as he led her to the shiny display window of the mercantile. Pointing at it, he leaned toward her. "Look at the reflections in the window."

The angle of the bay window reflected a clear image of the things behind her—including a man standing next to a tall chestnut mare tied to the nearest hitching post. "Donovan."

"He appeared just as I left you to walk to the livery. He seemed content to stay on his horse until you exited the mercantile…alone."

"He always does that. I think it's the only way he can work up the nerve to talk to me." She laughed at his skeptical frown. "He's harmless."

"Well, someone else might not be."

Her gaze shot to his hazel eyes. "Am I your latest

assignment, Lawson? And here I thought you'd left the Rangers."

"So did I." He tucked her hand in his arm and led her across the street. They both jumped at the sound of Maddie's joyful greeting through the café's large front window. The woman waved at her as though she'd just seen her long-lost best friend. *I understand that she's grateful that my list motivated Jeff enough to talk to her, but isn't this a little too much?*

The rest of the folks in the café turned to look. She could feel their eyes tracking her as she followed Lawson inside. She glanced around the room. Everyone was smiling at them. An entire table composed of Judge Hendricks, Mr. Potters and Joshua Stone lifted their coffee cups in a congratulatory toast. Lawson seemed just as bewildered as she did by the positive response. "Ellie, why is everyone smiling?"

"I don't know."

Maddie couldn't stop grinning as she led them to their table. "This is so wonderful! I don't know why no one thought of it before. You two are just perfect for each other. Y'all had us fooled into thinking you were just friends but now we all know better, don't we?"

Ellie felt her cheeks warm. She darted a glance at Lawson before she met Maddie's gaze. "What are you talking about?"

"Oh, you don't have to be coy, dearie." She patted Ellie's shoulder. "The whole town knows about your secret engagement. Don't worry. We haven't said a word to your families."

"Our secret what?" Lawson's question came out rather loud.

Maddie picked up the menu from the table. "Mrs.

Greene saw you propose, Lawson. It's been all over town for days."

Ellie's gaze flew to Lawson. She glared at him. "Mrs. Greene saw you propose." She couldn't imagine anyone worse to have seen Lawson's little prank. Mrs. Greene was, ironically, the biggest gossip in town and one of the strictest moralists. Not to mention that she'd always held a particular grudge against Ellie for all of her childhood pranks.

Lawson seemed to be at a loss for words but guilt was written all over his face. A quick glance around the room told her everyone was watching so she stood to her feet. "Everyone, please listen closely then spread the news like wildfire. Lawson and I are not, nor have we ever been, engaged."

Mrs. Cummins set down her coffee with a thud. "But Mrs. Greene saw him kneel down and ask you."

"I was joking."

Maddie frowned at Lawson. "What an awful thing to joke about."

Ellie sent him a look seconding that, then turned to the crowd again. "Mrs. Greene also should have noticed that I punched him in the arm afterward. That's obviously not how a woman says yes to a man."

Judge Hendricks cleared his throat. "Well, Ellie, you've always been sort of a tomboy."

"As a child, not as an adult…usually." She sank to her chair. Maddie studied the two of them. "So y'all aren't engaged?"

"No," they answered together, setting the whole café to rumbling.

"Well, don't that beat all," Mr. Potters muttered.

"A real shame, that's what it is," Mrs. Cummins announced.

"Well, folks, this just isn't right." Maddie put a hand on Ellie's and Lawson's shoulders. "These two would make a fine couple, wouldn't they?"

"The best!" someone yelled and others chimed in to agree.

Ellie rose to her feet again. "Now, hold on. I think I'd know if Lawson and I would make a fine couple, wouldn't I?"

People reluctantly agreed.

"Then you can trust me when I say we aren't a couple."

People adamantly *dis*agreed. Maddie held up a stilling hand to her patrons. "Ellie's right. We can trust her on this. You just tell us who you matched Lawson with on the list of yours and we'll let this all go."

"Oh." Ellie swallowed then glanced down at Lawson. His expression said they were done for, which was discouraging and slightly insulting at the same time. Her fingers clenched the side of her chair. "Well, he wasn't on the list so that can't be considered. Now—"

"That explains why you couldn't find the one meant for you." Maddie caught her hand. "He wasn't on the list, darlin', but he was *your* match."

"Don't I have something to say about that?" Lawson seemed more amused than he should have been in this situation, especially when a firm "no" echoed through the café. Ellie eyed him. Why wasn't he more upset?

"We can't abandon Ellie in her time of need." Maddie released them and turned toward her patrons. "Didn't Mrs. Greene say that Ellie deserves this after everything she's done for the town?"

"Mrs. Greene said that?" Ellie turned to Lawson. "Why would Mrs. Greene say that?"

"That *is* strange," he admitted with the beginnings of a grimace.

Maddie ignored them. "Well, that settles it."

Lawson jumped up. "Wait. That settles what? What's going on?"

Oh, now *Lawson decides to look nervous.*

"You just leave that to Peppin, folks." Mrs. Cummins said. "You just leave that to Peppin."

Just like that, it was over. Maddie promised to bring them each a special on the house. The other patrons went back to their food. Ellie and Lawson were left to stare about in shock.

Ellie spoke first. "I have chills and I'm not sure why."

Lawson understood her feelings exactly. He didn't have chills but he did feel a strange foreboding settle in his gut. He'd done his best to ignore what he'd convinced himself were just fleeting flashes of attraction to Ellie. Living in the old cabin on the Rutledge ranch for the past week or so hadn't made that easy. Especially since he tended to take his meals with the Rutledge family—and Ellie, train the horses with Nathan—and Ellie, complete barn chores with Nathan, Nathan's son Timothy—and Ellie. She seemed to be everywhere at once being helpful or kind or getting into mischief.

He'd almost wondered why Nathan hadn't just increased Ellie's responsibilities around the farm rather than hire him as foreman. After all, her talent for settling down high-strung horses was remarkable. Then he discovered that Nathan didn't only need the talented horse trainer he had in Ellie, but also the brawn her slim frame didn't carry and the business acumen she seemed to intentionally avoid.

Once he settled down into the new job and got used to being in Peppin again, his perception of her would go back to normal. It was obvious Ellie didn't see him as anything other than a friend, almost a brother. And that was the way it was supposed to be. He wasn't about to pin his heart on a girl who would no doubt reject him. The last thing he needed right now was for the town to bluster in and make things even more confusing. Unfortunately, it looked as if that was exactly what was about to happen.

He shook his head. "Well, Ellie, it looks like all of your matchmaking efforts are about to be repaid to you."

"Courtesy of Mrs. Greene. Why does that sound so threatening?" She shivered. "I think she incited this on purpose. Probably because she knows you'd never..."

He almost let that comment slide before deciding against it. "I'd never what?"

She lifted her chin to continue solemnly, "No matter how hard matchmakers might try, you're the one man who'd never fall in love with me. You're the only man in town unrelated to me who has a legitimate reason to treat me like a little sister."

"Ellie." Not knowing what else to say that wouldn't make them both feel more awkward, he covered her hand to comfort her.

She shook her head as her large green eyes filled with tears. "No, it's true. I tell you, it's true. She saw me punch you afterward. She knew what that meant. She did this on purpose to get back at me for who knows what."

"Then don't let her." He handed her his handker-chief in case one of the tears tried to escape. "Don't let her know it bothers you. Just go about your life as if it doesn't matter to you. We won't let it determine our behavior one way or the other."

She nodded. She pulled in a deep breath, seeming to will back her tears. Maddie approached to serve their food and eyed their clasped hands. They immediately pulled apart. She smiled, as the town's plan was working already. Lawson's gaze flew to Ellie when she gasped. "What's wrong?"

She straightened abruptly. "There's Mrs. Greene. I should talk to her."

"I don't think that's a good idea." He stared after her as she strode out the door. It clanged shut with a plaintive cry of the bell. He suddenly realized everyone was watching him. He stared right back at them. Maddie gathered Ellie's plate. "I'll box it up for her and she can eat it on the way home."

"Thank you."

"Fine way to start a romance," she muttered as she walked away.

Chapter Four

Ellie frowned as she hurried across Main Street toward where her childhood nemesis stood outside of Sew Wonderful Tailoring. For years, she'd assumed her antagonistic relationship with Mrs. Greene wasn't something worth contemplation. Now she wasn't so sure.

Perhaps if she'd apologized for her mischievous youth years ago instead of just letting the pattern continue, she wouldn't be in this mess now. The funny thing was that Ellie didn't believe it was entirely her fault. She'd sensed Mrs. Greene's disapproval for as long as she could remember. Once she'd realized nothing she did changed the woman's opinion of her, she'd decided she might as well live up to those low expectations and have fun while doing it. It had been a silly, childish decision for sure, and one that had gotten her into scads of trouble.

"When I was a child I spoke as a child but when I became an adult I put childish things away."

Isn't that in the Bible somewhere? Her heart beat rapidly in her throat even as her steps hastened in resolve. "Mrs. Greene, may I speak to you for a moment in private?"

The woman slowly turned from surveying the window to look at Ellie with a measuring stare. Her response came slowly but with precision. "Certainly."

"The courtyard is always quiet," she suggested. At Mrs. Greene's nod, she led the woman toward the courthouse then stopped beside one of the courtyard's benches. This was going to be either the wisest or the stupidest things she'd ever done. She cleared her throat. "I'd like to apologize for the way I behaved when I was younger—"

Mrs. Greene laughed. She laughed! "You must want something from me pretty badly if this is the approach you're taking. What is it, then?"

Taken off guard, Ellie pulled in a steadying breath before replying. "M-Maddie at the café says you've been telling everyone that I'm engaged to Lawson."

"Yes?"

"But I'm not!"

Mrs. Greene sniffed disdainfully. "Well, of course you are. I saw him get down on his knee and propose. It's pure nonsense keeping the engagement hidden when you know both families will approve. Why should I keep your secret for you?"

"It isn't a secret! I mean, it isn't an engagement!" Ellie shook her head to clear her confusion. "Lawson was just teasing me—he proposed as a joke. As soon as he was done, I punched him on the shoulder and then we both had a good laugh about it. That was it! Or it should have been, except that you had to go and tell everyone. Now the whole town has gotten the wrong idea."

"Have they?" Mrs. Greene tilted her head. "Are you sure?"

"Yes, I'm sure! I thought it was obvious we were joking and that you were just telling people it was real as a prank. You know, like the ones I used to pull." She probably shouldn't have reminded Mrs. Greene about the pranks. The woman's face turned a little red so Ellie rushed on. "I just thought that if we talked—if I apologized for the way I used to behave—maybe you could tell people that you were mistaken."

"Hmm." There was a long pause as Mrs. Greene pondered the matter. "No."

Ellie was so stunned that it took her a minute before she could speak. "No?"

"I don't believe I will." Mrs. Greene's laugh was tinged with pity. "Did you really think a half-sincere apology would fix everything? Oh, no. I think it's high time someone gave you a taste of your own medicine."

"What medicine? I don't spread false stories about other people."

"No. You prefer true ones," Mrs. Greene said before she paled slightly then hurried on. "Never mind, Ellie. I accept your apology but I doubt anything I say will stop this train now that it's on the tracks. Everyone will begin meddling in your life just as you've always meddled in theirs. We'll see how you like it."

Ellie surveyed the woman carefully then shook her head slowly. "That isn't what you meant about getting a taste of my own medicine. What true story do you think I spread?"

"I really must go."

Ellie stopped the woman with a quick hand on her arm. "No, Mrs. Greene. I think you'd better stay and tell me what this is all about. I've always sensed you didn't like me. I'd like to know why."

Mrs. Greene stared at her. "You really don't remember?"

She shook her head. "Should I?"

Ire momentarily rose in the woman's eyes. She gave a tight nod then sat down on the bench. "I daresay you should. I certainly do."

Ellie waited as Mrs. Greene gathered her thoughts. Finally, the woman met her gaze. "I used to be good friends with your mother. You remember that, at least."

"Vaguely." She took the seat at the far side of the bench. "I was only eight when they died."

"I know," Mrs. Greene said quietly. "Once I went to visit your mother. You were home from school because you weren't feeling well. You'd fallen asleep on the settee as your mother and I talked, so I felt it was all right if I shared a confidence. Your mother was so sweet. She even prayed that I would accept the fact that God's love had covered my sins. That was the end of it, or so I thought.

"The next day my daughter came home crying." Mrs. Greene surveyed her scathingly. "You hadn't been asleep after all. You'd heard every word and repeated it to your friends at school. The whole town knew in a matter of hours."

Ellie frowned in confusion. "Knew what?"

Mrs. Greene's words were quiet, steady, yet bore a trace of shame. "I bore my daughter out of wedlock."

Ellie gasped—not at Mrs. Greene's words but at what that meant about her. "You mean, I told everyone that?"

"You certainly did."

"Oh, no. I'm so sorry!"

The woman fiddled with her reticule. "Your parents came to me a few days later and apologized. They said you repeated the story without knowing what it meant. Unfortunately, the rest of the town did."

"My parents…" she murmured as she blinked away a vague semblance of a memory. It returned with vengeance. She remembered overhearing the conversation, telling the older girls and feeling so important when they gasped. She also recalled the disappointment on her parents' faces when she'd admitted it. The disappointment in their voices…

That vague feeling of guilt overcame her with startling intensity. Quickly, she pushed it away—blocked those memories from her thoughts. She didn't want to examine them. She didn't want to remember. She rose abruptly from the bench to look down at Mrs. Greene. "Don't tell me any more. I understand. I'm sorry. I—I don't want to talk about this ever again."

Odd, how Mrs. Greene didn't seem startled by her reaction. She just nodded slowly. As if she knew something Ellie didn't.

"Everyone has something to be ashamed of, Ellie," Mrs. Greene said quietly. "You exposed my secret and humiliated me and my family in front of the whole town. But you're not innocent, either. The things you've done have brought down terrible consequences on your family, too."

Ellie stared at the woman. What terrible consequences? What had she done that caused so much harm? Could it be possible that after all these years of suppressing it, that strange sense of guilt actually meant *something?* Was it something Mrs. Greene—and Mrs. Greene only—was somehow intimately aware of? It must have to do with her parents…with their disappointment in her. She swallowed. "I don't know what you're talking about."

"Perhaps not." The woman smiled ruefully. "Perhaps it's just as well you don't. We won't speak of this again. I have to go."

She watched Mrs. Greene walk away then sank onto the bench. She felt so guilty—almost dirty. She wasn't sure how long she sat there but she slowly became aware of the man standing before her. She shook the clouds from her head to meet the stranger's blue eyes. "I'm sorry. What did you say?"

"I said I'm new here. I just got off the train, in fact. I'm looking for the boardinghouse."

"The boardinghouse—" That's as far as she got before tears began to run down her cheeks.

A look of panic crossed the young man's face before he sat beside her and handed her a handkerchief. "There, now. If it's such a horrible place, I won't go anywhere near it."

She gave a watery laugh. "I'm sorry. The boardinghouse is a wonderful place. I just had an unsettling conversation, that's all. You mustn't mind me."

"Ellie, I've been looking all over for you."

She jumped up to greet Lawson. "I'm sorry for leaving you like that. I just had to speak to Mrs. Greene."

He eyed the handkerchief in her hand. "I'm guessing that didn't go well."

"She said some awful things. She also said that she thought the story was true when she shared it—but even now that she knows it isn't, she'll do nothing to stop it from spreading. I was right. She wants to get back at me for…everything."

"Well, let her have her fun." He caught her arms to give them a supportive squeeze. "We won't let it bother us."

A weak smile was all she could offer in return. After all, he wasn't the one with an ominous secret lurking somewhere in a memory. A throat cleared behind them. She followed Lawson's gaze when it traveled past her to the man standing patiently by the bench. "Oh, this man saw that I was upset and tried to cheer me up. I'd introduce y'all but I don't think I caught your name. I'm Ellie O'Brien and this is Lawson Williams."

The stranger's smile slipped into what almost seemed like alarm for an instant before he held out his hand to Lawson. "I'm glad to meet you both. I'm Ethan Larue. I'm sure y'all have a lot to discuss so I think I'd better get going."

Ellie managed to give him directions to the boardinghouse and he was soon on his way. "I'm sorry I was angry earlier."

He shrugged. "That's all right. I was angry, too— at the town, I mean. I hope they didn't offend you too badly."

"Offend me?" she asked with disbelief. "Why would I be offended? You're a wonderful person, Lawson. You're intelligent and funny and..."

His lips titled into that slow grin of his and he held up a hand to stop her. "I meant I hope they didn't offend you by suggesting you needed help finding a match— not that you may have been offended to be matched with me."

"Oh," she breathed, feeling her cheeks begin to warm. Why was it that she couldn't even have a simple conversation without making some silly mistake?

He eyed her. "It's kind of a crazy idea they have, isn't it?"

"Uh-huh," she muttered, in an effort to save face. "Plain crazy. That's what it is."

Lord, I just have the knack of getting myself into uncomfortable situations whether verbally or otherwise. It's just one of my many faults, I know, but if there's any way You can help me fix that I'd be forever grateful. She bit her lip. As for the town's matchmaking—well, she'd much rather focus on that than her altercation with Mrs. Greene and its mysterious implications.

Lawson ignored the sweat mottling his brow as he pounded another wooden stake into the ground. Nathan followed slowly behind him, digging the holes the new fence posts would soon go in. "We've got company."

He glanced up as a rider approached. It took him a moment to realize the rider was Chris Johansen. The distance between them dissipated, allowing Lawson to see him more clearly. The man's hair was slicked back and it was also obvious that he had taken special care with his clothing. However, it was the bouquet of wildflowers that gave away the true nature of the man's mission.

"It looks like you have some competition," Nathan teased.

Nathan and Sean had gotten a kick out of the town's decision to hitch him to Ellie, and his supposed "courtship" had been a running joke ever since. Sean laughed so hard that Ellie had been put out with him for the entire week. It was a little disheartening how against the whole thing she actually was. Not that he'd planned to do anything about the attraction that had started stirring in his chest during Founders' Day. He knew where stirrings like that eventually led—to a little white chapel and tiny booties.

Whether he'd really make a good husband and father was anybody's guess. He'd been willing to try with Lorelei but when she'd walked out on their wedding, he'd started to wonder if maybe God's will was involved in keeping him single. The past ten years of his life had been wonderful but he'd been branded by the first fourteen, and that scar wasn't going to go away. Even if he could somehow trust himself not to emulate his memories, he wasn't sure he would be enough to make a woman stay. His first mother had abandoned him. Lorelei had literally run from him. Despite Lettie's affection, he kept wondering when she'd reach her limit and decide she didn't want him. He'd spent a year away from home and she hadn't forgotten him. It was practically unfathomable.

Meanwhile, Lawson and Ellie had figured out the best way to avoid the town's tricks was to simply avoid the town itself. So far, so good, but now it seemed the town had come to them and not at all in the way they'd expected. Chris pulled his horse to a stop. Lawson drove the stake into the ground with one last swing then stood to greet the man since he was closest. "Hello, Chris."

Chris dismounted then turned to greet Lawson with a wary look. "Hello, Lawson. I'd like to see Nathan in private, if you don't mind."

Lawson nodded then turned to Nathan for direction. "Why don't you go get Ellie and tell her to meet us in the house?" Nathan suggested.

"Yes, sir."

"Thanks, Lawson."

Lawson waved off Nathan's thanks then made the long walk to the barn in search of Ellie. He found her near the back in the stall with a mare that was due to foal in the next few weeks. Her hands were carefully examining the mare's stomach. She looked up when he neared and he propped his boot on the stall's gate. "You have a visitor."

"I do?" She tilted her head curiously. "Who is it?"

"Christian Johansen," he said, carefully pronouncing each syllable.

"Why didn't he just come inside?" She gave the mare one last pat then climbed the few rungs of the gate until she was able to sit on top of it. She lifted her legs over the gate then pushed herself around to face him.

He tilted back his Stetson to look up at her. "It isn't that kind of a visit."

She braced her palms against the wooden railing beneath her. "What kind of visit is it, then?"

"Why don't you just open the gate and walk out?" he asked when she began to lean forward as if ready to jump down.

His question made her hesitate long enough to set her off balance. Her hands began to slip from the railing. He caught her around the waist and carefully lowered her down to keep her from tumbling the rest of the way. She found her footing then leaned back, accidentally trapping his hands between her waist and the stall gate behind her. Her green eyes sparkled as she looked up at him. "That wouldn't be nearly as exciting."

"Probably not," he admitted as he tried to ignore the way his heartbeat increased.

"What kind of visit wouldn't let Chris come to the barn?"

"A courting kind of visit." Grateful for the reminder, he shifted her weight forward just long enough to reclaim his hands, then took a large step back. Ellie looked positively perturbed.

"You're kidding me, right?"

"Nope. He's talking with Nathan and is going to meet you in the house. You should clean yourself up. You have a dirt smudge on your cheek." He gestured to the affected area. She lifted her shoulder and wiped her cheek on her shirt. That only left more residue. He grinned. "There's your problem."

He lifted her chin to the side then carefully wiped the smudges from her cheek with his handkerchief. He stuffed the handkerchief back in his pocket, released her chin and stepped back. "That's better. Now you'd better get in there."

Her green eyes sought his for a long moment before she smiled. "Yes, sir."

Ellie and Kate disappeared into the parlor to whisper together. Lawson figured he might as well stick around and get a drink of water before he headed back into the heat. He had just poured himself a cup when Nathan and Kate's oldest child, Timothy, burst through the back door. "I was digging up potatoes. That makes a man awfully thirsty."

"It sure does, partner." Lawson handed him the cup and poured himself another. "Slug that down. I bet it will help."

"Thanks." The dark-haired boy showed his gaptoothed grin and did just that.

The front door opened and Lawson heard Nathan and Chris enter. Chris went immediately into the parlor while Nathan joined them in the kitchen. "Looks like the men are taking over the kitchen. Kate's going to stay in the room with them."

"Chris, if you came about that silly list, you should know that I'm not going to talk about it anymore."

Lawson's eyebrows rose at the faint but clear sound of Ellie's voice, then he stared into the hall that separated the kitchen from the parlor. He looked at Nathan. The man shrugged. "There are thin walls in the old part of the house."

Lawson grinned. "No kidding."

Timothy frowned. "Who was that man you were walking with?"

"I didn't come here for the list, Ellie. I came here for you."

"That was Chris."

Ellie's voice sounded in response but Lawson couldn't hear what she said because Timothy started talking. "That didn't look like Chris. That looked like some kind of fancy man all gussied up."

Lawson laughed. Nathan shook his head. "Chris got all gussied up because he came to court Ellie."

Timothy turned to Lawson. "I thought you were courting her. At least, that's what the other kids say at school."

"Those were just rumors," Lawson said. "Don't believe them. You'd know for sure if I was courting your aunt."

"How?"

"You'd see me doing it, kiddo."

"I can't hear—" Nathan complained before he could catch himself. He turned to Timothy. "How about a piece of your ma's cake? You can have some if you're very quiet."

Lawson shook his head. "Shameless."

"Ellie, I've wanted to court you for a year now."

"Why didn't you?"

"I knew you thought we were only friends. I don't want to be only friends anymore. I know you're courting with Lawson and I respect that, but I couldn't go any longer without letting you know how I feel about you. I wanted you to know that before you did something you couldn't take back."

"For the last time, I am not engaged to Lawson." There was a pause, then her voice became gentler. "You've been such a good friend to me—"

"But it could change into something better if you gave us a chance."

"No, I honestly can't imagine us being anything more than just friends. I see you like a brother. Nothing more."

Nathan gave a nod of approval.

"You said the same thing about Lawson."

"I know, and I'm not going to marry Lawson, either."

"Does he know that?"

"Yep." Lawson nodded just as Ellie said, "Goodness, yes."

"Then why not—"

"Chris, let's forget all of this and go on as we always have."

"Poor man," Lawson said while Ellie said goodbye to Chris. "That has to hurt."

Nathan nodded. "That's about what I expected but I did warn him. I guess that means you and Ellie are still on the road to matrimony."

Lawson shook his head at Nathan's teasing. "For the

record, when I asked she said 'no' so there is no possible way we're engaged or courting."

Ellie breezed into the kitchen to grab Kate's mending basket. "It would have served you right if I had said yes. What would you have done then?"

He shrugged nonchalantly as he returned her challenge with his own. "Picked out a ring."

"Oh, sure." She breathed in disbelief but that uncertain look in her eye told him she'd picked up on that slight vein of truth in his voice. "We would have one-upped each other right to the altar."

"Probably."

"Well, if you gentlemen are done eavesdropping, you should probably get back to work." She sent them a knowing look over her shoulder before she breezed out of the room.

Yep, she had them figured out, all right. He turned to share a chagrinned grimace with Nathan only to find the man scrutinizing him thoughtfully. Lawson cleared his throat then decided he'd better follow Ellie's advice before Nathan asked him to explain that comment about the ring. He wasn't sure he wanted to explain it to himself.

Chapter Five

Ellie carefully slid her hand down Delilah's leg until she reached the mare's foot. She gave it a little squeeze and Delilah immediately kicked up her leg so Ellie could clean out her hoof. The horse leaned into Ellie's side then began nipping at the ribbon she'd used to tie back her hair. Ellie pushed the horse away with her shoulder. "Stop it, silly. You're going to topple both of us over."

She heard Nathan's confident steps pound toward her on the barn floor. "Ellie, you have another visitor."

She glanced up in surprise. It had been two days since her last visitor. Frankly, she'd been stunned by Chris's attempt to woo her. She hoped she hadn't hurt him with her reply. She knew how saddening it could be to discover that someone you were interested in saw you only as a sibling. After all, that was the story of her life in this town. She let out a world-weary sigh then released Delilah's hoof and straightened up. "Who is it this time?"

Nathan grinned wryly and opened the gate to the

stall, knowing better than to give her the option to climb over it. "I guess you'll find out when you see him."

She glanced back at him for some clue but he was already striding past her out of the barn. She followed him into the sunlight. It took a moment for her to realize the whole Rutledge family and Lawson had gathered to watch the proceedings. The man wasn't waiting for her inside like Chris had. Instead, he sat on the top of his wagon with a piece of hay stuck in his mouth. Ellie barely contained the urge to groan. "Hello, Mr. Turner."

"Call me Donovan." He jumped down from the wagon to grab her hand. He shook it up and down repeatedly as his eyes wandered across her face as though memorizing her every feature.

She carefully pulled her hand from his sweaty palm and attempted to smile sweetly. "I don't suppose you're here to buy a horse?"

"No, ma'am. I heard you got yourself engaged to this fellow, but I won't believe it until I see it." Donovan threw a frown at Lawson then grasped her left hand in both of his. He stared at it for a long moment before bursting into a grin. "There's nothing there."

Ellie sighed. "I know."

She jumped when he let out a whoop of joy then rolled her eyes, which caused her nieces and nephew to giggle. Suddenly he was herding her toward his wagon. Literally. He just turned toward her and started walking so she began backing up until he stopped at the front of the wagon. She glanced past him to meet Nathan's gaze. He stepped closer to the wagon to keep an eye on them.

Donovan reclaimed her attention by placing a hand on her arm. "Darlin', I've got something here that will make you wonder what you ever saw in that fellow."

"Really, Donovan?" She glanced past him to Lawson. He didn't look particularly concerned, with that poorly concealed half smile on his face. Then again, why should he be? He was just there to watch the show like everyone else.

"This is for you."

He reached under the wagon seat and pulled out a small, white piglet with black spots.

She stared at it for a long moment then lifted her gaze to Donovan's pale gray eyes. "You brought me a pig?"

"Yes, ma'am. I sure did." Her nieces squealed in delight but Donovan sent a glare over his shoulder at the sound of Lawson's disbelieving laugh. "It's the best of the litter. I thought you could use it on the farm."

She bit her lip to keep from laughing then couldn't stop the incredulous smile that followed. "That's very thoughtful, but I can't accept a gift like that."

"Sure you can."

She shook her head. "I'm afraid I can't because I'm not going to let you court me. You're a very nice man but I just don't feel that way about you."

He dropped his head and pulled the piglet closer. "Shucks, ma'am. I know that you feel that way now. I just had to take a chance and let you know how I felt so's I can try to change your mind." Each time he spoke, the sleeping pig's ears jerked toward the sound. The man lifted his head to stare at her. "I've watched you at church, Ms. O'Brien, and your faith is inspiring."

"That's nice of you to say." She glanced over his shoulder to meet Nathan's suspicious gaze.

"I watch you every time you come to town. Sometimes I even follow you a little. It always brightens my day to see you."

"That's…" She paused. *Very strange.* "Something you probably shouldn't do. Follow me around, I mean. You should stop."

"Yes, ma'am, I understand." He glanced down at the pig then thrust it under her nose. "You should still take the pig."

"I don't think—" She stopped trying to reason when he lifted one of her arms and slid the pig into it. "Oh, well, if you're sure."

"I'm positive. It's yours. No strings attached. Just because you're you." He smiled hopefully. "If you like, I can stop by to check on it—"

She cut him off with a shake of her hand. "If you leave it, that's it."

"I reckon that's all right." He patted the pig on its head. "Cute little fella, isn't he?"

She glanced down at the animal in her arms and smiled. "He is cute and very little. Thank you."

When she glanced up she found Donovan was still watching her. "Yes, sir. The man who takes you for a wife is going to be a mighty lucky man."

Nathan must have seen that as his cue because he stepped forward. "Donovan, I think you and I should have a talk about what's appropriate when it comes to young ladies."

Ellie slipped away just as Kate and her children stepped forward to look at the pig. Kate's wary eyes darted to Donovan as her children crooned to the animal. "He's a strange man. You'd do well to stay away from him. He may be harmless, but it pays to be careful."

"I've been doing my best."

"Well, Nathan will be on high alert, too, as I'm sure Lawson will."

"I appreciate that." She left the piglet in an empty stall under the watchful eyes of the children then went to finish Delilah's hooves. She found Lawson had beaten her to it. "You don't have to do that. I can finish what I started."

"It's fine," he said, but didn't glance up from his work. "Maybe you could start on Samson."

"Delilah was the last one." She propped her boot on the gate of the stall and watched him work, noticing the controlled power that surged through each motion.

"This will only take a minute." He released Delilah's hoof then straightened to meet her gaze. "It looks like our supposed engagement lit a fire under some of your suitors."

She crossed her arms along the stall's gate and leaned against it. "It's awfully silly."

"Silly?" He eyed her carefully, then turned away to run his hand down Delilah's back leg to get the horse to lift her foot. "You know I think I've got you figured out, Ms. O'Brien. The ruse is up."

She frowned at him in confusion. "What are you talking about?"

"You don't really want to get married."

"Of course I do. That's the most ridiculous statement I've ever heard."

"So you say." He finished cleaning Delilah's hoof and turned to face her. "Yet, over the past few days, you've managed to discourage two completely different types of men."

She shrugged nonchalantly. "So what if I did? I didn't like them, that's all."

Lawson rubbed his chin in thoughtful speculation. Delilah nudged him in the back, forcing him to take two steps toward her. "What about Chris?"

She narrowed her eyes. "What about him?"

"He said his feelings for you changed a long time ago." He braced his hands on either side of her arms and tilted his head. "Are you saying you really didn't notice?"

"I had no idea," she said honestly.

"I think that leads us to the crux of the matter."

She raised her brows expectantly. "Which would be?"

He gave a slow smile, and shook his head. "You, Ellie O'Brien, are afraid to take off the blinders you've fashioned."

"What blinders?"

"The ones that keep you from seeing yourself as everyone else sees you—as a kind, beautiful, spontaneous woman."

She stared at him in awe. He thought she was beautiful? Hadn't he always thought of her as one of the boys? Hadn't he always seen her as a surrogate little sister? Apparently, somehow that had changed. He now saw her as beautiful—a woman. She swallowed. Why did that send her heart galloping in her chest?

He carefully guided her chin up until she was forced to meet the knowing smile in his eyes. "You're the kind of woman who wouldn't have any trouble finding herself a husband, if she didn't try so hard to cross every suitable man off her list or give him away to her friends."

She didn't have anything to say because she'd suddenly realized why those relatively suitable men had seemed so unsuitable. She realized it because she was staring the reason right in the face. She, Ellie O'Brien, had a crush on Lawson Williams.

She barely withheld a groan. She had no idea how long this had been going on but she needed it to stop. Talk about embarrassing! He obviously didn't feel the same way. He thought proposing to her was so ridiculous that he'd turned it into a joke! Just because he said she was a beautiful woman didn't mean he considered her a woman he'd want to pursue. Goodness, he'd only been trying to encourage her. It didn't mean anything. As though to confirm her assessment, he stepped back and shook his head. "You need to give one of those men on your list a chance, Ellie."

She gathered her wits enough to lift an impervious eyebrow at his statement. "No, I don't."

He grinned. "Then I stand by my other statement. You aren't really searching for a husband. So what are you searching for?"

"Love," she said softly. "The kind of love that Nathan has for Kate and Sean has for Lorelei. I *do* want that, Lawson. I just haven't found a man who can love me like that or at least a man that I want to be loved by. I think if I had that, why, I might be a different person altogether."

He frowned at her. "What's wrong with the person you are now?"

"Do I really need to list my faults for you? I'd rather not." Especially since some of them she couldn't even admit to herself. Nevertheless, she'd been achingly aware of them lately…ever since Mrs. Greene mentioned consequences from the mistakes Ellie had made in the past—whatever they were.

"No, you don't have to do that," he said, then shook his head. "I still think you're selling yourself short in many respects."

She backed away from the stall's gate so he could walk through it. "Well, I think I just have a very clear view of my weaknesses."

A very *clear view,* she thought with a sideways look at Lawson as they walked to the corral. She planned to overcome one of them as quickly as possible to save both of them from embarrassment.

"Lawson, are you decent? Your parents came early to help set up for the party and want to see your cabin."

He froze at the sound of Ellie's voice as he glanced around in a panic at his messy cabin. Why hadn't he folded his clothes instead of dumping them in the chair near the cold fireplace? He probably should have swept out the dirt he'd tracked in. "Stall them for a minute, will you? This place is a mess."

An awkward silence seeped through the closed front door. He sighed and grabbed his shirt. "They're standing right next to you, aren't they?"

"Yep." Her muffled voice continued cheerily, "Lawson has been such a big help setting up for Maddie and Jeff's engagement party. I kept finding one more little thing for him to do so I'm afraid I've made him late getting ready."

He heard his parents respond but didn't bother to try to decipher what they were saying. Instead, he stuffed his clothes into the trunk at the end of his bed, straightened his bedding, pushed the chair under the table and hoped they wouldn't notice the dirt on the floor. He opened the door as he tucked his shirt into his pants. "Welcome to my humble home."

Lettie stepped inside wearing a pert little blue bonnet over her dark brown hair and carrying a basket that filled the cabin with the smell of freshly baked apple pie. "What a cute little cabin."

Doc chuckled as he clasped Lawson on the shoulder. "Lettie, that isn't exactly what a man wants to hear about his first home as a bachelor."

Ellie leaned against the doorway to peer inside. "Well, it should be cute. I picked out all the decorations."

"Did you?" Lettie asked with new interest.

"She did. I'm afraid all I added was the mud."

Doc nodded proudly. "That's the best part."

Ellie frowned, then stepped past him to sit at the table and pick up the planter filled with brown flowers. "You didn't water them."

"Was I supposed to?" He was quickly distracted when Lettie opened his cabinets to fill them with all sorts of colorful concoctions in glass jars. His stomach gave a low rumble of appreciation. "Preserves?"

"Of course." She set the pie on the counter next.

Doc sat in the chair now free of Lawson's laundry. "It's been a couple of weeks now. Are you're still happy you resigned from the Rangers?"

"Yes, sir."

Lettie looked relieved then straightened her shoulders in pride. "I think my boy is ready to settle down."

The significant wink she tossed Ellie's way wasn't lost on Lawson. He coughed to cover his laugh then shot a glance at Ellie to see her reaction. She rolled her eyes at them both. "Don't smirk at me, Lawson Williams. Talk to your mother."

He turned to Lettie and found her looking absurdly innocent. "Now, Ma, just because I came home doesn't mean I'll marry the first girl who asks me."

Ellie gasped and straightened in her chair. "Who's asking?"

"I haven't even thought about looking for a wife yet."

Ms. Lettie frowned. "Why ever not? Every man needs roots. Doc and I have done our best to provide some for you these past years but you deserve more than that. You deserve a family of your own."

Lawson met his ma's gaze directly. "Not every man is supposed to have a family of his own. I'd even go so far as to say that some men shouldn't."

Lettie shook her head at Lawson's statement. "Well, you are the type of man who *should* have a family. You'd make a wonderful husband and father. Isn't that right, Ellie?"

"I think I'd better go change before the other guests start showing up." She rose from the table to stand in front of him. Her dancing green eyes captured his. "Be on your guard, my friend. The whole town is coming to this shindig. This is just the beginning."

She handed him a clean sock she'd somehow managed to pick up, then waved at his parents before she sashayed out the door. Lettie delicately cleared her throat, making him aware that he was still watching that vacant door. He felt a dull heat creep across his jaw. He pulled another sock from his trunk then grabbed his boots to sit down at the table. As he put them on, Lettie served the pie. "She's getting to you, isn't she?"

He glanced up to discover that she was enjoying a

lot more about this situation than the pie she was eating. He glanced at Doc for help. The man was watching him over the top of his spectacles as he would a patient in an examination room. Lawson stomped his foot into the boot a little harder than necessary. "Come on, Pa. Y'all can't gang up on me here."

Doc walked over to stand behind his wife and gave her shoulder a little squeeze. "It's obvious you and Ellie have a special connection. Don't tell me it's just because y'all are friends. There's more to it than that. The whole town can see it, even if y'all can't admit it."

He leaned onto the table with his elbows and rubbed his jaw. "Fine. I admit that I'm attracted to her but I wasn't planning on doing anything about it. Why do I get the feeling that y'all think I should?"

"Eat your pie, dear." Lettie pushed the plate closer to him as she'd done many times in the past. Since there was never a problem that a slice of one of her pies couldn't help solve, he did as he was told. She set her plate aside and leaned closer. "I know that Ellie thinks she has the corner on matchmaking in this town but what some people, Ellie included, may not realize is that she learned everything she knows from me. Therefore, the true question here is not 'What do we think *you* should do?' but rather 'What can *we* do for *you?*'"

His fork lowered to his plate. His eyes widened then flew from Lettie to Doc then back again. "Are y'all suggesting that I— That we—"

He didn't want to finish his question because the answer was on their faces as plain as day. They wanted his permission to matchmake. No, they wanted more than that. They wanted his full cooperation. An echo of Lettie's words whispered through his heart. *You are*

*the type of man who should have a family. You'd make
a wonderful husband and father...*

He wasn't sure if he could believe that completely
but if he ever wanted those words to describe him, he'd
have to start somewhere. Maybe this was that place.
Maybe this was the start of the "someday" he'd always
longed for where he'd have his own family—a real family with someone. They weren't talking about a vague
"someone," though. They were talking about Ellie. This
was the same girl he'd pushed off the top of the waterfall more than once. The girl who'd helped him study
for school. The woman who could suddenly make his
heart race with a mere touch.

"She doesn't feel that way about me." He wasn't even
aware that he'd stated that out loud until Doc responded.

"How will you know for sure if you don't take a
chance?"

"I don't want to ruin our friendship."

"Son, you've always made me proud with the way
you haven't let fear hold you back from doing the right
thing," Doc said gently. "Don't give in to fear now. Any
relationship worth having is worth taking a risk."

Quiet descended as everyone waited for him to make
his decision. He swallowed then gave a shallow nod.
"All right. I'm going to do it. I'll pull back the moment
I sense she's the least bit uncomfortable but I want to
see where this goes. Does that make me crazy?"

Lettie shook her head. "That makes you brave."

The rich timbre of Chris Johansen's fiddle filled the
air with a lively melody that nearly drowned out the low
crackle of the fire. One last drop of juice from Ellie's
piece of sausage sizzled in the flames before she pulled

out her skewer. She skirted the fire to sit next to Lorelei on a wooden bench and fanned her food to help it cool. An odd look crossed Lorelei's face. "You do know where that's from, don't you?"

"The kitchen."

"I mean—originally."

Her gaze trailed down to the kebab. Suddenly, she realized she was probably eating one of her piglet's cousins. She set the skewer onto a discarded plate. "I think I'm full."

Lorelei giggled. "I'm sorry. I shouldn't have done that."

"Don't worry. I've had too much food already." Ellie pulled in a deep breath as she surveyed the happy scene in the field around her. Folks stood or sat in groups while Maddie and Jeff shared a kebab near the outskirts of the firelight. Lorelei leaned toward her. "I heard Chris came calling. How did that go?"

She pulled the list from her pocket. "I crossed him off the list."

"So...not well."

"It wasn't that bad. It just wasn't right." She bit her lip and glanced around the field. "When I cross someone off I try to match them with someone else, but I haven't figured out Chris's match yet."

"It will come to you." Lorelei leaned over to steal a peek at the list. "It looks like the field is narrowing."

"Rapidly. Most of the men left are the ones I don't know as well."

"Who is that man who came with Amy?"

Ellie glanced around until she found the man talking with Lawson a bit closer to the house. "That's Ethan Larue. He's staying at the boardinghouse—that must be how Amy knows him. I met him in town the other day. He seems nice but I don't think he's planning to stick around long so I didn't put him on the list."

"Is Lawson on it now?"

She shook her head then changed her mind and shrugged. "I guess it's only fair to add him. He deserves to find a good match as much as anyone else— maybe even a little more."

Lorelei set her elbow on the back of the bench and rested her cheek in her palm as she leaned in. "Who would you match him with? Sophia?"

Ellie's gaze darted to Chris's sister. "I had Sophia in mind for someone else."

"Helen?"

Ellie shook her head. The schoolteacher would be a good match for someone with children. *Of course!* She smiled then put the woman's initials by a name on her list. "No."

"You?"

She stilled. Her eyes shot to Lawson. The firelight painted him in shades of gold simultaneously softening and contouring his handsome features. He caught her watching. Their eyes held for a moment before he flashed a grin and winked. Her heart lurched down a few rib bones before fluttering back into place. "I don't remember him being quite so…"

"Attractive?" Lorelei laughed softly. "So you don't mind if your family and friends do a little matchmaking?"

"For my part, I'll admit that I wouldn't mind. But what makes you think he'd want to be with me? Everyone in town's all but thrown me into his arms and he hasn't shown any interest yet."

"Hmm. Do you think we're taking the wrong approach?"

Ellie started to argue that that wasn't what she'd meant, but then she stopped to think about it. "Well, that may be part of it. Blatant suggestions like we've been getting tend to make couples more resistant—at least when they're together. Now, if they're apart, then it helps to encourage the idea of a romance. Mainly, y'all just need to be less obvious about pretty much everything."

"Got it." Lorelei gave her a parting smile then hurried away as if she couldn't wait to start coordinating everything.

Ellie chuckled. *Well, Lord, I asked for a little help in finding a match for myself and You sent me an entire town. I sure do appreciate it. Now if only I could convince myself it will do any good.*

Chapter Six

Lawson drowned his bemused smile with another gulp of lemonade as he glanced at the man beside him. He had no idea what Ethan Larue was talking about. He'd stopped paying attention the moment Ellie looked up and smiled at him from across the fire. Her golden hair was swept up and away from her neck, leaving her shoulders bare save for the pale green cap sleeves of her dress. He wasn't used to seeing her all fancied up like this. Normally she wore a simple blouse and split skirt around the ranch and left any fancier fare for Sunday services. He'd called her beautiful when they were in the barn, but now she was truly stunning. And very distracting.

Guilt pulled his focus back to the conversation just in time to realize that Ethan was staring at him expectantly. Lawson grasped for some clue of what the man had been saying. He came up empty. He cleared his throat. "Well, now. I couldn't say."

Ethan nodded thoughtfully. "It would probably be hard to tell without an official census. There are plenty of interesting people here, though, and they've all been so kind and welcoming. It makes a man think about settling down and starting a new life."

"Are you planning to settle here, then?"

"No. I'm not exactly the settling type." He glanced out at the field and frowned as if looking right into his past. "My mother died when I was eight. I lost my father when I was thirteen. I was put in an orphanage a few years before I was able to leave. I learned a long time ago that it's pointless to put down roots."

"I understand. I'm—"

"You understand?" Ethan gave a bitter laugh. "I appreciate your sympathy but—"

"No." Lawson met his gaze unflinchingly. "I said I understood and I meant it."

"Really?" A slightly victorious smile pulled at the man's lips for an instant before he tempered it. "Tell me about it."

Lawson stilled. Why did he just feel as though he'd just walked into a trap? Had Ethan been waiting to hear Lawson's story? But why would he? Lawson scanned the man's features, looking for anything familiar in them. As a Ranger, he'd made his share of enemies. Enemies who'd do a good deal to learn his background and find out where he was vulnerable. But Lawson couldn't find anything there to legitimize his suspicions. He'd give Ethan, if that was his real name, what he wanted for now.

He began with a grim smile. "I don't remember a time when my parents weren't drinking or fighting. When I say fighting, I don't just mean yelling or screaming words no child should hear. I mean…" He swallowed against the emotion that rose in his throat. "Let's just say there was a lot of abuse involved. Most of that time is just a blurry memory. I try to keep it that way."

Ethan gave a curt nod but didn't try to interrupt.

"I must have been about nine or ten—maybe eleven—" he hated that he could never be completely sure "—before they left me."

"What do you mean, 'they left me'?"

Lawson was startled awake by a banging on the door. He sat up and watched the shadow of his mother's petite frame race across the white sheet that separated his little corner from the rest of the cabin. His father's shadow staggered into the room. His familiar walk seemed a little off—almost listing. His mother gasped and guided his father into a chair. "What happened? You're bleeding something fierce."

He groaned. "You aren't drunk, are you, woman?"

"I had a couple but I'm not drunk yet."

"Good. I need you to bandage me up then we've got to get out of here."

"The job went bad?"

"Course it did. Why do you think I'm bleeding like a stuck pig?"

"I guess that means you won't get paid. The rent's due in the morning. Maybe you should have thought about that before you messed up whatever you were supposed to do."

"The rent! I could have the sheriff on my tail and you want to talk to me about the rent!"

Lawson sighed and snuggled back under the thread-bare cover with no other choice than to listen to another argument. "You get that look out of your eye. Don't even think of hitting me tonight or I'll push you out the

*house and let you die on the street where you belong!
Do you really think the sheriff is after you?"*

*"Probably so. They couldn't pin anything on me,
though. I wasn't sloppy enough to leave evidence."*

*"Don't be a fool. That hole in your side is all the
evidence they need."*

*"That's why I say we've got to leave here and tonight.
I'm in the clear if no one sees this."*

"What makes you think I'm coming with you?"

"Do you want to be put in jail as an accessory?"

*"Accessory to what? No, don't answer that. I'm com-
ing. Let me get the kid."*

"No. The kid stays."

*Lawson's eyes flew open. He saw his ma pause be-
fore she set the suitcase on the table. "Are you crazy?
We can't just leave him here."*

*"He'd slow us down. Have you looked at the boy
lately? He's skinnier than a ragweed and twice as puny.
We can't even provide for ourselves in the best of times.
How are we going to provide for him on the run? Send
him to your family. They'll take him in, won't they?"*

*"I suppose they'll have to. I know, I'll write a letter
and pin it on him. That will explain everything. Have
you got any money I can leave with him?"*

"I've got a dollar."

*Lawson pretended to be asleep when his mother
stepped through the sheet. It only took a second for
her to pin something on his raggedy shirt. She paused
then whispered, "I know you're awake. You have to
trust me. This is for the best. You know how mean your
pa gets when he drinks and you know how silly I get.
Neither of us is getting better. Look at me, Lawson."*

He slowly did as she commanded. Her bright blue

eyes stared as though she was memorizing his every feature. "I'm no good but I love you. That's why I'd rather see you gone than bleeding to death from a beating one day. Promise me you won't be like your father or me. Promise."

"Yes, Ma," he whispered.

He watched her sweep from the room. Her shadowy form grabbed the suitcase then disappeared. He jumped from the bed and slipped around the white sheet in time to see his father turn to close the front door. The man caught sight of him and hesitated for just a moment. Their eyes held. "You stay inside tonight. You hear me?"

Lawson leaned against the wall then gave a single nod in response. The door closed. He stared at it for a while. His gaze swept the disheveled but empty cabin. Then, turning on his heel, he slipped back into his cot, pulled the covers over his head and waited for daylight.

"I don't think I ever believed my mother's reasons for leaving me behind." He shrugged. "Whatever they used to justify it in their own minds, they abandoned me."

"That's awful."

"That's just the beginning. The landlord was a big man and I was scared of him so I ran before he could come for the rent. I couldn't read the note they left. I was afraid if I showed it to someone else they'd send me to an orphanage like the one my father said he'd take me to if I was bad. I wandered from town to town doing whatever jobs I could manage and stealing food when I couldn't get work. Let me tell you, Ethan, you lived a charmed life in that orphanage. People don't treat children well in bawdy Western towns. I've got the scars to prove it. Some of them are still visible."

He stared at the man who would no longer meet his gaze. "Is that enough or do you want to know more?"

"That's enough."

"Good." Lawson was quiet for a moment then decided to take a risk. "Now, who are you going to give that information to next?"

Ethan tensed, his startled eyes flying back up to meet Lawson's.

Lawson smirked in satisfaction. Man, he was good. He leaned forward to press his advantage. "You're pretty good but you aren't professional. Your face gives too much away. You should work on that."

"I don't know what you're talking about."

Lawson laughed. "Oh, come on, Ethan. I know you're digging around for someone. Tell me who it is."

Ethan just stared at him. "I'm not digging for anyone. I shouldn't have asked. I didn't know it would be so painful for you. Don't let it ruin your evening. I'm not going to let my past cheat me out of a dance with one of those lovely ladies over there. Excuse me."

Lawson didn't believe him for a moment, but Ethan ignored his silence and walked toward Amy and her sisters. Meanwhile, Lawson valiantly pushed away the heaviness that settled around his soul. He never went through a visit to his past unscathed.

Sean appeared at his side with Lorelei in tow. "I convinced Chris to play a few more dances before putting away his fiddle. The rest is up to you, my friend."

It took Lawson a moment to figure out what Sean was talking about. "My parents told you about our conversation in the cabin, didn't they?"

Sean grinned. "Why do you think they brought it up?"

"Of all the—" He shot a frown at his parents then slid his wary gaze to Ellie. "That was supposed to be private."

Sean slipped an arm around his wife as she swayed in time with the lively music. "You agreed to let us help so they had to tell us."

"Don't worry. Ellie won't know a thing about it." Lorelei winked at him as she tugged her husband toward the circle of dancers. "Now, go get her before someone else does."

"What have I gotten myself into?" he mumbled as he searched for Ellie in the crowd. He found her already dancing with Clayton Sheppard, a young farmer who was a good friend of Jeff's. However, when Clay caught sight of him, the man led Ellie closer to Lawson. Clay sent him a questioning look, which Lawson returned with a nod. Clay gave Ellie one last twirl, which placed her right in front of Lawson.

They both stilled along with pretty much everyone else on the field. Ellie's gaze held his before it slid away to take in the fact that everyone was waiting for something to happen. "What? Are they expecting me to kiss you or something?"

He swallowed a chuckle. "Well?"

Her eyes widened until she realized he was waiting for her to place her hand in his. "Is that an offer to dance?"

"It is."

She frowned. "We're giving people all sorts of wrong ideas. You know that, don't you?"

"Can't give people something everybody already has so I reckon we might as well have a little fun."

She considered this for a moment then made a show of resting a hand on his shoulder and placing the other in his. His free arm went around the small of her back. They waited for the right moment in the music before he led her into a quick two-step to Chris's robust rendition of "Cotton-Eyed Joe." A cheer echoed across the field but it was Ellie's warm smile that chased away the heavy memory of his past.

Ellie pulled in a refreshing breath of dawn air as she urged Starlight into canter through the woods toward the farm. It still smelled like rain from the heavy deluge that had lulled her to sleep last night. She had awakened before dawn and finished her chores in the barn early so she would have time to ride Starlight before getting ready for church.

She burst from the woods near the old cabin where Lawson was staying. She didn't see any movement inside of it so she assumed he must already be doing his chores. She guided Starlight across the cleared land toward the barn. Suddenly a small white object dashed from the barn toward the pasture. She leaned over the saddle horn to stare. Was that her pig? It was. Her breath caught in her throat. It must have escaped. She urged Starlight faster. Her shout pierced the still morning air. "Lawson! Lawson!"

She pulled Starlight to a stop outside the pasture fence then vaulted over it. The pig streaked toward her, running in a zigzag pattern. She heard Lawson call her name and glanced up in time to see him running out of the barn. Good. She needed help catching it. She refocused her attention on the pig. The little thing slowed to a trot and stared up at her with a wary eye. She took a calm step toward it. It took off again. She whirled and chased after it.

It ran straight toward the tree line. Her eyes widened. If it went into the woods she would never find it. Suddenly the pig turned and ran straight up the middle of the field away from the woods and the few horses Lawson must have already let out to pasture. Relief filled her. Mud began to cling to the bottom of her skirt, making it harder to walk. She stopped for a moment to catch her breath. The pig stopped almost immediately. She narrowed her eyes. The pig stood frozen. She stepped toward it. The pig began walking away. She stopped. The pig stopped. She let out a huff of frustration. "Great."

"Ellie, stop!"

She glanced behind her to see Lawson closing in on her. Three horses followed on his heels. "Good," she yelled back. She motioned him to her left. "You go that way."

"No."

She frowned at him over her shoulder then started running. The pig started running. It veered sideways so she tried to cut it off. She was getting closer. "Now, Lawson! Go that way quickly."

A hand caught her arm and she screamed. She'd been so focused on the pig she hadn't realized Lawson was behind her. He pulled her to a stop. She fought to free herself from his grasp. Finally, she pinned him with a glare. She said between gasps, "You were...supposed to...go that way!"

He shook his head. "I'm trying to tell you. Don't chase it."

"Of course I'm going to chase it." She pulled in a

deep breath. "It's my pig. I don't want it to escape." She swallowed. "Now stop talking and help me."

"But Ellie, I'm trying to tell you that the silly pig—"

"The pig." She gasped. She turned from him to scan the field for the pig. It had stopped running to wallow in a mud puddle about ten feet away.

"Ellie—"

"Hush!"

"Fine. Do it your way."

"I will," she breathed as she carefully approached the pig. It was apparently too busy wallowing in the mud puddle to notice. Mud began to creep up the sides of her boots. It dragged at the hem of her skirts. She hiked it up several inches. Each time she pulled her boot from the mud it made a loud sucking sound.

She froze as the pig's ears jumped. She took another large step as it gave one last good wallow, then turned onto its stomach to stare at her. It was so close. She diverted her eyes so she wouldn't threaten it. Then she knelt. The pig stood to its feet and took a step toward her. Her eyes widened. This was too easy. She reached out to it very slowly. The pig took another step toward her.

Suddenly it tried to bolt past her. She lunged in a twisting motion toward it. She managed to get one hand on it before it slipped through her fingers. She landed facedown in the mud. She lay there for a stunned second before she managed to push herself onto her forearms. She glanced up in time to see its curly-tailed behind racing back toward the barn.

She closed her eyes. She heard the squish-pop of Lawson walking toward her through the mud. Finally, he stopped in front of her. She eyed his muck-covered boots for a moment. Pushing her stomach away from the mud, she didn't even bother to stand up. Instead, she plopped onto her bottom and braced her arms behind her to look up at Lawson.

She lifted her eyebrows, daring him to comment. He did an admirable job of keeping his laughter in check, though he couldn't stop the way his golden eyes danced. He knelt beside her as a smile barely tilted the corner of his lips. "I let your pig out every morning. He runs around the pasture for ten minutes then comes back to the barn on his own. He likes the exercise."

"Oh, no." A smile rose unbidden to her lips. A giggle slipped out without her permission. Lawson started chuckling and that just made everything funnier. Her sides began to ache as the tension of the past week seeped out of her. She finally gathered herself enough to send Lawson an expectant look. "Well, don't just sit there. Help me up."

He rose to his feet then extended a hand down to her. He gave a powerful tug that pulled her from the puddle. Mud oozed between their palms, causing her hand to slip from his. She gasped as she nearly tumbled back into the mud, but at the last moment his other arm stole around her waist. He hauled her to his chest and set her feet on the ground.

"That was entirely too much trouble," she muttered against his shirt.

"What?"

She pushed away slightly to look up at him just as he lowered his head to hear her more clearly. They both stilled. Lawson's eyes flashed to hers. Her eyes widened. His arms tightened around her. Her gaze fell to his lips before resting on the top button of his shirt.

The still morning air filled with the sound of slightly winded breaths. "I just... I said—trouble."

"Oh," he said as if her statement made a lick of sense. "You lost your shoes."

It wasn't the best line to give the girl he'd almost kissed but it was the only thing Lawson could think of at the moment. It was a wonder he'd been able to come up with anything at all with her hand pressed against his chest, her lips inches away. Despite the cold mud seeping into his shirt, she felt warm in his arms. He released her and retrieved her boots as slowly as possible to give himself time to think.

Telling his parents—and apparently the whole town with them—that he didn't mind their matchmaking didn't mean he should haul off and kiss the woman two days later. He had to let the matchmakers do their job and warm Ellie up to the concept, first. The idea of pursuing something with Ellie still sent a bolt of fear straight to his chest. His relationship with Lorelei had been easy. They'd both been so disengaged. He'd only experienced a few surface feelings.

That would not be so with Ellie. She was so open with her thoughts and feelings, so full of emotion. She would expect the same warmth and openness from him, which would mean he'd have to let down his guard completely. His past had taught him being that invested in someone wasn't wise. He knew better than to hand out even a piece of his heart without thoughtful consideration. If he did decide to approach Ellie with his heart in his hands, it would be after prayerful deliberation. For now, he'd just handed her the boots.

The question in her eyes made him wonder if she'd

felt the same powerful tension between them or just wondered why he was acting so strange. He needed to pull himself together. "I guess we'd both better get cleaned up."

A confused frown flashed across her lips before she took her boots and began to walk away. She turned to smile at him as she walked backward. "Thank you for trying to stop me."

"That's what—" *friends are for*. He couldn't quite get himself to complete that statement so he just finished with, "You're welcome."

She gave him a jaunty wave and picked her way across the field toward the house. He grabbed his Stetson from the mud where it had fallen a few feet away, hit it against his leg to clean it off then turned to watch her go. He'd learned a long time ago that he could trust God with his heart, but could he trust Ellie? More important, could he trust himself to be the man she deserved—the kind of man she wouldn't walk away from?

Chapter Seven

Kate hadn't even asked why Ellie showed up at the kitchen door covered in mud. She'd just ordered Ellie to wash in the creek and return in her Sunday best in time for church. She'd washed away the mud with little difficulty but she couldn't rid herself of the memory of being in Lawson's arms. She'd been there many times in the past for a hug, so why did that one feel so different? Why did it feel so real? She even imagined for a moment that he might erase the distance between them with a kiss.

Wishful thinking—nothing more, nothing less. That was the same kind of thinking that had led their families to sandwich him next to her in this pew through some rather crafty maneuvering.

Lawson leaned over to whisper beneath the closing hymn of the church service. "Did you say something?"

Had she said that out loud? She just smiled and shook her head. A small hand tugged her skirt. She glanced down at her four-year-old niece, who whispered, "I want to see Aunt Lori play."

Ellie obediently lifted her niece onto her hip so she

could see around the grown-ups to where Lorelei played the piano at the front of the church. Grace rested her curly red head on Ellie's shoulder as Pastor Brightly gave his closing prayer. "Lord, give us the strength to meet life's challenges. Give us discernment as we seek Your will, and courage to perform it. Help us to be a demonstration of love to those around us and to remember that the greatest love of all is found in You. Amen."

Ellie looked up and frowned at Pastor Brightly, then quickly bowed her head when he opened his eyes to smile at the congregation. "Go in peace."

She put her niece down but kept hold of her hand as they followed Lawson and their families toward the sanctuary door. Donovan stood as she passed the aisle where he sat. He held her gaze for a moment then smiled when he looked at Grace. "Do you like children?"

"Yes."

"That's good."

Why can't you be a little less strange? She frowned at him before hurrying on. Mrs. Brightly, the pastor's wife, pulled her into a warm hug when they reached the door of the church. "I hope you're going to help us with the box social next week. You were indispensable at the Founders' Day celebration."

She released Grace to go play with the other children. "I was already planning to come early."

"Perfect!" The woman stepped aside to continue her conversation with Ellie. "Lorelei mentioned you might be willing to help with the children's Sunday school we're trying to start."

"Yes, I told her I was interested in serving as an alternate."

"You'll be wonderful with the children. I'm afraid

we still need one more person. Do you think Lawson might want to help?"

"Lawson?" She looked at Mrs. Brightly a little more closely and realized… *She knows. I wonder who else is aware that I've sanctioned the matchmaking. Probably the whole town.* She felt a telling heat begin to warm her cheeks. "I'll ask him."

Mrs. Brightly gave her arm a squeeze then moved on to the next parishioner. Ellie found Lawson and was surprised when he immediately agreed to help with the Sunday school. Before she had time to question him about it, Rhett appeared in front of them. "Ellie, is Lawson in the Bachelor Club?"

"In the—" She shook her head and blinked at him. "What?"

He passed his hat back and forth between his hands. "I don't know. I made it up because I wanted to know if it's all right to talk about the Bachelor List in front of Lawson."

"Yes!" Lawson's response was entirely too quick and enthusiastic. "I would like to be admitted into the club."

"There is no club."

"As the club's founding member, I welcome you," Rhett replied, ignoring her.

"Please don't make a club." Her protests were in vain because the two men shook hands heartily.

"Thank you. I'm honored." Lawson tipped his head toward Ellie. "We'll need a president."

Rhett grinned. "I nominate Ellie O'Brien."

"No!"

"I second the motion."

"Carried."

Her mouth opened and closed without any sound before she finally managed, "You can't—"

"Madame President," Rhett drawled then gave a slight bow, "I'd like to discuss the match you gave me."

"Who did you get?"

"Amy."

Lawson tilted his head for a moment then nodded. "I could see that happening."

"Well, it isn't. That's the problem. Amy doesn't even know I'm alive."

Ellie glanced at Lawson expectantly.

"Oh, no. I'll leave the advice giving to you, Madame President."

She sighed. "Have you tried talking to her?"

"No." He grimaced at his shoes as though it was all their fault. "I *can't* talk to her. When she's around, my mind freezes up and my words come out all wrong. Do you know what I mean?"

"Yes," she said with certainty as her mind replayed the difficulty she'd had that very morning. Lawson shifted slightly and she suddenly remembered that he was *right there*—listening to her every word. Her eyebrows rose, she bit her lip and dared to slide her gaze to his. He had a bemused expression on his face. She swallowed. "I mean everyone experiences that at some point. After all, it's just a nervous reaction. It doesn't only happen with romantic relationships and…"

When a hint of a half smile played at Lawson's lips, she decided it was best to stop talking altogether.

"How did you overcome it?"

Apparently, I haven't. "I suppose you just have to push through it. Practice. Talk to her about something small and keep it short. Then each time after that, try to increase the length of conversation and the depth of the topic. You'll grow more comfortable over time."

"I can do that."

Ellie smiled. "Yes, you can."

"Thank you, Ellie." He reached down and gave her a hug then shook Lawson's hand before heading across the church lawn. She watched as he hesitated a moment then gathered his courage enough to speak briefly with Amy and Isabelle. She hadn't even realized that she and Lawson had moved closer together, smiling like proud parents as Rhett made his move, until she heard the disapproving sniff behind her.

Ellie knew that sniff—she'd had its disapproval aimed at her through most of her childhood. She pulled in a steeling breath then turned to face Mrs. Greene with a smile. "Good morning."

The woman's eyes darted back and forth between Ellie and Lawson. "Well, isn't this a cozy scene? Are y'all sure y'all aren't hiding an engagement? You can tell me. I'm good at keeping secrets. Isn't that right, Ellie?"

A sick feeling filled Ellie's stomach but she stood taller and lifted her chin. "No, ma'am. It's plain wrong, but thanks for the offer. Have a good day."

She escaped Mrs. Greene's intimidating frown with Lawson in tow. He caught her arm to slow her flight and leaned toward her to ask, "What was that about?"

She shook her head and began walking toward the church without even making a conscious choice to do so. Lawson followed her. "Why is she always rude to you? She seems to get along well enough with the rest of your family these days."

"She hates me." She skirted the church door to walk

around the side to the peaceful grounds behind it. "She's hated me for a very long time."

"Is there a reason for this hatred?"

She glanced at him. "There is but please don't ask me what it is."

They both stilled when they realized where they'd ended up after their brisk walk. Shafts of warm sunlight poured through the canopy of tall oak trees that shaded the quiet cemetery. She didn't have to walk far down the cobblestone path before coming to her parents' headstones. Their deaths were one of the young town's earlier tragedies. She closed her eyes and the storm that had taken their lives raged once more in her memories.

His voice was as hushed as their surroundings seemed to demand. "Ellie, what is going on? What was Mrs. Greene talking about?"

"I don't know. I think it ties back to something bad I did—something about my parents."

"She could be making it up just to make you uncomfortable."

"It's real." Her breath rushed from her lungs with a sigh, leaving her with nothing but a whisper. "I know it's real but I can't remember. I don't want to remember."

"Then don't." His hand gently caught her arm and he turned her away from the grave to face him. "We forget things because we have to in order to move on. It's more than a necessity. It's a gift."

"It doesn't feel like a gift."

His eyes deepened to a troubled olive-brown. "I've tried to forget so many things in my past, Ellie, but the memory of it is like a bruise that never fully healed. Don't wish that on yourself. Let Mrs. Greene live with her memories and her hate while you leave them buried."

A soft smile gradually rose to her lips while his hand fell away. "This reminds me of Pastor Brightly's sermon."

"It does? All I remember is him mentioning something about the sins of the fathers not being visited on the sons."

"Right, but there was something after that. Oh, what did he say?" She pursed her lips as she tried to remember. "It was something like, 'God's grace is experienced…fully experienced…when we have the courage…to believe that the past no longer defines us.'"

He began to lead her to the front of the church. "I've never been that courageous."

"Neither have I." She glanced over her shoulder once more before the cemetery was hidden from her view. "Do you think our lives would be very different if we were?"

"I know mine would be."

She let that answer rest for a moment but her curiosity got the better of her. "How?"

He stilled as a slow revelation seemed to overtake him. For some reason, it twisted the side of his mouth into a frown. Her eyes widened with intrigue. He just looked at her, gave a funny little smile and left her wondering.

Lawson hefted the thick wooden board then held it in the right position for Nathan to pound it into place with his hammer. Thankfully the field had dried enough that they were able to keep working on the new corral fence. Lawson was glad to have a task that didn't take much thought, since his mind was full of Ellie. He'd learned something valuable after that mud bath yesterday. Ellie was attracted to him. Her response to Rhett's question hadn't clued him in to that as much as her reaction to having said it. She'd looked guiltier than a cat swimming in a bucket of milk and just as uncomfortable. That made things infinitely more complicated because if the attraction was mutual, he might have to stop thinking about being brave and actually take a real step in that direction.

Nathan's mind seemed to be on a similar track because he asked, "So what happened in the field yesterday between you and Ellie?"

Lawson tossed him a sideways glance. "What makes you think something happened?"

"You were up to your knees in mud and Ellie was covered in it." Nathan paused his hammering to glance up in amusement. "There has to be a story in there somewhere."

Lawson told Nathan about the pig's morning run and how Ellie reacted to it.

Nathan laughed and shook his head. "That girl. She's something else."

"She sure is." Lawson grinned.

"So did you kiss her?"

The question was asked so casually that it took a moment for it to process. When it did, Lawson nearly dropped the board he was holding then glanced at Nathan with a frown. "What kind of question is that?"

"A perfectly normal one." Nathan wiggled his eyebrows. "Did you?"

"No." He paused then murmured, "Almost."

"How do you *almost* kiss someone?"

Lawson knew right then and there that letting that slip had been a bad idea. "You realize what you're about to do in time to be sensible."

"Well, then." Nathan pushed against the fence to test its stability. "I guess I'd better ask—what are your intentions toward my little sister-in-law?"

"Nothing I'm ready to declare."

That didn't mean he hadn't thought about developing some. He had. He'd thought about it when he'd gotten home and proposed. He'd thought about it in that café when she'd bemoaned being paired with the one man who would never love her. He'd thought about it yesterday when she'd asked how his life would be different if he believed his past didn't matter.

"Why don't you have any intentions toward my little sister-in-law?"

Lawson froze and stared at Nathan in shock. "Did you really just say that?"

Nathan grinned then crossed his arms. "Look, I don't want to pressure you, but if you have feelings for Ellie I hope you'll pursue them."

"You *are* serious," he said with a bemused smile. "Why?"

"Your personalities fit together like puzzle pieces. Where she's weak, you're strong and vice versa. What I notice most is that she lightens you up and you keep her grounded. She's a dreamer so she needs that. Your past weighs on you at times so you need her, too." Nathan shrugged. "Maybe I'm just being selfish, but I like the idea having you in our family."

Lawson lifted his brows. "You really mean that?"

"Sure I do. I couldn't think of a better man for her."

He pushed against the fence post to test its sturdiness. "You have my blessing if you ever want it."

Of course he wanted it, but that fact raised so many questions. *What if this just ends up like other important relationships have in the past? What if I'm not enough to make her stay? If it doesn't work out, what would happen to my relationship with the O'Briens?*

His shoulders straightened in determination. Hadn't he told himself over and over that he was nothing like his birth parents? He was supposed to believe it by now. And like Doc had said, any relationship worth having was worth taking a risk. Ellie was worth it.

A burst of joyful laughter pulled Ellie's attention from the strawberry bush to her six-month-old nephew. He waved a dandelion then laughed as the seeds vanished into the air. Ellie caught his gaze and grinned. "I don't think I've ever seen anyone have so much fun with a dandelion before."

Kate watched her son lunge toward Ellie. "Pretty soon he'll be crawling and getting into everything. That's when the real fun will start."

Ellie dropped another berry into the large pail then picked up her nephew and deposited him in her lap. He squirmed until his back rested against her stomach then smiled up at her. "You're like a ray of sunshine, aren't you, little Matthew?"

She glanced up to find Kate watching her curiously. "You've been pretty quiet until now, Ellie. Is everything all right?"

"I was just thinking about how Ma used to take us berry picking." She reached a bit deeper into the bush for more berries.

"That was fun, wasn't it? I'm a little surprised you remember it. You were so young."

"Not too young to cause trouble," she said, then wished she hadn't when it immediately made her think of Mrs. Greene.

Kate laughed. "No. You were never too young for that."

Ellie bit her lip. She hated that Mrs. Greene seemed to know something about her that she didn't know about herself. Or rather—something she'd tried to keep from knowing. Surely, those mysterious "consequences" of her actions couldn't have been that bad. Then again, telling the whole world Mrs. Greene's secret had been bad enough. What could top that?

She steeled herself before quietly asking, "Kate, did you ever get the feeling that our parents might have been disappointed in me for some reason?"

"What? No. Why do you ask?"

She shrugged. "Oh, I don't know. It's just a feeling I get sometimes. Or maybe it's a memory."

Kate frowned and surveyed her searchingly. "Our parents were just as proud of you as they were of Sean and me."

I don't think she knows. She'd finished school by that point so she wasn't there when I spread the rumor. Sean might remember it happening but I don't think he knows I started it, either. My parents and Mrs. Greene were the only ones who knew where it originated. But what were the consequences for my family?

"There you go looking pensive again. What are you thinking about now?"

She groped about for some other subject and went with the first thing that came to mind. "Just that I need to start planning what I want to achieve as a maiden aunt for the rest of my life, since my Bachelor List scheme didn't work."

Kate rested her berry-stained hand on her knee in exasperation. "You don't need to give up on a husband. You just need to be patient and stop worrying about it."

"I'm not worrying. I'm planning for the next practical step." She grinned teasingly. "I figure I'll need to find a house in town and take in a few cats to keep me company."

"Stop it, Ellie. This is serious." Kate's fiery blue gaze met hers. "We are long overdue for a talk. I have a few things I need to set straight with you."

Matthew dropped his dandelion. "Uh-oh."

Ellie picked it up for him then eyed her sister as she whispered, "Brace yourself, Matthew. Your ma's on the warpath."

Kate ignored her but narrowed her eyes. "You are twenty-one years old. That is entirely too young to start planning a life alone. Can you look me in the eye and tell me you know without a shadow of a doubt that God called you to be single?"

"No."

"Then you need to start praying that God will lead you to the right man or make it clear that you aren't supposed to have one." Kate leaned forward to catch her hand. "Ellie, dear, I want you to be honest with me about something."

Ellie decided it was best to stick to one-word responses. "Anything."

"I know what Ms. Lettie thinks and I know what the town thinks, but what are your feelings toward Lawson? Tell me the truth. There is no right or wrong answer."

Ellie sighed. Of course Kate would ask that. She was getting plumb tired of it being mentioned and having to think about it so much. Yet, as she stared back into her sister's eyes she didn't see laughter or teasing, she saw only concern. She tightened her grip slightly on Kate's hand then shrugged lightly. "We've always been friends."

"I know," Kate replied softly as Matthew used both of his hands to pat theirs.

"It's only since he returned that…" Ellie searched Kate's face for a moment, wondering if she should let her sister in on the emotions she'd barely acknowledged to herself. "That I've started to like him as more than a friend."

Kate's eyes widened and a slow smile spilled across her face. Her voice was low as though they were sharing secrets. "You aren't pulling my leg, are you?"

"No!" She covered her mouth then laughed at her vehemence. "I'm not saying I'm in love with the man."

"But there's potential." Kate glanced past her at the sound of girlish giggles. "Grace and Hope, y'all are not too far away for me to see you throwing berries at each other. Pick up each one of them and put them in the pail where they belong."

"Yes, ma'am," the sisters chorused.

Ellie shrugged. "I'm afraid I'm just being silly."

"You aren't."

"Oh, but I am! You don't seriously think he'd be interested in me, do you? I certainly don't. I thought for a moment he was going to kiss me the other day but now I think I was just imagining it."

"If he might have almost kissed you, why don't you think he'd be interested in you?"

"I have no delusions about myself. I know what I am and what I'm not. I'm not nearly as beautiful as Lorelei. I don't have it all together like you. I'm not nearly as nice as Ms. Lettie." She brushed an errant tear away and frowned. "I have no idea why I'm crying."

"You're crying because you're being too hard on yourself. Stop comparing yourself to other people. You are a wonderful person, Ellie O'Brien. I can't believe you don't know that."

"You have to say that because you're my sister."

"I have to say it because it's true. I ought to know *because* I am your sister. I raised you, for goodness' sake. I know you. I know you mean well even if what you do only seems like mischief to others. I know you have a wholesome beauty that you haven't stopped long enough in front of a mirror to notice. I know you haven't had a beau because you've been too busy trying to plan everyone else's love life to care about your own."

Ellie gave a watery laugh. "Why do you always say exactly what I need to hear?"

Kate smiled gently. "It's not my words you needed to hear, silly. It's God's. You need to figure out what He says about you in His words because I know it doesn't match up with any of the things you just said. His opinion is what's really important—not mine or some man's, right?"

"I guess," she said with a frown. She should believe that. It just didn't seem true. At least, it didn't feel true.

"As for moving into town with a bunch of cats, I think we both know that's just silly. This farm is Ma and Pa's legacy. They left it to you and Sean as much as they left it to me. That means you have every right to stay here for as long as you want. Nathan and I are happy to have you here. I never meant to make you feel unwelcome."

"You didn't—I was just being silly."

Grace bolted past them. "Papa!"

Ellie glanced up in surprise to see Nathan heading toward them on his mount with Lawson beside him on his own. Grace stopped abruptly as though suddenly realizing how she was supposed to approach the horses. Hope joined her as Nathan dismounted a few feet away. Kate stood to greet her husband. "You have perfect timing. We've filled all our pails and could use some help carrying them to the house."

"We'd be happy to help." Nathan's gaze flashed to Lawson then slid to where Ellie still sat with Matthew. "Wouldn't we, Lawson?"

Ellie narrowed her eyes suspiciously at Nathan when Lawson quickly agreed. What was going on with those two? Lawson approached her with his hat in his hands. "How can I help?"

"Hold him for a minute."

He looked a little panicked but took Matthew from her hands while she stood to her feet. She settled her nephew on her hip. Lawson picked up the huge pail before grabbing the reins of his horse. Kate and Nathan strolled ahead of them. The girls shared the saddle while Kate led the horses and Nathan carried the two large pails.

Nathan said something to Kate, who glanced back to look at them in surprise. A smile flashed across her face before she turned back around. Kate responded to Nathan. He actually winked at them. Ellie nearly winced, then risked a sideways glance at Lawson. He caught her looking. She wrinkled her nose. "Subtlety doesn't exactly run in the family."

He chuckled. A beat of silence hovered between them before Lawson cleared his throat. "There's going to be a barn raising at the Sheppards' place next weekend."

"Yes, I heard Clay mention it."

"I was wondering if you'd do me the honor…of going with me."

It took a moment for the meaning of his words to process. By that time, they'd both stopped walking and she found herself in danger of getting lost in hazel eyes that shone with cautious hope. "Are you— Do you…"

"Maybe the town and our families aren't entirely crazy. Maybe they are." His chest rose and fell with a deep breath that rushed out in one sentence. "I think we should find out."

"What does that mean?" Her heart was beating at a full gallop but her mind couldn't seem to catch up.

"I'm not sure. We could just see what happens. If you don't think that's right then we can forget the whole thing—"

"No." She bit her lip when the word escaped a bit too quickly and she forced herself to slow down. "I think that's fine."

"You do?"

She nodded.

"All right. Then we'll just see what happens, I guess."

"I guess so."

Their eyes held for another moment before they started walking again. She wasn't exactly sure how to classify the agreement she and Lawson had just come to. They weren't exactly courting—or were they? Either way, it looked like the matchmaking might be starting to work, so she kept her mouth shut and played with the baby. Perhaps Kate was right and she didn't need to give up on finding that transformative love she longed for after all.

Chapter Eight

Ellie stood outside the door of the church's storage room while she waited for the arrival of the first entries into the box social. She saw Mrs. Greene arrive and hoped beyond anything the woman wouldn't approach her. Of course, she had to be the first to follow Marissa Brightly's instructions to check the picnic baskets in with her. Ellie greeted her pleasantly and tried to act as if nothing had happened that day by the courthouse. Mrs. Greene managed to do the same except for that knowing glint in her eye.

Ellie felt that look right to the pit of her stomach. She'd allowed her courtship with Lawson to become a welcome distraction from her fears but they were still there—taunting her when she tried to go to sleep. She couldn't stand it anymore. She'd figure this out as soon as she could. Otherwise, Ellie would have to live not only with that feeling of guilt, but with Mrs. Greene lording over her with whatever special knowledge the woman had.

Amy Bradley and her younger sister, Isabelle, were the next to arrive. Ellie forced a cheerful greeting to her lips and ushered them inside the room so she could write down their names and a description of their lunch baskets for Pastor Brightly. Isabelle watched the proceedings with a curious smile. "Why are we being so secretive this year?"

"We're just trying to liven things up. We're also trying to spark some competition to raise a bit more money," Ellie explained. "That schoolhouse roof needs a lot of work."

"I think it's a wonderful idea," Amy said as she set her basket down on the table.

Isabelle rolled her eyes. "You're just happy Rhett won't know to bid on yours."

Ellie's gaze shot to Amy. "What have you got against Rhett, anyway?"

"Nothing in particular," she said with a vague wave of her hand.

"It's just something in general," Isabelle informed Ellie wryly. "Amy here has sworn off men since that Silas Smithson character left town without a word. I gave that resolve about two weeks but it's lasted for a year now."

"Amy, why didn't you tell me?" Ellie must be slipping. How did she not already know this?

Amy shrugged and sent her sister an unappreciative look. "Well, I haven't exactly been shouting it from the rooftops. Thank you, Isabelle. You don't think it's silly, do you, Ellie?"

"It isn't my place to judge."

"Isabelle, please take note of that statement and apply it the next time you want to give advice." Amy squeezed Ellie's hand gratefully then left the room.

Isabelle sighed. "I wish you would have said something in Rhett's favor. She hasn't been any fun lately. She wouldn't have even entered a basket if Mother hadn't insisted."

"What's wrong with her?"

"I wish I knew. She's been in love with someone for the past few years and now it's as though she feels nothing."

"Who has she been in love with?"

"Who hasn't she been in love with? My sister has fallen in love more times than I can count."

Ellie chuckled. "Well, then, it's good that she's taking some time out from love. Perhaps it will help her figure out who she really loves."

"Maybe so, but I'm rooting for Rhett."

A few other women entered the room as Isabelle left, so it was a few minutes before Ellie stepped outside the door. She was surprised to find Chris waiting for her. He held up a basket. "This is Sophia's."

She frowned. "Why didn't she bring it herself?"

"I wanted to talk to you."

She almost asked why, then remembered what he'd said the last time he'd tried to talk to her. She glanced around for any sign of Lawson but he'd said he wouldn't be able to come early. "I'm not sure that's a good idea."

"We've always been good friends, haven't we? I thought that meant I could at least have a conversation with you."

Her shoulders relaxed and she smiled. "You're right, Chris. I'm sorry for being prickly. Let me check in that basket while you tell me what's on your mind."

"Are you really courting Lawson?"

She glanced up from her list to meet his gaze. "As far as I can tell."

He frowned. "What does that mean?"

It meant she wasn't sure. They were more than friends but less than a couple. As far as she could tell, that meant he liked her but didn't want to be her beau yet. She couldn't fault him for that exactly. No one else had shown even half as much interest in her…until now, apparently, when men kept coming out of the woodwork.

She eyed Chris thoughtfully. "Why do you want to know?"

"I was hoping that since you just want to be friends with me, you might be willing to tell me who my match is."

She let the tablet fall to her side as she tilted her head. "Aren't you moving on a little too fast for someone who's supposed to be in love with me?"

His jaw tightened. "Don't tease me, Ellie. It's cruel."

"I'm sorry, Chris. I didn't mean to be." She sighed then leaned back against the door frame and crossed her arms with the tablet in front of her. "I haven't figured out everyone's match yet."

"You mean I don't have one."

"Yet."

He lowered his head in disappointment. "Did you give Amy one?"

"Did I give…?" she echoed, then met his gaze when he looked up. "Amy," she breathed in realization. "Didn't you two go to the harvest dance together last year?"

He crossed his arms and lifted his chin to stare down at her. "She threw me over for that fancy out-of-town fellow who broke her heart."

"I remember." She frowned. "Wouldn't that have

been right around the time you said you started developing feelings for me?"

Either her eyes were playing tricks on her or her friend was blushing. "Maybe."

Her mouth fell open for a moment. She clamped it shut then placed her hand on her hip. "Tell me the truth, Chris Johansen. You were settling for me, weren't you? I was your last choice."

He just stood there, not giving an inch, then his arms slowly relaxed to his side. "I don't suppose you could talk to her for me?"

"No!"

"I didn't think so." He handed her the basket then walked away.

She glared at his back for a moment then placed the basket inside the room, muttering to the Lord, "Of all the nerve, expecting me to fall at his feet when he doesn't even care a whit about me and is in love with someone else entirely."

"Who's in love with someone else?" Lawson's deep voice asked from the door. "I hope you don't mean me."

She gave a startled jump then whirled to face him. He lifted his eyebrows to prod an answer from her and she realized she hadn't given him one. "I don't."

"Good, because it wouldn't have been true." He surveyed the room filled with baskets. "Are you going to tell me which one of these is yours?"

She shook her head. "It's against the rules. Why don't you help me move all of these to the sanctuary? It's almost time to start."

After Ellie handed Mrs. Brightly the list of entries, she wandered back over to the seat Lawson had saved for her on the same pew where Nathan and Kate sat with Ms. Lettie and Doc. When the third basket came up for sale, Lawson leaned over to her conspiratorially. "I recognize that basket. It's my ma's."

With that, he lifted his hand to place the first bid. Doc immediately leaned over to challenge. "Are you trying to steal my woman, Son?"

Lawson grinned, but before he could answer, Chris yelled, "I bid a dollar."

She turned to stare at him in confusion. He just met her gaze with a grim nod. Suddenly, another man yelled, "One dollar and ten cents."

She whirled around to face the front of the church to find Donovan standing with his hands obstinately on his hips. "They think it's mine."

Doc finally had a chance to bid. Donovan hesitated a moment then sat down. No one else spoke up after Doc so he won the basket. Lawson sent her a sideways glance then rubbed his hands together. "This is going to be fun."

Lawson randomly started bidding on many of the baskets after that. Chris and Donovan followed suit, which drove the prices up until Lawson dropped out. After that, Chris and Donovan would stop, which allowed the person who really wanted the basket to step in and purchase it. Finally, Isabelle's basket came up. Lawson continued to bid on it more intensely than he had the others.

People began to whisper their speculations on whether or not it was Ellie's basket or someone else's. Chris dropped out of the running so it was just between Lawson and Donovan. Lawson stopped bidding, leaving Donovan with the prize. Isabelle stepped forward and did not look pleased. For that matter, neither did Donovan.

Pastor Brightly held up the lunch Ellie had prepared next. It was packed in a medium-size picnic basket that had been whitewashed and covered in bright yellow fabric. "I'm told this cheerful basket is filled with fried chicken, hashed potatoes, fruit and chocolate cake. Let's start the bidding at fifty cents."

Ellie waited for Lawson to start the bidding. He didn't. This was obviously going to be one of the baskets he didn't bid on. Unfortunately, no one else did, either. Embarrassing silence permeated the air. "Who will make the opening bid?"

She bit her lip.

Pastor Brightly cleared his throat. "Why don't we start at thirty, then?"

Her fingers clenched. Clayton Sheppard raised his hand. She had a bid. One bid. That was better than nothing. She unclenched her fingers and felt her shoulders relax. Lawson's arm pressed against hers. She glanced up to find him watching her carefully. He smiled slowly. "I thought so."

He raised his hand. "Sixty."

Just like that a bidding war erupted. Chris jumped in the game. Nathan put up a bid, then Sean tried to make things interesting. Finally, Chris and Lawson began duking it out for the highest bid. Obviously, Lawson was serious about this one. Pastor James was desperately trying to keep up. A third bid from Donovan threw him for a moment before he paused. "Donovan, I told you three times now. You can't bid anymore once you've won a basket. Why don't you and Isabelle find a spot to eat? Now, where were we?"

Lawson stretched his arm so it landed on the pew behind Ellie. "You were just about to sell me that basket."

"A dollar fifty," Chris yelled from the pew behind her.

"This is ridiculous," Ellie murmured. She turned to look for Amy and found the girl seated with the rest of her sisters. Amy was only paying cursory attention to the drama unfolding on the auction block. She seemed more interested in exchanging furtive glances with Rhett. Ellie hissed to Chris, "Would you stop it? I promise you're not doing yourself any favors with this."

He followed her gaze to Amy then hesitated. "I withdraw my last bid."

"Then the last bid was from Lawson for one dollar and thirty cents. Going. Going—"

"Two dollars!"

A mixture of gasps and groans filled the church at the sound of the new voice from the back of the church. Ellie turned in her seat with the rest of the congregation to find Ethan Larue leaning nonchalantly against the back wall.

Lawson turned to find Ethan's gaze settled on him in open challenge. Who was this man and why did he keep inserting himself into Lawson's affairs? Granted, Lawson had willingly bared his past to the near-stranger but that didn't mean he trusted him. Far from it. He still believed Ethan was up to something underhanded. Rhett hurried across the aisle to ask lowly, "Is he in the club?"

"Not a chance."

Rhett nodded like a Ranger receiving his first assignment. "Put your hand up and leave it there. We'll do the rest."

Ellie leaned over as he did just that. "What are y'all whispering about?"

"Why is he bidding on your basket?"

"I don't know why anyone does anything these days," she moaned.

Lorelei's father, Mr. Wilkins, leaned across the aisle to slip something into his hand. Lawson glanced down and realized he now held three rolled-up dollar bills. Ellie nudged him. She opened her hand to reveal more than a dollar's worth of coins. "Mrs. Cummins passed us this. It's from her row."

Lawson shook his head in amazement. The town was giving Lawson the money to up his bid. Once Ethan realized what was happening, he bowed out with a grin that said he'd never intended to win in the first place. The man was starting to get under his skin. One of these days, when there wasn't a crowd of people watching, Lawson intended to find out why. For now, though, he had four dollars and fifty cents worth of a lunch basket to eat. He stole a glance at Ellie's flushed cheeks and knew it was worth every penny.

Tap. Bam. Tap. Bam. Lawson reached for another nail but it rolled off the end of the roof of the unfinished barn and fell two stories to hide in a bush. He picked another nail, tapped it into place and drove it through. He'd gotten so used to building things in the weeks he'd been home that he could probably save himself time by driving the nail through the board in one blow. He just didn't trust himself to get it right the first time.

"Lawson, why are you still here?" Rhett's yell sounded loudly over the noise of construction and the distant sound of singing. "Your shift is over. Go find that pretty girl of yours and give someone else a turn up there!"

Laughter and hoots echoed through the new walls of the building. Lawson smiled in case anyone was watching, although he wanted to groan. Bringing Ellie to the barn raising seemed to have given the town the last piece of evidence they needed to convince themselves that he and Ellie were meant to be. Pretty soon they'd convince themselves he'd proposed again. By next month, the town would have them married and living in his cabin. The way everyone was rushing things made him nervous. Didn't they realize he needed to take this slow, make sure everything was going to work out before he put his heart on the line completely?

"I hear you, Rhett. I guess I got a little distracted, but I'm leaving now." His feet hadn't been on the ground floor for long before Ethan Larue approached him. Lawson took a deep drink of water then gave the man a suspicious look. "Is there something I can help you with?"

"I need to talk to you. It's important."

"What is it?"

Ethan's gaze swept the rafters of the barn and the crowded area outside before he shook his head. "We'd better find someplace quieter."

He reluctantly followed Ethan away from the ruckus of the barn raising toward a quiet spot near the Sheppards' house. Lawson took stock of his opponent. The man wasn't armed as far as he could tell. "I think you'd better sit down," Ethan said.

Lawson frowned but complied by wrangling a wooden crate. "I think you'd better tell me what this is all about, Ethan."

"You were right at the party. I did come here to find

out about you. I wasn't given permission to reveal why until yesterday." Ethan sat on the crate across from him and watched him intensely. "I lied about my last name. It isn't Larue. It's Lawson."

Lawson placed his elbows on his knees as he leaned forward. "Your last name is my first name?"

"Actually, your first name is your mother's maiden name."

"How would you know that?" He shook his head in confusion. "I don't even know that."

"Your mother, Gloria, was my aunt."

"My…" Lawson stared at him. "That means you're my cousin."

"That's right."

He had a cousin. He stared at Ethan blankly for a moment as he went over the facts he'd just heard. "You said *was*. Is she dead?"

"I don't know. She'd run off by the time my father died and your father took me out of the orphanage."

"My father is Doc Williams." Lawson's firm tone brokered no question. His thoughts stumbled about as he tried to figure out what to call the man Ethan knew. "This other man—he took you out of the orphanage and you lived with him?"

"Yes."

"I'm sorry."

"Don't be. He treated me well." Ethan ignored Lawson's disbelieving scoff. "You don't have to call him *this other man*. You remember his name, don't you?"

He shook his head.

"Well, surely you remember your own last name."

"It's Williams."

Ethan frowned but his tone was patient. "No."

Lawson ran a hand through his hair and suddenly realized it trembled. His words came out harshly. "I don't remember."

"It's Hardy."

"Hardy," he whispered before another blow landed across his small jaw. He reeled but the stranger's rough hands held him upright.

"Speak up, boy. I want my friends to hear you. What's your last name?" The drunk slurred then shook him until his brain rattled.

"I said it's Hardy!"

The man's bloodshot eyes held his. "Your father's name is Clive."

"Yes, sir." He whimpered when the man let him fall to the ground, then carefully rubbed his jaw.

"I told you, friends, I told you. That's the kid. His father will pay big to get him back." The man whirled toward him. "Don't move. We're taking you back to Papa...right after I finish this drink."

Lawson pulled his knees to his chest and crossed his arms around them. His pa didn't want him. What were these men going to do when they found that out?

One of the painted ladies came down the stairs and frowned at the blood on his face. She shot a look toward the men who were too deep in their cups to notice when she offered him her hand. He hesitantly took it and allowed her to lead him into the kitchen. She cleaned his face before handing him a sack. "I know those men. They don't mean well by you. Take this and run."

He stared at her in shock. She didn't want him, either. "You promised I could stay on and wash dishes."

"I know I did but if you stay, they'll hurt you worse. I can't stop them. You run away and don't ever come

back to this town. Too many people here know you're Clive's son. With that reward on his head, there will be plenty more like those men wanting to use you to get to him. Promise me you'll run."

"Yes, ma'am."

"Oh, and Lawson, you've got to protect yourself in the next town. You can't tell anyone who you are. From now on you don't have a last name. If anyone asks, you're just Lawson. You hear me?"

"Lawson!"

He snapped back to reality to find Ethan watching him in concern. "What?"

"I said he wants to see you."

"Who does?"

"Your father."

"No."

"At least think about it."

"I don't have to think about it. The answer is no." He shot to his feet, nearly overturning the crate in his haste. He searched the crowd for Nathan and found him sitting next to Sean. "Nathan, I need you to take Ellie home. I'm not feeling well."

"You look pale. Maybe I should drive you," Sean offered.

"No." The word came out louder than he intended. He thanked them then turned away. He realized it would be rude to leave Ellie without saying anything but it couldn't be helped. He needed to be alone. He needed to think. So this was it. For the past ten years, he'd been waiting for the other shoe to drop. It finally had.

The world seemed to slow down yet rush with color and sound—memories that he had to fight back. He had a cousin. His mother was probably dead. His father wanted to see him. He was filled with disbelief. There had to be a way to salvage this. He'd just ignore it. Ethan would go away. Lawson would go back to the life he'd created. He'd go back to hope, to Ellie's pure smile, to moments when he'd thought maybe his past could be erased.

Somehow he knew it wouldn't be that easy.

Chapter Nine

The incessant hammering from the barn raising rooted Ellie on as she held her breath and gulped down a full glass of water. She placed a hand on her stomach as she waited to see if her hiccups had been sufficiently drowned by the deluge. Her next hiccup was followed by a frustrated groan. She'd spent the past five minutes trying everything she could think of to get rid of the annoying condition she was in.

"Miss Ellie, you sure look pretty today!" She jumped and turned to find Donovan Turner standing a bit too close for comfort. He leaned even closer in concern. The piece of hay in his mouth bobbled as he asked, "What's wrong?"

"Nothing." She waited for a moment then smiled. "You scared the hiccups right out of me, though."

He grinned. She scanned the crowd for Nathan and found him talking to Sean and Lawson. Donovan fiddled with the Stetson in his hands. "How is Hamlet?"

She shifted out of the way of a passing woman, which conveniently placed her farther away from Donovan. "Who?"

"The pig I gave you."

"Oh, I didn't know it already had a name."

He nodded. "It's Shakespeare—one of his tragedies."

"Yes, I know."

"You know Shakespeare?"

"Not personally." He didn't seem to think that was funny so she bit her lip to hide her smile. "I read a few of his plays in school."

"Did I ever tell you that I was an actor in a troupe?" He shifted closer as though her surprise gave him permission to do so. "We toured the panhandle and made a lot of money."

"How did you end up running a pig farm?" She nearly winced when she realized she'd gotten him started on his favorite subject. He'd trapped her good this time. She cast a pleading look over his shoulder to where her oblivious brothers stood before he blustered on. Where had Lawson gone? He'd asked her to come with him. Didn't he care that she'd been cornered?

Something in her question must have hinted at disapproval because Donovan shifted into more of a combative stance. "What's wrong with my pig farm? You've never been there so how could you have formed an opinion?"

She suddenly remembered Kate's warning not to encourage the man or be alone with him. She glanced around the bustling activity of the barn raising. Well, she wasn't alone with him. However, it was probably best if she moved along. "I'm sure your pig farm is just fine."

"I'm glad to hear you say that." He ducked his head then decided to peer at her instead. "The truth is I like you a lot, Miss Ellie, more than that dandy you're spooning with now. Anyone can see he's just going along because the town's making him. And, where is he now?"

Donovan's words hit a little too close for comfort. She shifted farther away from him. "I don't know, but I'm afraid I don't return your feelings, Mr. Turner."

His eyes narrowed. "It's because of my pig farm, isn't it?"

Why couldn't he understand that she just didn't like him? She'd already said it once. Did she need to tell him that he made her uncomfortable or that she didn't trust him? Her pause must have lasted too long. She jumped when he abruptly slammed his Stetson on his knee, somehow managing to make a loud popping sound in the process.

"Doggone. It is the pig farm. If I'd known, I never would have bought— Oh, here comes your brother. I'll see you later." He hurried away like a cat with its tail on fire.

Nathan placed a protective hand on her shoulder as he stared after Donovan with a frown. "Was he bothering you?"

She squeezed his hand appreciatively. "I find him slightly annoying, but other than that, not really. He scared my hiccups away at any rate."

Nathan crossed his arms. "Well, I told him to leave you alone and he ignored me. That doesn't bode well. The next time he tries that, be curt with him. He has to get it through his head that you're off-limits."

"He always seemed so harmless before."

"A rattlesnake seems harmless until it starts to shake."

She shivered at the analogy. "Aren't you descriptive?"

"I'm supposed to tell you Lawson left because he wasn't feeling well. You'll ride home with me and Kate."

Ellie looked at him in concern. "Do you think we should send word to Doc?"

"Doc's delivering a baby."

"Even so, someone should check on Lawson."

"I know. We won't stay here much longer. You can check on him yourself."

Nathan kept his promise and less than an hour later, Ellie knocked lightly on the door of Lawson's cabin. He didn't respond. She shifted the large basket Kate had filled with anything and everything Lawson might need to cure whatever ailed him, and knocked again. Finally, his voice called from deep inside the cabin. "Who is it?"

"Ellie."

A moment later he opened the door with what seemed to be reluctance. Her eyes widened at his disheveled appearance. His short brown wavy hair looked as though he'd combed it with his fingers in myriad directions. He wore the same cream-colored shirt from earlier but it was half-unbuttoned and haphazardly tucked into the waistband of his brown pants. He didn't bother to meet her gaze. Instead, he stared down at his bare feet. "Sorry for leaving early."

"That's all right," she said, looking everywhere but the expanse of his exposed chest. "I understand why."

His gaze jerked to hers. "Ethan told you?"

"No, Nathan told me you were sick. I didn't see Ethan." His eyes lowered but not until she saw a hint of relief there. "I'm sorry if I awakened you. Are you feeling any better?"

He shrugged then leaned against the door frame. "I suppose."

"It must have come on suddenly."

He hardly seemed to hear her. He stared unseeingly at some distant object. "I'll be fine."

She wasn't so sure about that. He certainly seemed dazed. She remembered Nathan acting the same way when he'd had a high fever. "You don't have a fever, do you?"

He shook his head but she lifted her hand to his forehead, anyway. Suddenly, his hazel eyes focused on her. For the first time since he opened the door, he seemed exactly like himself, only somehow more intense. Her hand drifted back to her side. "Kate sent this basket. I don't even know what's in it."

He reached out and caught her arm to pull her closer.

"She threatened to send Nathan with the shotgun if I didn't come back in ten minutes."

His gaze captured hers. His other hand cradled her jaw while his thumb brushed her cheek.

"I told her that wasn't funny but she…" She stopped trying to talk the moment his forehead touched hers. How she'd managed to speak at all as breathless as she felt was beyond her. They stood there for a moment, neither of them speaking or moving. Finally, he lifted her chin and kissed her. She immediately began to pull away from the new sensation then hesitated. His hand pressed gently against her back and she allowed him to guide her into another kiss.

It seemed to take him a moment to gather his thoughts. His gaze finally found hers. "You didn't slap me."

She let out a breathless laugh. "Did you think that I would?"

"I wasn't sure."

She pushed away from his chest slightly to look up at him and dared to ask, "Lawson, what is happening here? I can tell you aren't sick but obviously something is wrong. Won't you tell me what it is? Maybe I can help."

"You can't help, but thank you." He leaned down to kiss her once more then set her away from him. "You'd better go. Tell Kate I'll be fine in the morning."

He quickly took the basket then shut the door behind him, leaving her with no choice but to walk away. Nathan was still unhitching the horses from the wagon so she wandered into the barn and found him in the tack room. "How is he?"

She watched him put away the last harness. "I don't think we need to send for Doc."

"That's good." He closed the tack room door and grinned. "You and Lawson seem to be getting pretty close these days. I'm really happy for y'all, Ellie. I told him courting you would be the right thing to do."

"Thank you. I…" Suddenly, her heart gave a little hiccup of disappointment. "Wait. You *told* him that he should do it?"

"I sure did. I also said he would be perfect for you and that we'd love to have him in our family if things progress."

"Oh." She tilted her head to watch him closely. "Was that before or after he asked your permission?"

"Well, he didn't ask for my permission exactly."

"I see."

"Did I say something wrong?"

She squeezed her brother-in-law's shoulder to try to chase the furrow from his brow. "No, you were very sweet. Lawson hasn't officially said that we're courting, which is fine. I just wanted to make sure I was reading the signs right."

"I'm sure you are. Be patient. Lawson tends to hold his feelings close to his vest." He led her out of the barn and closed the door behind them. "How about a game of checkers before dinner?"

"Thanks, but I think I'll take a walk."

A few moments later, the few horses out in the pasture ran up to greet her when she reached their fence. Starlight was the only one who stayed when they realized she hadn't brought them any treats. She rubbed the horse's strong neck. "I wish I could be as sure as Nathan is, Starlight."

Instead, Donovan's words sifted through her mind to reveal the doubts she'd been afraid to face. What if she was mistaken and he was right? What if Lawson was only expressing an interest in her to please the town and their families? If so, then it was her fault because she'd encouraged everyone to matchmake on her behalf. Essentially, that meant that poor Lawson had the whole town pressuring him to be in a romantic relationship with her. Even the people who he normally went to for advice, like his parents and Nathan, had gotten caught up in the matchmaking fever.

What if I made the wrong choice in encouraging the matchmakers? Did I even stop to consider how Lawson might feel about that? No, because I wanted to feel important. I wanted to feel wanted. Isn't that exactly how I made an enemy out of Mrs. Greene? What if the same thing ends up ruining my relationship with Lawson?

She shook her head to rein in those thoughts. It was too much to take in. Maybe it wasn't true. Maybe the town wasn't the driving force behind his decision to court her.

She pulled back to look into her horse's large brown eyes. "He kissed me, Starlight. That has to mean something, right?"

Starlight gave a low nicker of agreement. A flash of color in the woods that led to the creek drew Ellie's attention for a moment until Starlight nuzzled her shoulder. When she looked again there was nothing there, so she patted her horse's shoulder. "I know you love me, darling. That wasn't in question."

Her gaze slid to the cabin and she bit her lip. *At least now I know to keep my eyes open. I'll find out the truth and if I've made a mistake—if I've made him feel obligated to court me—then I'll fix it. Even if it hurts me to do so.*

Lawson sank onto the chair realizing he'd nearly frightened Ellie away during that little interlude at the door. He glanced down at his shirt and grimaced at the sight of the collar hanging open. He'd been changing when he'd heard her knock. He'd become so afraid that Ethan might have followed him that he'd forgotten what he was doing. Then he'd gone off and kissed her.

That kiss had been building inside of him since their muddy foray in the field, but he wasn't sure if he'd done right to give in to it. Lawson didn't kiss women often but when he did, it meant something. Usually that something was that they were eventually going to hightail it out of his life.

He pulled in a calming breath as he continued unbuttoning his shirt. A metal button broke from its place and tumbled to the ground. He placed his boot over it to keep it from rolling away then froze.

His raggedy boot covered the gleaming metal coin that rolled his way. He tried to look nonchalant as the gentleman stopped to look around. The man muttered about hearing something fall before he continued on his way. Lawson picked up the coin with a satisfied grin.

A moment later, he ducked under the swinging doors of the nearest saloon. No one seemed to notice him stop and stare to get his bearings. None of these rowdy places had exactly the same layout. He spotted an empty stool at the bar so he climbed it and placed his elbows on the shiny wood. The bartender did a double take then ignored him. Lawson frowned at him. "Hey, I'm thirsty. I found five cents and I want a drink."

The man next to him glanced down and pushed away from the bar. "Starting them a little young, aren't you, Cal?"

The burly bartender turned to greet him as though unsure whether to laugh or snarl. "You're chasing away my customers."

He held up the shiny nickel. "How about it, Cal?"

"You've got a smart mouth." Cal didn't seem to think it was a bad thing because he grinned. "How old are you, anyway?"

"I don't know."

A man sidled up to the bar and winked as he slid a few coins toward the bartender. "Give the boy a drink on me."

"Sure, Lem." Cal quirked a brow. "What'll it be, son? Whiskey, Scotch or gin?"

Lawson shrugged. "No one ever asked me that before. They usually just give me water or sarsaparilla."

"Whiskey," Lem said.

Lawson's eyes widened as everyone began throwing money on the counter in front of him to place bets on whether he'd drink it or not. The tension mounted as he took the cup into his hand. He wrinkled his nose dubiously at the smell of the liquid, then lifted the glass to take a sip. Suddenly, a man on his left snatched the glass from his hand and threw its contents in Lem's face. "You no good—"

The man didn't get to finish before he reeled from Lem's punch. Lawson suddenly found himself in the middle of a brawl. Noticing everyone was distracted, he gathered all the money and crawled out on his hands and knees.

He stuffed the money in his pockets and grinned. He was rich! He could buy himself a sandwich, some new clothes and maybe even some new boots. Not in this town, though—the next one. It wouldn't do to get caught. He glanced back at the saloon to make sure he was in the clear, then started making tracks...

Lawson clenched the button tightly in his closed fist. He leaned back against the chair and closed his eyes. His memories would have their fun for a while. There was no avoiding that. He'd grit his teeth and bear it because they wouldn't last forever—not when he'd finally found someone in the present he might be able to hold on to. The choke hold of his past couldn't be as strong as it seemed...or could it?

Chapter Ten

Nathan had told him that someone was interested in buying a few of their horses and that he wanted Lawson to help with the deal. But when the next morning rolled around, Lawson could hardly keep his mind on his job. To say that he'd had a rough night was a bit of an understatement. He hadn't been able to shake those memories or the feelings they inevitably brought with them of anger, abandonment and fear. Between that and the preparations for the important buyer coming today, he hadn't had time to speak with Ellie. He wanted to make sure that he hadn't hurt her feelings by refusing to tell her what was bothering him.

In the meantime, he needed to get his head together enough to show the buyer the horses' full potential so he wouldn't make Nathan lose the sale. He finished the last exercise near where the buyer—who'd insisted they call him Alex—stood talking to Nathan. Alex nodded in appreciation. "Nathan, you have some of the finest horses I've seen in a long time. I'd like to buy the three you showed me today."

Nathan shook the man's hand. "Let's go inside and talk specifics."

Lawson finally found himself alone with Ellie. He circled the arena on Sheba a few times to cool the mare down then stopped the horse in front of where Ellie stood. "I'm sorry about yesterday."

"What are you sorry for?" She stepped onto the bottom rung on the fence and peered up at him with what seemed to be trepidation. "Kissing me?"

"What do you think?" He leaned across the saddle horn to kiss her pert nose. Her cheeks turned rosy and a hesitant smile tugged her lips but she stepped down from the gate leaving a big gap between their heights. Lawson dismounted. "I just wanted to make sure I didn't mess anything up with my strange behavior."

"Your strange, *unexplained* behavior." She lifted a prodding brow.

"Right. So we're fine?"

She held his gaze long enough to tell him that she was aware of his not-so-artful avoidance, then gave a single nod. "I am if you are."

He covered the hand she'd placed on the fence between them. "Good."

"When did all of this start between us, Lawson?" She placed her other hand on top of his. "Was it at the café when the town suggested it? Or maybe at the engagement party?"

"I don't know. I kind of think it started that first day I got back."

"You do?"

He smiled at the strange tone of hope in her voice. "Sure. Of course, it took me a while to figure it out, and

I probably wouldn't have done anything if our families hadn't encouraged it."

Her gaze dropped from his and she pulled her hands away. "They were pretty convincing, weren't they?"

Before he could respond, they spotted Alex ambling toward them from the house. Ellie smiled at him. "Did you want another look at them, sir?"

"No need. The contract is signed." The man propped his boot on the fence and trained his gaze on Lawson. "I'd like to speak to this young man alone for a minute."

Ellie sent him a curious and questioning glance. At his shrug, she left him alone with the man. Lawson absently tied the horse's reins to the fence as he watched her go. Alex shifted slightly. "You haven't been able to keep your eyes off that gal since I got here. I looked at your ma the same way before she ran off and left me."

Lawson's entire being stilled. He slowly turned from the closed door of the farmhouse to pierce the shadowed gaze of the man before him. Alex removed his Stetson and met Lawson's eyes straight on. "I guess I should introduce myself properly. I'm Clive Alexander Hardy."

"Clive Hardy." The words came out in a disbelieving echo.

Clive nodded as a slight smile briefly appeared on his lips. "I'm your father."

Lawson stared at the man in shock. He had the strangest sense that those words should make him feel something, but he couldn't seem to feel anything at all. Finally, he spoke as though from rote memorization. "No, you aren't."

"I can prove it."

A slow leak of anger began to drip from his soul to his tongue. "I don't care if you can prove it."

Lawson suddenly realized that the man didn't have to. If someone looked, really looked, it was obvious. They were practically the same height and build, though Lawson was a bit taller and Clive was stockier. The man had remnants of the same brown hair in his silver hair and beard. The shape of their eyes was different but the hazel coloring was the same. His jaw tightened. "You should go."

Clive shook his head. "I didn't come all this way just to purchase a few horses. I want to talk to you."

The frayed thread he'd been holding on to for years suddenly snapped. "How dare you? How dare you possibly think you can just waltz into my life like this? I told Ethan I didn't want to see you but you ignored that completely."

"I was already on my way." Clive held his gaze urgently. "I wanted to see you."

"Why? How did you expect me to react? Did you think this would make me happy?"

"I guess not," Clive drawled. "I thought I'd at least try to start a relationship—"

Lawson shook his head in disgust. "I don't want anything from you and you're too late to give it. I think you'd better leave."

Clive stared at him for a long moment, then smiled wryly as he put his Stetson back on. "I guess I have no one to blame but myself for the way you turned out— just like me."

His eyes narrowed. "What does that mean?"

Clive shrugged lightly. "You've got the same anger, same stubborn mindset, apparently the same weakness for pretty women, and from what I hear, you'd make a pretty good outlaw."

"I'm nothing like you." The crack in his voice belied the firmness he was searching for.

"Sure you are. Don't fool yourself into thinking otherwise. You're a Hardy, from your hazel eyes to that smile you flashed when you met me. I think it's about time you figured that out."

"I asked you to leave."

Clive tipped his hat. "Sure, for now. But this isn't over, kid."

Lawson hardly waited for the man to head toward the house before he mounted Sheba and pointed her toward the woods. It was only when he dismounted at the creek that he was able to reel in his racing thoughts and breathe. It wasn't fair. After all this time and all the ways he'd struggled to distance himself from his past, he'd wanted to believe that he was finally free of it. He wasn't. It kept reaching out to pull him back—forcing him to remember who he was, where he'd come from, what kind of person he could expect to be. He'd never truly forgotten, but having his father come and point it out seemed like the stamp in the wax that sealed his fate.

He'd even thought that he might be able to create a new life with Ellie. Oh, he hadn't let himself truly plan that far ahead, but the intention had been there all along. He'd been working up his courage bit by bit in preparation for that final plunge. Too bad it was all for nothing. His father's sudden appearance served as a stark reminder of what usually happened when he let people too close—they left.

He picked up a rock and tossed it into the lazy creek. It was his parents' fault. When they left him, they'd left some sort of invisible mark that warned others off or so it seemed. Maybe it was the Hardy family curse—

abandoning or being abandoned by the ones who were supposed to love you the most. Whatever caused it, the result was the same. He was still lacking, still missing that special ingredient that would make him worthy of the family he'd always wanted.

"Who am I fooling?" he muttered above the low grumble of the waterfall. He wasn't enough. It was time he realized that.

Ellie placed a stilling hand over her nieces' to end their exuberant hand game when Alex stepped back into the parlor with his hat in his hands. "It's been nice to meet all of you but I think it's time I head back to town. Nathan, would you mind if we left now?"

"Certainly not." Nathan set Matthew in Kate's arms and picked up his Stetson.

They followed him outside and Ellie's gaze immediately went to the corral. "Where's Lawson?"

Alex put his Stetson on and tugged its brim low as he walked toward the buggy. "I don't know. He took off on one of my new horses."

Ellie shot a concerned look at Nathan before hurrying to keep pace with the man. "What? Why? What did you say to him?"

The man stopped to frown down at her. "That's a private matter."

She surveyed him in confusion. What private matter could a stranger have to discuss with Lawson? The man looked pale in the sunlight and the twitch in his jaw showed that he was upset about something. "What happened?"

"Ellie," Nathan cautioned.

"Well, something must have."

Alex looked at her with new interest. "Why do you care? Who is my— Who is he to you?"

"He's..." She glanced away to search for the right word. Her what? Could she say he was her beau? She wasn't sure. Her friend? Somehow that didn't seem appropriate or meaningful enough. She met Alex's gaze again. The color of his eyes seemed to change from green to gold. She suddenly realized they were hazel, just like... She caught her breath as she took in his height, his build, his age. She stepped back. "Perhaps I should ask who he is to you."

His gaze faltered. She didn't wait for further confirmation before bolting for her mount. It took her nearly thirty minutes to find Lawson skipping rocks at the creek. The wildflowers from weeks ago had withered away and a new batch hadn't yet come in to replace them, so the only contrast to the greens and blues of the creek and surrounding forest was Lawson's dark shirt. He turned at the sound of Starlight's hooves. Their eyes met for a moment before he sent another rock skittering across the surface of the slow-moving creek. "Did he tell you?"

"I guessed." She dismounted and pushed away the tendrils of her hair that had managed to come loose during her ride. "What are you going to do?"

He shrugged as his gaze transferred back to the creek. "I told him to leave. What else is there to do?" Panic filled his voice. "He is leaving, isn't he?"

She stepped slightly closer to place a comforting hand on his arm. "He was the last time I checked."

He nodded then sent another rock hopping with a bit too much force. "I'm so angry, Ellie. I told Ethan I didn't want to meet him, and Clive completely ignored that. He just came, anyway. I should have known. He never respected anyone's choices but his own."

Confusion lowered her brows. "What does Ethan have to do with this?"

His gaze leapt to hers. "His real name is Ethan Lawson. He's my cousin."

She stared at him in awe. "You have a cousin."

"Apparently, I have a lot more than that."

Her hand slipped from his arm. She picked up a smooth, round rock and studied it as she turned it over in her hand. "How long have you known about this?"

"Since the barn raising."

Well, that explained his mysterious behavior. She sent the rock skipping across the water. "What did your father want?"

"I think he wanted to build some sort of relationship with me."

"And you didn't want that?"

He threw the last rock into the creek then turned to face her defiantly. "Why should I?"

"Maybe you should at least consider it." She lifted one shoulder in a slight shrug. "You know my parents died when I was eight. I hardly remember them. Sometimes I wonder what it would be like if I could just sit down with them at least once to find out who they were, what they wanted out of life…" Anxiety filled her but she continued, "What they think of me."

"My parents were nothing like yours. I wish I could forget everything about them and I've certainly tried." He frowned. "I remember all too vividly who that man is and what he's like."

"Maybe he's changed."

"Maybe he hasn't." He set his jaw stubbornly. "Either

way, I don't intend to find out. For so long, I've been trying to prove I'm not like him. I became a Ranger to show I'd uphold the law and not break it like he did, but even that didn't work. They called me Lawless and said I'd make a better outlaw than a Ranger."

She wasn't sure what to do about that or what to say to comfort him. He made the decision for her by turning away and stuffing his hands in his pockets as he stared at the creek. "Why are you here, anyway?"

"I thought… I thought you might want me to be with you."

"I don't. Not anymore. Not the way it has been." He turned to face her, his intense gaze arresting her. "I want us to go back to being friends and nothing more."

"But an hour ago you said—"

"I said what I thought you wanted to hear. That doesn't make it true."

This shouldn't surprise her. It was just what she'd suspected. Still, she had to hear it from his own lips to believe him. "It's because our families and the whole town pressured you into it, isn't it?"

Confusion flashed across his face an instant before realization took hold. Some of his intensity left him but determination tightened his jaw. "They did—I can't deny it."

"I suspected as much. I'm sorry. I shouldn't have encouraged them." She let out a short laugh. "You must have thought me so desperate. I needed a whole town to make you consider courting me and even that—" She cut herself off with a shake of her head. "Well, that's one thing you don't have to worry about anymore, at least. I'm willing to stay with you as a friend, if you like. However, you probably want to be alone."

He gave a short jerk of a nod then turned away. "You should leave."

She stared at his strong back for a moment, wanting to protest, but she wasn't going to force her presence on him if he didn't want it. She mounted Starlight and turned to look at him once more before she was swallowed by the woods. His head was bowed, his shoulders low—he looked defeated. He wasn't the only one.

She forced her gaze forward. *I knew this was a possibility. I should have prepared myself.*

Tears flooded her vision and fell in large drops on her skirt. "Lord, why am I always making these stupid mistakes and messing everything up? Please, don't let my willfulness ruin our friendship. I have no idea what he is going through right now but I ask that You work things out for Lawson. He needs to know You have good plans for his life.

"As for me…" She sighed. "I think it's time I stop trying so hard to figure out everything happening around me and just figure myself out."

That meant gathering enough courage to get to the bottom of the guilt she'd always struggled with. She'd at least gotten off to a good start by asking Kate about her parents a while ago. Of course, she hadn't gained anything from her inquiry—no information, no peace. Just the fearsome realization that the answers she needed must lie within her own mind. She just prayed she'd have the courage to find them.

Chapter Eleven

Lawson rested his forehead on the warm hide of Rosie, one of the milking cows, as he stole a glance across the aisle where Ellie patiently waited for her pesky piglet to mosey out of its stall for its morning jaunt. She turned toward him so he trained his gaze back on the bucket. She walked toward him, anyway. "Good morning, Lawson."

"Good morning."

"You missed breakfast." She placed her hands on the stall railing and leaned back as she surveyed him. "Aren't you hungry?"

He finally lifted his head to meet her gaze. "No, I ate something at my cabin."

"Oh." She stilled as though contemplating the fact that he'd never done that before. No doubt she was trying to figure out if he was avoiding her or just people in general. The answer was both.

She'd given him a convenient excuse for ending things between them yesterday. He'd wanted to keep himself from feeling the pain that might one day accompany her leaving but he hadn't planned on hurting her to do it. He hadn't truly realized how much using that excuse would hurt her until she'd laughed at how desperate and unwanted she must have seemed to him. He'd been both of those things before and Ellie was neither. He hated that he'd made her feel that way, but there was nothing he could do now. The deed was done. He had to make sure it accomplished what he needed it to because in the end he was probably saving them both from heartache.

She leaned against the stall gate. "Aren't you going to talk to me, Lawson?"

"There's nothing to say."

Her voice was quiet and sincere. "Please don't push me away. I know I made a mistake by trying to change our friendship into something it wasn't. I'm sorry for that but I don't want to let it ruin our friendship."

"You're right." He wouldn't have to lose her completely if they could just stay friends. "I'm sorry. I'm not sure how to deal with all of this."

"Neither am I."

She looked so miserable that he halfway rose to take her into his arms, then sat down with a thud. *Friends,* he reminded himself, *nothing more and nothing less.* He swallowed against the sudden lump in his throat. "Give me time, Ellie. I'll be back to my old self soon enough."

She gave him a compassionate smile then nodded once before walking away. A moment later, he glanced up to find Nathan standing in her place. His boss crossed his arms. "Do you want to tell me what's going on between you and Ellie?"

"There's nothing going on." His gaze dropped down to the pail between his boots. "We called it off."

A moment of silence stretched between them. "That's

a shame. You're going through a rough time, Lawson. This may not be the best time to make major decisions."

"The decision has been made."

"Fine, but I don't think we need that much milk. Give Rosie a rest, will you?"

He suddenly realized the pail had quite a bit more milk than they usually used. He grimaced, then stepped away from the cow with an apologetic pat. "Sorry, girl."

"Timothy," Nathan called as his son stepped into the barn. "Come take the milk to your ma. I need to talk to Lawson."

"Yes, sir." The boy skipped over and took the pail from Lawson.

Lawson smiled dubiously. "It isn't too heavy for you, is it?"

"No, I'm strong. See?" The boy grinned over his shoulder as he left.

"We need to talk about the Hardy contract." Nathan held up an official-looking document. "It was signed with a stipulation."

Lawson took the contract from him. "What kind of stipulation?"

"The full payment will be collected when the horses are delivered, which has to be within two weeks."

Lawson nodded, realizing he hadn't even considered the fact that Clive would need to come back for his horses.

"He also paid for one week of training with the horses and his men." Nathan sat down behind a modest desk and looked up at Lawson. "I'd like you to do this, Lawson. It's part of your job. Besides, one of the main reasons I hired you was so I wouldn't have to leave my family to make deliveries like this. However,

I understand that the circumstances surrounding this particular contract are unusual. If you don't want to go, I won't make you. I hope you will consider it, though. Not for the job, but for yourself."

He shifted uncomfortably. "What do you mean?"

"I mean that the past has a funny way of creeping up on us." Nathan shook his head and Lawson knew he was speaking from experience. "Trust me. Sometimes you can't truly move on until you deal with the problems you left there."

Lawson tried to ignore the chills that raced down his arms at that statement. "My first instinct is to say no but I'll consider it."

"Good." Nathan eased the moment with a smile. "You should know that I'm giving you a few days off. Let's see. Today is Thursday. Once you finish today, you don't have to report in until Monday."

Lawson frowned. "What? Why? I didn't ask for time off. I want to work."

"Then work hard today. I think you could use a few days with Doc and Ms. Lettie. Besides, this would be a good opportunity for you to decide about that contract and get a bit more perspective on your relationship with Ellie."

Lawson stared at his longtime friend-turned-boss and frowned, realizing the only answer Nathan would accept was yes. He shrugged and gave in. "All right, Nathan, if that's what you want I guess I need to make the most of my day here. I think I'll go find something to throw."

Nathan's dark eyes began to twinkle. "The stalls could use some new hay."

He rubbed his hands together. "That sounds perfect."

He climbed up to the loft and began tossing the heavy bales into disorganized submission on the barn floor. That allowed some of the pent-up aggression to ease out of him. At least, it did until he was interrupted.

"You look like you're spoiling for a fight."

Lawson stilled then turned to find his cousin peering over the loft floor with a knowing smile on his face. He watched Ethan scale the last few rungs of the ladder to stand a few feet away with his Stetson in his hands. "Who let you in here?"

"Ellie."

"Figures." Lawson grunted, then turned to push another hay bale over the edge. "You have a lot to answer for, Ethan. I thought I told you I didn't want to see that man."

"*That man* doesn't often take no for an answer."

Lawson paused to glance at him. "What do you want?"

"I thought you'd like to know Uncle Clive went back to the ranch this morning. He was pretty broken up. Not that it would matter to you." Ethan took a seat on one of the bales.

"Is that all?"

Ethan was quiet for a moment. "You should have taken a swing at him and gotten it out of your system."

Lawson turned to stare at him. "Whose side are you on?"

He gave a careless shrug. "Uncle Clive was the only family I had until I found you. We're cousins and in my book that means something. Besides, if you got some of that anger out of your system, maybe it would leave some room to let your family in."

Lawson frowned at him skeptically.

"We could go a round or two if you want." Ethan sized him up. "I think I can take you."

Lawson narrowed his eyes. "You couldn't, but it doesn't matter. I'm not going to fight you."

"We probably would have more than a few times if we'd grown up together."

Who is this man? Lawson couldn't figure him out. He knew nothing about his cousin except that they were related by blood and that didn't bode well. The unnerving thing was that Ethan seemed to know more about him than he knew about himself. He cleared his throat and decided to start digging for clues about both of them. "You're younger than me, aren't you?"

"By a few years." Ethan frowned. "Please tell me you know how old you are?"

Lawson shook his head. "Do you know?"

"I'm twenty and you're twenty-three."

"Are you sure?" At Ethan's nod, he tilted his head. "I'm younger than I thought."

Ethan laughed. "How old did you think you were?"

"Somewhere around twenty-five." He hesitantly took a seat near Ethan but not close enough to be friendly. "I guess I've had a lot of life experience."

"You were nine when they left you. From what I've gathered, that would have made you about thirteen when you came to this town. They took good care of you here, didn't they?"

He nodded. "Better than I deserved."

"We could compare stories, if you like."

"I'd rather not."

Ethan grabbed his Stetson and stood. "I'm staying at the boardinghouse in town. If you change your mind about swapping stories or have any other questions, just stop by and see me. I've given my notice at the livery so I'll be here for another two weeks."

Lawson nodded. He returned Ethan's wave before the man disappeared down the ladder. He moseyed over to the window in time to see Ethan pause to talk with Ellie, then ride off. One of these days he might take Ethan up on that offer. Until then, he had work to do.

Ellie shaded her eyes from the sun and seemed to look directly at him. Even from this distance, he could feel the concern telegraphing from her. He swallowed. Nathan was right. A little time away from the farm would be good for him.

Ellie probably should have told her family that she and Lawson had called it quits. Oh, wait. She had. It just didn't seem to change her family's perception of them as a couple or the seating arrangements at dinner. She realized that as soon as her fingers slid their usual path across Lawson's warm palm to settle in his grasp for grace that evening. When Timothy's lengthy monologue came to an end, she tried to divert her thoughts from the man beside her but failed miserably.

She passed him the sweet potatoes while gleaning a sideways glance. He caught her watching him and captured her gaze before she could look away. His hazel eyes deepened to a dark shade of olive. The corners of his mouth softened into an almost smile before an unreadable mask slipped into place and he glanced away. He'd made it clear that he'd lied about wanting to be more than friends. Odd, it hadn't felt like a lie. It had felt natural and right.

She pushed those thoughts from her mind. She wouldn't do this to herself. It would be foolish to pine for a man who didn't want her—had never wanted her. She might make a lot of mistakes but never the same one twice.

Supper passed in a flurry of chatter, though neither she nor Lawson added much to the conversation. Afterward, the men moved to the sitting room with the children, which gave Ellie the opportunity to talk freely with her sister. Kate must have realized it, too, because she glanced up from the bowl she was washing. "It's strange to see how things have changed between you and Lawson."

"Yes," Ellie admitted as she swept a dry towel across the wet plate in her hands. "It's for the best."

"Is that really how you feel?"

She absently accepted the bowl Kate handed her. "All I know is that I should have accepted that he wasn't interested in me from the start and left it alone. Instead, I messed up our friendship. The silliest part is that now I can't imagine myself with anybody else."

A moment of quiet descended around them, interrupted only by the sound of the game taking place in the sitting room. Kate's voice softly filled the void. "Are you in love with him, Ellie?"

She finished drying the bowl before setting it aside and leaning back against the counter with a sigh. "Am I? I can recognize it in everyone else but when it comes to my own feelings and Lawson's, I seem to be lost. I'm beginning to think I wouldn't know love if it came up and bit me. If this is it, then I guess I was expecting more."

"More what?"

"Oh, I don't know. More of a difference in me and the way I feel about life in general."

"Ellie, loving someone doesn't make your problems

go away." Kate shook her head wryly. "If anything, it just adds the other person's problems to the mix. The benefit is that you are able to solve them together."

"I see." So did that mean she should try to help Lawson with his problems? She could support him and encourage him even if it was only as a friend.

Kate smiled at her discouraged tone. "Have you ever heard the saying 'Love is friendship set on fire'?"

"No."

"Well, I think it's true. I had to learn to appreciate Nathan as a friend before I was able to consider him as anything more."

"But Lawson and I have been friends for years."

"Yes, and I've never seen a more romantic friendship in all my life. That's why I say going back to that might help you both. Give it time. He's dealing with a lot right now and it looks like you have a lot to figure out, too. Don't give up yet."

Ellie wasn't entirely sure that was wise. She just kept hearing that familiar refrain explaining why he'd really sought her out. The whole town had been fooled into thinking their "romantic" friendship should turn into more. The whole town—including her. How could she move past her feelings if she let herself slip right back into the old routines? "What if Lawson can't love me?"

"Then you'd have to let it go, but I think it's worth finding out. Don't you?" Kate handed her the last dish then wiped her hands on a dry towel. "Didn't you say something about giving Nathan and me a child-free evening for once? The children finished their homework and there is a bit of time left before bed. Why don't you and Lawson play with them?"

Ellie rolled her eyes then laughed. "What? Are you

charging for advice now? I wish you'd told me before I asked."

"You don't have to—"

"I want to. It will be fun," she said as she carefully put away the dishes. "Besides, I can take a hint."

"What hint?" Kate asked innocently.

"I know I didn't offer, though I should have." She lifted a coy eyebrow at her sister. "You must really want to be alone with Nathan."

Kate sent her a mischievous look. "Like I said, don't forget to invite Lawson. He might want to go along and he could definitely use a bit of fun."

It took Ellie a moment to catch on. "Oh, you're still matchmaking, aren't you?"

Kate shook her head piteously. "You're right. You really are lost when it comes to love."

Ellie popped her with the damp towel, then skedaddled out the kitchen before Kate could retaliate. Everyone looked up when she abruptly danced into the sitting room. She glanced behind her once more to make sure she hadn't been followed, then smiled. "Who's up for a game of tag?"

Lawson gave an approving nod sending Timothy sneaking through the trees toward Ellie. She gasped and whirled in the opposite direction, which happened to be directly into Lawson's path. He sidestepped her tumbling strides but caught her arm and somehow managed to keep them both upright. A small hand slapped Ellie's back, then his. "Freeze, both of you!"

They automatically froze in their somewhat awkward positions. Suddenly, Lawson's gaze snapped to

Ellie's nephew. "Wait. What just happened? I thought we were partners."

Timothy stepped away from them to scan the landscape. "No more teams. It's every man for himself."

Ellie shifted to frown at the boy in protest. "You can't play freeze tag without teams. Who is going to unfreeze us?"

Timothy's eyes lit up as he spotted his prey. "Hope. You have to stay frozen until she tags you."

That is not going to happen, he thought with a glance at the woman practically in his arms. Once Timothy ran off, Lawson stepped away before he could change his mind and do something foolish. He'd almost refused to help Ellie mind her nieces and nephew. However, he'd decided to leave for town first thing in the morning to stay with his parents as Nathan had ordered, and if he hit the hay too soon he'd just spend hours sorting through stacks of old memories.

He'd told himself a game of tag would be far easier than that. After all, the children would provide a buffer. He stared at the three small retreating forms and shook his head. *Some buffer they are.*

"Great. Now they're just hitting each other." Ellie stepped up beside him.

"I'd say it's more of a spirited tap."

She laughed. "I guess I'll let them run around a bit more then call them in."

"I think I'll go to my cabin. I have some packing to do before the morning."

"You're leaving?"

"Yes…" He watched a strong breeze suddenly toss her hair into disarray, hindered only by the single ribbon that kept her golden locks from her face. He glanced away and struggled to regain the vein of conversation. "Nathan practically insisted I take the weekend off. I'm going to spend some time with my folks."

"That will be nice." She finally corralled her hair enough for her to catch his gaze. "That means I won't see you again until church on Sunday."

He cleared his throat softly. "I guess not."

Disappointment seemed to settle in her eyes and a strange warmth filled his chest at the sight of it. He stepped away to grab his Stetson from where he'd tossed it on the grass earlier. He managed to ease the tenuous moment with a nod and half smile. "See you later."

He walked away and that should have been the end of it but it wasn't. He still had the sense that they were connected—tethered together almost. The rope wouldn't break no matter how far across the field he traveled. It just seemed to stretch along with him.

As he stopped to say goodbye to the children, he managed a quick look back at her. She must have felt his gaze for she lifted her hand in a wave. He returned the gesture before his long strides ate up the rest of the distance to his cabin. He wasn't sure what was worse—watching her walk away later or having to do it himself every day.

Chapter Twelve

Lawson leaned back on the cushioned wicker bench on his parents' porch with a discontented sigh at his cousin's stubbornness. "So you really won't try to convince your uncle to cancel that clause of the contract?"

Ethan shrugged from his perch on the matching wicker chair. "I told you, the main reason he bought those horses was to make sure you'd come to the ranch. He isn't going to cancel any clause."

"Surely, if you reason with him—"

"Not a chance, cousin."

Lawson's lips edged upward in amusement. Ethan had a habit of reiterating their relationship to each other. He'd managed to sneak that word in multiple times over dinner. Lawson wanted to find it annoying but he actually almost liked the sense of belonging it gave him. "Fine. There are some things a man has to do for himself and this might be one of them."

Ethan's eyebrows shot up in surprise. "Are you coming to the ranch, then?"

He pressed his lips together to keep from speaking an answer he didn't want to give one way or another.

He had no problem traveling to a ranch for business purposes. He could even stomach going to a ranch his father owned. The problem was that once there, another reckoning with his father seemed inevitable. He'd won the first round but he wasn't sure he'd come out on top in the next one.

"I don't want to," he said as the door opened and Doc joined them with a tray of after-dinner coffee, obviously prepared by Lettie. Lawson felt relief unwind his tense shoulders. "You're joining us, aren't you?"

The distinguished-looking gentleman smiled as he put the tray on the table next to the chair. "I was hoping for an invitation, hence the coffee, but I don't want to intrude."

"You're no intrusion, Pa." Lawson used the term purposefully with a quick glance at Ethan to see how his cousin processed that. His parents had been as stunned as she was at the news of Clive's visit, but their support and encouragement had left no doubt in Lawson's mind about who truly deserved the titles "Ma" and "Pa."

Ethan shifted uneasily but didn't protest when the older man settled onto the other end of the bench. "Lawson was just saying he didn't want to go to Uncle Clive's ranch."

Doc nodded. "It isn't a decision to be made lightly."

"I'd be more willing to go if I knew that Clive wouldn't try to—"

Ethan's blue eyes snapped. "Get to know his only son?"

Just like that, anger began to simmer in his chest. "He had a chance to do that and he lost it. That was his choice. I don't feel the need to make things easier on him by walking into his lair."

"He isn't a villain."

"To you."

"Villain or not," Doc said, calmly easing the tension, "ignoring his existence, his wishes or the past won't make any of this go away. Maybe you need this, Lawson."

"I don't want to go," he repeated, then shook his head. "I just have this awful feeling that seeing him again is inevitable, and you're right. I have to face this."

"Have you prayed about this?"

"Besides praying I wouldn't have to go?" Lawson shook his head. "No."

"I'll call your mother out and we'll do it as a family."

Lawson began to agree but paused when Ethan stood to his feet. "In that case, I think I should leave. Please tell Ms. Lettie I said thank-you for a delicious meal. It was nice to meet you, Doc. I'll be around."

Lawson stood. "Where do you think you're going?"

Ethan froze. "The boardinghouse."

"Are you a praying man?"

Ethan nodded, then shrugged. "On occasion."

Lawson glanced at Doc. "Think that will do?"

"I'm sure the Lord will be happy to hear from him."

"Pa said *family,* Ethan." He crossed his arms. "I'm pretty sure that somehow means you, unless you need to call me 'cousin' a few more times to make sure."

Ethan didn't seem to know how to respond at first. He cleared the emotion from his throat a few times before he nodded. "I reckon I can manage an *Amen* as well as anybody. I practiced in church last Sunday so I'm not that rusty."

"I heard there's going to be a prayer meeting," Lettie said as she preceded her husband onto the porch. "We should have started the evening this way but I think it's a good way to end it, too. 'Pa,' will you lead off?"

"I'd be glad to." Doc waited for Lettie to settle on the bench next to Lawson before he sat in the chair beside Ethan and bowed his head. "Heavenly Father, first and foremost, Lettie and I want to thank You for entrusting us with Your son Lawson."

Lawson swallowed as his ma's hand found his and squeezed in agreement.

"When Nathan asked if we'd give a young man a chance at a better future, I had a feeling we were giving ourselves the best possible future as well, and I was right. Now, we ask that You give Lawson the strength, wisdom and courage he needs to face his past. Give him peace."

After a moment of silence, Lettie took her turn. "God, I pray for Clive right now."

Lawson couldn't help but tense at her words.

"I can certainly understand him wanting to get to know Lawson. I pray that if it's Your will, it will happen in Your time and in Your way. Whether he knows You or not, let this situation draw Clive closer to You."

It was Lawson's turn. He knew it, so he cleared his throat of the emotion clogging it. "I just want to do the right thing, Lord." For some reason, that made him think of Ellie. He was doing the right thing by letting her go, wasn't he? "Help me to be strong. Help me to make the right choices. Help me to know what those are."

Ethan was quiet for so long that Lawson wondered if it might be best to let him off the hook. When Ethan finally spoke, his deep voice was quiet but entreating.

"All I ask is that You teach us—all of us—how to be a family."

Family. Was it made of blood? He stole a glance at his cousin. Or law? He rubbed his mother's cool hand. He closed his eyes and saw Ellie standing in the field with the wind blowing in her hair. Or love? Was any of it enough to truly bind people together? Ten years ago, that downtrodden boy without a last name would have said no, but tonight—tonight, he wanted to say yes more than anything. Would this feeling of belonging disappear if he surrendered to it? Maybe. Maybe not. It was too precious for him to take that chance, so he settled for the next best thing. He pushed that desire into the corner of his heart where only God could see it, then allowed his whisper to blend with the voices that echoes around him in a final "Amen."

Ellie snuggled deeper into the cushions of Ms. Lettie's comfortable settee with her eyes closed against the morning sunlight in an effort to doze. The corners of her mouth tipped upward slightly when the settee sank to the right a few moments later. Lawson's deep voice drawled in amusement, "You look like you either need a nap or a cup of coffee."

"Probably both." She kept her eyes closed to concentrate on the rich tone of his voice.

"Why are you so sleepy?"

"I stayed up most of the night reading. I didn't even look at the clock until it was too late—literally and figuratively." She lifted her lashes to meet his gaze with a wry smirk. "Of course, I also woke up an hour earlier than normal to teach Sunday school to imaginary students."

"'What Sunday school?'" he asked, quoting Pastor Brightly's exact words.

She shook her head. The man had wandered into the church to find them waiting for their pupils to arrive. After twenty minutes without anyone coming, they'd been ready to give up, anyway. Pastor Brightly had informed them that Sunday school had been canceled due to a lack of attendance last week. Apparently, children didn't like the idea of going to school an additional day of the week.

"I can't believe no one told me." She shifted more to the left for a better view of Lawson, who sat at the opposite end of the settee with his ankle propped on his knee.

He placed his arm on the back of the settee. "I guess I should warn you that the town isn't taking the news that we broke things off very well. They're actually pretty up in arms about it."

"I assumed they would be." She fiddled with the fringe on the pillow resting between them. "They were the ones who convinced you to pursue me in the first place so they're bound to be disappointed that their efforts weren't enough."

Lawson shifted slightly away. "Where are my parents? We should leave soon."

Ms. Lettie made a timely entrance into the parlor with Doc right behind her. "We're ready when you are."

"Thanks for letting me rest here until the service." Ellie corralled her slightly mussed hair back into place as she stood. "I don't know what else I would have done with myself."

Doc smiled fondly at her. "You're always welcome here. Shall we go?"

Doc offered his arm to his wife and the two set off,

leaving Lawson and Ellie to follow. They walked the rest of the way to the church in silence where they confused the gathering parishioners by arriving together, then immediately separating. Ellie managed to avoid anything more than a few concerned and curious glances as she wound her way to her sister-in-law. They barely had time to exchange a hug before Lorelei sent her a warning look. "Don't look now, but the Peppin Inquisition is on its way."

She barely had time to turn around before Maddie, Sophia, Amy and Isabelle appeared at her side. Maddie immediately pulled Ellie into an embrace. "Oh, my dear, dear friend. We are so sorry to hear about you and Lawson. You must feel awful."

"Thanks, girls," she said when she could breathe again. "I'm fine. We weren't even officially courting so you don't need to worry about me."

Amy searched her face with a frown. "Don't tell me you're the one who broke his heart and not the other way around?"

"Hardly." She glanced at Lawson who was across the churchyard no doubt getting the same treatment from Sean, Jeff, Rhett and Chris. "It seems that all the matchmaking from the town and our families made him think he needed to pretend emotions he wasn't feeling. I shouldn't have encouraged y'all. It was all a big mistake, nothing more."

Silence followed her statement as the girls exchanged significant looks with each other. Maddie finally broke the silence. "Ellie, did he say that was the reason he broke things off?"

"Yes." She couldn't interpret the strange looks on her friends' faces. "What?"

Lorelei stepped closer and whispered as if Lawson might overhear, despite their distance away from him. "It just can't be true, that's all. He encouraged us to matchmake the same as you. Oh, he didn't give us pointers like you did at Maddie and Jeff's engagement party, but he told his parents that he was willing to cooperate. I promised him myself that you wouldn't find out he was in on it."

Sophia smiled. "You see, Ellie? You didn't make a mistake."

She felt a weight lift off her soul as those words settled into her mind. Her words came out more as an exclamation than a question. "Why would he lie to me?"

Amy shushed her, throwing a quick glance over her shoulder at the men. "He was probably trying to hide the real reason. That's the way men are. He's probably upset about something else entirely."

Sophia nodded. "Whatever the reason, we know for sure that it isn't what he told you."

"I don't know. He isn't usually one to lie. And come to think of it, he didn't actually say that was his reason. I brought it up, and he just agreed. Maybe he doesn't want to tell me the real reason because it's something worse. Either way, I'm not sure the reason matters if the bottom line is that he doesn't want to be more than friends with me."

"Of course it matters," Lorelei protested.

Ellie glanced around the circle of her friends who nodded adamantly. "But, even when we tried being more than friends, he didn't seem that serious about me."

"Serious?" Maddie asked. "The only other girl he ever expressed interest in he was willing to marry."

Lorelei laughed. "He wasn't half as interested in me as he has been in you, which proves to me that he knows he has a shot at creating something incredible with you. For some reason he doesn't want to admit, he's willing to walk away from that. All I can say is don't make it that easy for him."

The church bell rang to announce the service would start in a few minutes, so the girls dispersed, save Lorelei, who lingered for a moment. "Did you ever finish that list you were making?"

"Actually, I forgot about it. I guess I've been distracted."

"Perhaps you should finish it." Lorelei gave her a little wink then left. Ellie spotted Kate, Nathan and their children arriving, so she excused herself to meet up with them. Someone started matching her steps. *Donovan Turner.*

"Hello, Miss Ellie. You'll be pleased to know that I sold my farm."

She stopped abruptly to face him. "You did what? Why?"

"It was keeping us apart." He removed his hat.

She stared at him in shock. "Please tell me you didn't sell your farm because of me."

He puffed out his chest proudly. "Sure I did. Now that you're no longer with Lawson there is nothing to stand in our way."

"My goodness!" She glanced around and though no one seemed to have noticed their interlude, she kept her voice quiet but urgent so as not to embarrass him. "You've got to get your farm back. No, don't shake your head. Please stop smiling at me and listen. I am not interested in you, Mr. Turner. It has nothing to do with whether or not you're a pig farmer. You won't seem to heed my brother-in-law but you need to listen to me. You have to stop this. You're making me uncomfortable. I don't want you to seek me out anymore. Do you understand me?"

As she spoke, the smile on his face slowly faded to confusion then disappointment. "But, there's no other girl for me. We have to be together."

"There is another girl somewhere who's right for you but I'm afraid it isn't and never will be me."

His eyes seemed to harden.

She softened, realizing her words must have wounded him mightily. "I'm sorry if I hurt your feelings. I'm not trying to. Honest, I'm not. Just please find someone else. Oh, and talk to Judge Hendricks. Maybe he can help you get your farm back."

She hurried away holding her breath until she was sure he wasn't following her. When she reached Kate and Nathan she told them what happened. They both assured her she'd done the right thing. Even so, the look in Donovan's eyes after she told him they'd never be together was not one she'd soon forget.

The end of Lawson's match burst into flame a moment before he led his mount through the barn door. He turned to light the lantern that normally hung inside the door, but realized it was missing just as he spotted its golden glow reflecting off the window near the south side of the barn. It illuminated a rather familiar feminine form that slept cuddled uncomfortably on a wooden chair. His lips pulled into a slight smile before he trained them into a curious frown.

A few moments later, his horse properly settled for

the night, he surveyed Ellie's slumbering features. She looked pure, innocent in the pool of light that spilled across her features into her golden hair and down her yellow dress. The open dime novel in her hand had slowly slipped from her lax fingers to dangle perilously toward the ground. As he watched, it broke free from her grasp. He instinctively tried to catch it before it could fall and awaken her but it didn't do any good for she startled awake.

He stepped back and closed the book. "I didn't mean to frighten you."

"That's all right." Her hand sleepily rubbed across her cheek then slipped into her hair. "I wasn't supposed to be sleeping, anyway."

"What are you doing in here this time of night?" He handed her the book.

"Abigail is foaling. It's her first and Nathan wants to make sure there aren't any complications. I'm supposed to keep watch until eleven o'clock, then he's taking over."

He eyed the mare that appeared to be sleeping. "Did you tell Nathan that you didn't sleep much last night?"

"No. It's my own fault for staying up late. I'm not going to shirk my duties because of that."

"I see." He wandered down the aisle until he found a stool, then carried it back to where Ellie sat. "I'll keep watch until Nathan gets here. You go on to bed."

Her eyes widened but she shook her head. "You don't have to do that. Besides, I'm awake now. Perhaps you could stay a while to keep me awake."

He stared at her, thoroughly confused. She'd been sending him mixed signals since the day after they'd broken things off. He should have rejected her invitation. He should have gotten up and walked away or insisted she leave. He knew that so why did he nod? Why did he straddle the stool and allow a companionable silence to fall between them? It was probably because he was a little bit crazy and very foolish. Or, maybe he was just curious about how she managed to read her book upside down without knowing it. He glanced at Abigail. "Are you sure that horse is foaling?"

He'd managed to startle her again. Had she fallen back to sleep? She set her book aside. "She was before I went to sleep. You don't suppose she already had it and I slept through it?"

"I don't think so."

She went back to reading her book upside down. He wondered how long she could keep it up then she lifted her green eyes to his. "Have you decided about the trip?"

He nodded but glanced away. "I'm going."

She let that answer stand for a moment before she softly asked, "Why?"

He rolled his shoulders in a shrug. "I've always had that one fear lurking in the back of my head that I was like my father or would somehow end up like him— them, really…my parents. No matter what I do I can't seem to make it go away. Until now, I've never had the opportunity to know—really know how we're similar or different. Now I do."

He glanced up to meet her gaze with intensity. "The only thing I want less than to see my father again is to live with that thought haunting me for the rest of my life. Either way, I've got to know."

"I know what you mean about having a fear hanging

over you." She rubbed her arms and frowned. "Only I'm not sure I'm brave enough to face up to mine."

"What is it?"

"I don't know. Isn't that the strangest thing?" Her voice quieted as she stared into the distance. "Mrs. Greene knows part of it. Maybe she knows all of it but I don't want to ask her. It has something to do with my parents."

"I remember you mentioning this at the graveyard."

"Yes, and you told me to forget about it but I can't. You see, I don't remember much about my parents but I do remember that they were full of life and laughter. Then one day they were gone. They just died. They were too young to die." She bit her lip. "Ever since then, in the back of my head, I've always had this fear—this nagging sense that I did something to make them go away."

He frowned. "That's hard to imagine from what I've heard of your parents. They didn't choose to die like my parents chose to leave."

Her eyes refocused on his, and a wan smile touched her lips. "My head says you're right but my heart isn't convinced."

"I understand." He would have continued the conversation but Abigail decided to remember that she was going to have a foal. Lawson watched her carefully as she began to pace. Everything seemed to be progressing normally. As Lawson kept an eye on the nervous mare, Ellie subtly turned her book right side up and began to read. It wasn't long before the book was drooping in her hands again. He shook his head. "Aren't you ready to give up yet?"

She didn't respond so he whispered a promise to Abigail that he'd be back, then managed to lift Ellie from the chair into his arms. She stirred but he was fairly certain that she was too sleepy to realize he was taking her to the farmhouse. He mounted the steps to the porch, then called her name to awaken her. "Do you think you can stand?"

"Mmm-hmm."

He glanced down to meet her mischievous eyes with a frown. "You little faker. You were awake the whole time."

She didn't go far when he set her down. In fact, she left her arms around his neck and leveled her deep green eyes at him in the evening shadows. "All right, I'm a little faker. I admit it. I think you'd better admit something, too."

"What?" He thought about removing his hands from her waist but got distracted when she poked him in the chest.

"You are a faker, too."

He released her. "What are you talking about?"

One of her hands slipped to her hip as she lifted her chin. "You agreed with me when I said that you only courted me because everyone was pressuring you, but that's not the truth. You didn't feel pressured by the town's matchmaking. You *encouraged* it. You wanted to be more than friends just like I did."

He should deny it but the hurt in her eyes after he'd ended their fledgling courtship kept him from doing that. He rubbed his stubbly jaw and turned his gaze to the star-covered sky so he wouldn't have to look her in the eye. "Who told you?"

"It doesn't matter. The whole town knew." She tugged him slightly closer, arresting his attention once more. "Why did you let me believe something that wasn't true?"

"I didn't know it would hurt you as badly as it did. I just…I thought it would be simpler than telling the truth."

"What is the truth?"

He lifted his hand to cradle her chin and swept his thumb against her smooth cheek as he faced it for the first time himself. He cared for Ellie as a friend but his feelings went far deeper than that—so deep that they were dangerously close to love. It wouldn't be a weak sort of love, either. At least, not according to the feelings she'd inspired so far.

His past told him that if he let her that close—closer than he'd let anyone before—she was bound to leave. Maybe not tomorrow or in a year, but one day. Somehow he had to make her understand.

"The truth is that I'm not the man for you, Ellie. You deserve so much more than what I have to offer. One day you're going to realize that I'm not enough and you're going to walk away. I don't want my broken heart trailing behind you."

She barely let him finish before she shook her head. "The only one walking away from this is you, Lawson. Not me. Maybe that's saving your heart but it's breaking mine and I won't stand by and watch it happen."

He tensed at her declaration. The last thing he needed was for her to make this more difficult than it already was. His hands found their way to her arms. "We agreed to go back to being friends."

She leaned into his touch and tilted her head back to meet his gaze in a challenge of temptation. A hint of a smile touched her lips. "Is that what this is? Then by all means, Lawson, let's be friends."

"Ellie," he groaned. "You're not being fair."

She swayed onto her tiptoes to give him a soft but lingering kiss. "Good night, Lawson."

He'd never heard anyone say his name like that before. Her voice caressed those two simple syllables as if they were something precious—as if he was something important and dear. It took him a moment to realize that he was the one holding on to her. He released her. "Good night, Ellie."

Chapter Thirteen

Ellie went into the house, hurried up the stairs to her room and peered out her window to see Lawson standing just where she'd left him. No doubt the shocked look on his face hadn't changed, either. A smile tilted her lips when he slowly walked toward the barn. She lit her lamp, then grabbed her nightgown and spun in a joyous circle. "I didn't make a mistake. I didn't! I actually did the right thing for once. Thank You, Lord!"

She changed into her nightgown, marveling at how close she'd been to letting him go without a fight. That *really* would have been a mistake. She still had a chance. She'd seen it in his eyes and heard it in his voice even as he'd told her he wasn't the man for her.

She pulled the Bachelor List from beneath her mattress, then settled onto the stool in front of her vanity to look at it. She'd given a match to nearly everyone on her list except Lawson. From the way he talked, he probably wouldn't give himself a match at all. He seemed to think love would expose something inside of him that would frighten her away. Didn't he know that wasn't the way romantic love worked?

What about God's love? she asked herself, then wondered where that thought had come from. She knew she had God's love. She knew that Lawson had it, too. Didn't he realize that it covered a multitude of sins? God would never leave him…and if Lawson gave her a chance, then neither would she.

She found a pencil, then proceeded to circle Lawson's name before placing her initials beside it with a deliberate flare. *I won't let him cheat himself and some fortunate woman out of a beautiful future—especially if that woman might be me.*

She blew out the lamp and slipped under the covers. Sleep beckoned her, lowering her defenses. A wisp of a memory fluttered through her mind. She could almost hear her mother's voice. *"You did a bad thing, Ellie. A very bad thing."*

Her sleep-laden lashes flew open as she instinctively pushed the thought away. She swallowed. Gathering her courage, she closed her eyes and allowed the memory to wash over her.

She looked up at her mother through tear-blurred eyes. Her father knelt beside her. "Do you know what you did wrong?"

"I told a secret."

"We have to fix this," her mother said.

Her father nodded, but looked doubtful. "There's a storm coming in."

"I know, but she's ruined Amelia!"

Her parents scolded her once more and she sulked off to the settee to watch the flurry of activity as her parents got ready to leave. She refused to say goodbye to them because she was smarting from their rebuke. They left and they never came back.

Ellie gasped as realization filled her then left her breathless. The guilt that she'd always felt in the back of her mind settled in the pit of her stomach and tripped up to her lips. "It's my fault. They left that day because of me…my stupid mistake… I wanted to feel important by telling others about Mrs. Greene. It's my fault they died."

These were the consequences Mrs. Greene had mentioned. And yes, they were just as awful as she'd promised. How could she face her siblings now knowing the truth? She couldn't tell them. Not after all these years. She didn't want to see them try to disguise their feelings to make her feel better. They'd tell her it wasn't her fault. They'd be lying.

I think I knew the truth all along. I was always afraid it was true—afraid I was right.

She could no longer hide from the memory or the disappointment she remembered hearing in their voices. They had been so disappointed in her—had died while still upset over what she had done. And if they had lived, she would have upset them so many more times with her endless stream of mistakes—except for Lawson. Despite her earlier fears, she hadn't made a mistake with him. It wasn't enough to rectify her earlier mistakes, but it was a start.

Pushing away her covers, she settled on her knees beside her bed in a position she only assumed when she desperately needed help. "Lord, I prayed that You would reveal what happened to me and You did. I don't know that I'm particularly grateful for that but I finally know. What am I supposed to do now? I'm so tired of feeling guilty and dirty. I thought knowing might relieve me of that but I just feel worse. Will You help me, please? Show me what to do."

She paused, realizing that was the first time in a very long time that she'd actually prayed for direction instead of just handing out an order. She grimaced. All right, so maybe she had a little to learn about walking with God instead of running ahead of Him. At this point, her sense of direction was so confused that she had no idea where she was, let alone where she was supposed to be going. Perhaps she'd try to let Him lead for a while just to see how it felt. Anything would be better than this.

Lawson ran a nervous hand through his hair. He hesitated for a moment then stepped into the Rutledges' kitchen for breakfast. A quick sweep of the room revealed that it was empty of everyone except Kate. She glanced up from the pancakes she was frying and placed her hand on her hip. "It's about time you showed your face in my kitchen, Lawson Williams. I was starting to get offended."

He grinned. "You know I can't stay away from your cooking for long."

"The laces fell out again, Ma." Timothy clomped into the room in his untied boots and stopped in his tracks at the sight of Lawson. "How come you don't eat breakfast anymore? Don't you get hungry?"

"I'm hungry today." He gestured the boy closer. "How about some help with those boots?"

As he helped Timothy straighten out the tangled laces, Nathan arrived in the kitchen with baby Matthew in his arms and chuckled when he spotted Lawson. "I wondered how long it would take you to get sick of your own cooking."

Timothy stopped him when he began tying the shoes. "Thank you, but I like to tie them."

Lawson settled into his chair just as Ellie entered with her nieces in tow. Surprise painted her features just as it had the rest of her family's. All right, so he couldn't blame them for being surprised. He'd been taking meals with them less often lately. Today he settled into his normal place at the table because for the first time in a long time he hadn't battled against his memories to win a few hours of sleep. No, last night he'd stayed awake thinking about Ellie.

He'd thought about the silly way she'd read her book upside down. He thought about the concern in her voice when they'd talked about his upcoming trip. He'd thought of the way she'd belittled her own courage. He'd thought about the words they'd shared at the door and the kiss she'd given him.

Ellie's familiar hand slipped into his. He stilled for a moment before he realized Nathan was praying a blessing over the meal and over the day. She promptly removed her hand from his once the prayer was over. As breakfast progressed he couldn't help but notice that Ellie seemed much more subdued than normal. He stole a glance at her to discover that her cheeks lacked their usual bloom and her eyes their usual sparkle. Had his rejection done this to her? She hadn't seemed discouraged last night. She'd seemed eager—even excited—to face the challenge of winning him over.

When nearly everyone was finished, Nathan cleared his throat. "Well, before everyone rushes off, you might all be interested in meeting the new addition to our ranch."

The whole table stilled except Grace and baby Matthew. Ellie leaned forward with the eagerness previously missing from her person. "Abigail had her foal."

"She had a healthy colt."

Kate grinned. "Now we get to name it."

After breakfast the entire family walked out to the barn to welcome the new addition. As soon as Ellie's pig caught sight of them, it gave an attention-grabbing screech. Lawson veered his path to open the pig's pen. "Demanding little thing, aren't you?"

Ellie paused to watch the pig hightail it toward the field at a brisk trot. "He isn't very little anymore. He's growing fast."

"That only means he's becoming even bigger trouble."

She wrinkled her nose at him. "You never did like Hamlet."

"I don't mind the play or the pig. It's the man who gave it to you that I have a problem with."

"Donovan Turner?"

"Nathan informed me of his latest maneuver."

She rolled her eyes. "Nathan worries too much."

He quirked a dubious brow. "The man sold his farm."

"I know." She couldn't deny a grimace. "So he's a little crazy and a little strange. That doesn't mean he's dangerous like Nathan seems to think."

"No, it doesn't. But there's no harm in being cautious. Don't let your guard down around him, and don't go places alone." Having delivered his words of advice, he would have rejoined her family, but she caught his arm to keep him from leaving.

"I have something for you." She held up a folded piece of paper that she'd pulled from her pocket. "Let's call it a declaration of intent."

He caught her wrist to still her waving hand and took

the paper from her. He opened it, trying his best to ignore the way she leaned against his arm to get a look at it, too. "What is this?"

"You'll figure it out."

He did. It didn't take him long once he realized it was a list people who all had one thing in common—they were bachelors. Most of the names were lightly crossed out and were accompanied by a set of initials. His name was last on the list. It wasn't crossed out. Instead, a bold circle set it apart from the others. He swallowed. "Those are your initials, aren't they?"

"Yep." She took the list, then folded it before placing it safely back in her pocket. "I thought you might like to know that I'm serious about this."

"I guess it doesn't matter that I still don't think it's a good idea."

She patted his arm as she led him toward the barn. "Of course it matters. It just doesn't change what I'm going to do."

"It won't work."

"I think you're just afraid that it will. One thing is certain…I'm going to have a whole lot of fun trying."

He should be angry at her for ignoring his wishes. He should make her give up this game right here and now. He didn't for one very simple reason. He was a man with a history of being abandoned, and being sought out might be a welcome change—even if he knew it wouldn't last. He would be leaving for Clive's ranch in a couple of days, anyway. He just had to stay strong until then.

A sharp whistle and a hiss of steam from the black iron giant announced the arrival of the ten-fifteen train into the station. As it lumbered to a stop, Ellie saw Lawson's face turn a couple of shades paler before he set his jaw and stood a little straighter. For a moment she wished Nathan hadn't trumped up a reason for her to accompany Lawson to the station instead of him. While she appreciated the few minutes she'd have alone with Lawson, Nathan might have had a better idea of what to say to make this trip easier on Lawson.

She hadn't even realized she'd reached out to hold his hand or that he was holding it right back until she saw him staring down at it. He released her under the guise of collecting the lead ropes for the three horses he was taking with him. "Ethan better get here soon. I'm not doing this alone."

"I could always go with you."

The skeptical look she received told her just how likely that was to happen. "The town would love that. We wouldn't step more than a foot off the train when we returned before they'd make us get married."

She lifted a brow. "Maybe I should come then."

"That isn't funny."

"It wasn't a joke."

She realized it probably wasn't attractive to smirk, and glanced away from Lawson just as Jeff Bridger stopped to greet them. The metal deputy's badge on his chest barely outshone his smile. "Don't tell me you two are eloping?"

Her laughter clashed with Lawson's exasperated tone. "We aren't eloping."

Jeff's eyes twinkled. "A man can hope, can't he? Well, it's good to see you two together again."

"We aren't together," Lawson corrected. His gaze

brushed her before he continued quietly. "At least, not the way you mean."

"Why are you two unchaperoned folks heading off by yourselves, then?"

"Lawson is taking those horses to a buyer. I'm just seeing them off." Her fingers tightened on Starlight's reins as she lifted her chin to indicate the horses under Lawson's control. It was always hard to say goodbye to them after she'd spent so much time helping raise and train them. Starlight seemed to sense her mood and shuffled closer until Ellie was able to lean against her.

Jeff eyed the other horses and whistled. "They sure are beautiful. I wouldn't want to handle all three of those horses alone, Lawson. Maybe you should take Ellie with you."

"No. Ethan Law—Larue is going with me." Lawson's brow lowered into a weary expression. "His uncle is the one who bought them. There's Ethan now. We'd better get these horses loaded."

They said goodbye to Jeff and met Ethan near the stock car. Lawson stepped forward to speak with the man in charge of loading the horses, so she turned to meet Ethan's blue eyes with a smile. "I have a surprise for you."

"For me?"

"Yes." She opened her reticule and pulled out his freshly laundered handkerchief. "I bet you thought I'd stolen it for good."

He chuckled. "To tell the truth, I'd forgotten all about it. Thanks for returning it. I'm glad to be leaving you much happier than I found you."

Lawson returned and tied the horses to a nearby hitching post. "Ellie, Wesley says Ethan and I should take our seats. Seems he's particular about loading the horses himself. Will you watch to make sure they get on all right?"

"Sure."

"Thanks. Time to go, Ethan."

"Bye, Ellie. I'll leave you two to say goodbye."

"Goodbye, Ethan." She returned his parting smile then turned to Lawson. "Well, I guess this is it."

"Yep. Remember to have Sean see you home." His gaze met hers for an instant before it darted away. "See you in a week."

She blinked and he was already hurrying to catch up with Ethan. There was no way he was in that much of a hurry to start this trip, which could only mean that he was trying to avoid her. She should have expected that since he'd had plenty of practice at it over the past three days.

She narrowed her eyes, tied Starlight's reins to a post and rushed after him. "Lawson Williams, stop right there."

He frowned at her and didn't stop but slowed his pace. "Ellie, I have to catch the train."

"You know I care about you even if you refuse to admit that you return my feelings. You're leaving for a week. Can't you muster up something better than that pathetic excuse for a goodbye you just gave me?"

"You mean like a kiss?"

She froze in surprise. "Yes, if you're offering it."

"Well, since I'll be gone a whole week, I reckon one kiss wouldn't hurt." He slipped one arm around her waist and the other behind her back to dip her back slightly. He placed a gentle kiss on her forehead before setting her upright. "Goodbye, Ellie."

"You aren't half as funny as you think you are." She wrinkled her nose at his wink, then placed her hands on her hips and watched him walk away laughing. "We'll see who gets the last laugh when I buy my ticket and get on that train."

He sent her one last warning look before he mounted the steps and disappeared into the railcar. She rubbed her forehead. "I guess something is better than nothing."

The conductor gave another call as she wandered back to where she'd left her horse. Starlight was gone. She glanced around the bustling train station. An ominous bang announced the closing of the last stock car. She turned to face the train with a dreadful sense of foreboding. She rushed to the attendant that had been helping Lawson. "Wesley, where is my horse?"

"How should I know?"

"You've seen my horse. She's white with a gray mane. I left her tied right there."

He washed his hand over his face. "Lawson told me to put all the horses tied there on the train."

Her frantic gaze flew to the stock car. "You have to get her off that train."

"That's impossible. The train will be leaving any minute. There's no time."

"But the train can't leave with my horse on it!" She glanced around for help and caught sight of Jeff standing nearby. "Deputy, please make this man take Starlight off that train."

"I told her I can't do that." The attendant shook his head. "Lawson said he was coming back. I'm sure he'll bring your horse."

She turned to Jeff entreatingly. She couldn't be sure but she thought she caught the tail end of a wink. "I saw the whole thing. You loaded that horse into a different stock car. Lawson will never know Starlight is there."

Wesley scratched his head. "Come to think of it, you might be right."

"You saw the whole thing? Why didn't you stop him?"

Jeff shrugged. "Maybe you're supposed to go on this trip after all. The Lord works in mysterious ways."

"Oh! You can't blame this on Him." She panicked as the train began to move. "What do I do?"

Jeff caught her arm and rushed her toward the passenger car. "You're going to get on that train. You can get off at the next stop and collect your horse, then ride back to town. Maybe you and Lawson will part better farther down the road."

"I don't want to see him. I just want my horse." The plan sounded crazy, but she didn't have time to think of an alternative. She hopped onto the moving train with his help. Bracing herself, she turned toward Jeff and yelled, "I don't have a ticket!"

He just waved and smiled. She wanted to throw something at him. This was ridiculous. She should jump off. She stared at the ground passing by in front of her. Too late to go back now. She gritted her teeth. "I've been bamboozled!"

Chapter Fourteen

There was nothing she could do but climb the stairs and open the door to the train car. She scanned it for Lawson and Ethan and found them seated at the very front of the car. They hadn't seen her. Her first instinct was to rush over to them and demand they do something to help her. Then she remembered her foolish jest to Lawson about joining him on the train. She quickly slid onto the nearest open seat. *He's going to think I'm trying to trap him into marrying me.*

The man across from her grinned. "You almost didn't make it."

She smiled weakly. "Did the conductor pass through here yet?"

"No, miss," he said before he disappeared behind his newspaper.

"Oh." She swallowed. "Good."

She probably only had a few minutes before she would be kicked off the train in high style. She closed her eyes. Well, that would be fine with her. She just wanted to get her horse and leave. She bit her lip nervously. Would the conductor be more or less lenient if she was traveling under the protection of two men?

She shifted in her seat to peek at them, then abruptly sank down in her seat when the conductor entered the car. Five minutes later, he made it down the aisle to stand in front of her. "Ticket."

"I don't have one," she said quietly as though a lack of volume might lessen the seriousness of her offense.

His lips turned down into what seemed to be a familiar expression to his face. "What did you say?"

She winced at the censure of his question and the weight of her traveling companions' glances. "I'm sorry. It really isn't my fault. You see, the man loading the livestock car accidentally put my horse on the train and he wouldn't let me get it off."

"So you thought that entitled you to a free ride?"

"No. I was still trying to figure out what to do when my friend took action and practically forced me on the train."

His eyes narrowed suspiciously.

She held up her right hand as though swearing on a Bible. "I'm telling the truth. I promise. You can let me off right now if you want. Please, just let me get my horse. Her name is Starlight. I've had her since she was born. The poor girl is probably scared crazy."

The man across from her lowered the newspaper and eyed first her, then the conductor. "If you stop this train, I'm getting off, too. It's already running late. I have places to be even if the rest of these folks don't."

The conductor frowned harder. "The next stop isn't for another fifty miles. I can't keep her on the train that long without a ticket."

"I can pay my fare—"

"I don't take money. I just take tickets."

The woman next to her shifted forward to enter the fray. "I hope you aren't seriously considering putting this young woman off the train. Look out the window. There's nothing out there but open land, rattlesnakes and probably a few outlaws. Anything could happen to her."

"Let her stay," the newspaper man said, as though that settled it.

The conductor crossed his arms. "All right, missy, you can stay until we get to the next stop. At that time I will personally see to it that you take your horse and yourself off this train. Do you understand?"

"Yes, sir."

"I will also report you to the company so they'll know what to do if you take any unplanned trips in the future."

Ellie let out a sigh of relief when he turned to the other side of the aisle. She waited until he left the car to thank her traveling companions. The man across from her sent her a conspiratorial wink before returning to his newspaper while the woman sitting next to her patted her hand comfortingly, and started a conversation that lasted for nearly the entire fifty miles.

The train finally stopped at the next station, and the disembarking passengers began to file past her. She started to rise but the man across from her shook his head. "Wait for the warden. He wanted to see you off personally, remember?"

"Oh, right." She perched on the seat again while her gaze combed the aisle for a sign of the conductor. She was greeted instead with the sight of Lawson and Ethan rising from their seats. This was their stop, too. She grimaced. If they didn't see her, she could return home without Lawson ever knowing she was here.

The man across from her began to fold his paper and set it aside. She impulsively reached toward it. "I'm sorry. Do you mind if I borrow this?"

"Go right ahead," he said. "Though I'm pretty sure the conductor will recognize you, anyway."

"That's fine, but tell me when those two cowboys pass."

The woman next to her leaned in. "This is Texas, honey. You'll have to be more specific."

She glanced at the woman. "There are two young, particularly attractive ones."

"I see them." The woman smiled. "If I was you, I sure wouldn't hide from them."

Ellie bit her lip to keep from laughing and drawing attention to herself. A few moments passed before the woman told her she was safe. She let out a relieved sigh. She carefully folded the newspaper and handed it to the man just in time for the conductor to appear at her side. "This is your stop, miss."

She grabbed her reticule and stood. The conductor gestured with the Stetson in his hand for her to precede him. She hid a smile of confusion at his hat then started walking toward the exit. She stopped abruptly, realizing she should at least say goodbye to her new friends. The conductor grumbled at her to keep walking so she did—backward...just for a moment as she said goodbye. That was all it took to slam into someone.

The air rushed out of Lawson's lungs in a whoosh, stirring the curls of the blond woman who'd backed into him. He found it strange that the conductor reached out to steady him, not her. "Are you all right, sir?"

"Yes," he managed. The woman stiffened, murmured something unintelligible that could hardly pass for an apology, then kept her back turned as she moved past him. He returned his focus to the conductor. "I left my—"

His voice stopped abruptly as he reached out to catch the arm of the woman trying to sneak down the aisle. He tugged her around to face him. The woman bit the corner of her pink lips while her cheeks flushed, enhancing their rosy hue, and her large green eyes trailed up to meet his. *Ellie.*

His brain stopped working for a moment as he tried to reconcile that the woman was standing in front of him after he'd left her at the train station fifty miles back. He suddenly remembered her threat to follow him, so they'd be forced to marry. *No, she wouldn't do that.*

But why else would she be here? Why was she being escorted by the conductor? What was going on? He should ask her any or all of those questions but they fled when her mouth teased into a smile and she innocently quipped, "Hello."

"Hello." She was here but she shouldn't be and that pretty much summed up the past several days of his life. He'd avoided her, purposefully annoyed her, tried to discourage her, but she kept turning up just when he needed her—like right now when he was about to face his past head-on once and for all. He wasn't supposed to need her. He shouldn't be the least bit glad to see her and yet he couldn't deny that a little part of him was. *Just because she's here now, doesn't mean she's going to stay in my life forever. It's only been three days.*

He knew that, so why didn't he let her go? His thumb stroked her arm even as his heart seemed to dislodge just enough to connect with hers. Was it his imagination or did she lean into his touch? The conductor cleared his throat. "You said you left something?"

"My hat." His gaze flew to the conductor's before settling back on Ellie's.

"Here it is. I was going to take it to the lost and found."

A nearby passenger snickered. "It looks like he found something better."

"Wish I'd found it first," another drawled.

Lawson suddenly became aware of the gaping railcar of travelers. He took his Stetson and guided Ellie off the train. Ethan was waiting just where he'd left him. She explained how she'd ended up on the train as they collected the horses and recovered Starlight. He shook his head. "Why didn't you just wire ahead and tell me?"

She stilled. "I didn't even think of that. It all happened so quickly."

Ethan slid a sly glance his way before turning to Ellie. "You should stay. It will only take a week—"

"That isn't a good idea." Lawson frowned.

"You know just as much about these horses as Lawson, if not more."

He crossed his arms. "You mean I could have sent her instead?"

"It would be fun." Ethan tipped his head toward Lawson. "This fellow could use another ally, anyway, if you know what I mean."

Ellie's gaze stumbled back and forth between them. "Oh, I couldn't do that."

Lawson nodded firmly. "No, she couldn't. Come on.

We have to wire Peppin to let your family know you're safe, then get a ticket for you to go back home."

"You'd let her travel unaccompanied?" Ethan asked, his disapproval apparent.

"Why not? She rode all the way here without—" He almost said "without incident" then caught himself when he realized it wasn't true.

"Just a minute," Ellie objected as she crossed her arms suspiciously. "Why couldn't I stay if I wanted to? Ethan is right. I'll get into all sorts of trouble if I go back alone—just see if I don't. Besides, there is a chaperone at Clive's ranch, isn't there?"

Ethan nodded staunchly. "Ruth, the housekeeper and cook, will keep everyone in line."

"You could use an ally. I'd be a great one, I promise." Her green eyes turned slightly desperate and very hopeful. "Besides, I wouldn't mind getting away from the ranch for a little while. A change would be good for me."

She was right. He could use another ally. Still, he wasn't sure it was an idea Nathan would approve of— Ellie by herself with only a housekeeper to protect her from any wayward ranch hands...and Clive. He shook his head. "I said no."

Ethan grinned as if that sealed the deal for Ellie to stay, and Lawson fought the urge to groan. Telling Ellie no, flat-out, was the best way to bring out her obstinacy. Lawson watched as her chin lifted and knew that she wouldn't back down now. "Haven't I mentioned to you once or twice that I make my own choices? I'll just wire home to make sure it's all right. What do you say to that?"

Lawson hid his smile at the ridiculous statement. "Your stubbornness is showing."

"Where's the telegraph office?"

Ethan offered her his arm. "Right over here."

She took his arm, then lifted her eyebrows at Lawson as if to say, *So there*. Lawson frowned. "Hold on, Ethan. I want to talk to you. Ellie, go on and send your telegram."

"What is it?" Ethan asked once Ellie left them.

"I am not comfortable bringing Ellie along to meet Clive. He never thought twice about hitting my mother. I'll not subject her to that."

Ethan's face paled slightly. "Uncle Clive isn't like that anymore. I've never seen him raise a hand to anyone, not even an animal. Ruth has never borne a scratch and she's lived with us for eight years. He's a different man than you remember."

"I hope so for your sake but I'm not willing to trust him that far."

"Then trust me," Ethan said quietly. "She'll be safe. I give you my word on that."

Lawson eyed his cousin. "If Clive so much as looks at Ellie wrong—"

"I'll personally buy her ticket home and see that she gets on the right train with Ruth to accompany her."

"Fine," he agreed. They joined Ellie inside the telegraph office and less than thirty minutes later, she received permission to stay from Sean. Her triumphant smile was quickly followed by a sigh of relief, leaving him to wonder if more than just a desire to be with him motivated her not to return home.

He put his hat on as they exited the office, and let out a deep breath. If he was being honest, he'd admit he was grateful for the distraction of Ellie's presence. His stomach had slowly but surely begun to climb toward his throat those last few miles into town. He felt like Daniel being led toward the lion's den. He swallowed. *Maybe it won't be that bad. Yeah, and maybe I can get away with "accidentally" leaving my Stetson somewhere again.*

It was too bad stalling didn't actually change the destination.

Lawson was relatively certain he'd seen this little meadow before. Just to make sure, he leaned forward to rest his wrists against the saddle horn and catch Ethan's attention. "How long would it take to get to Clive's ranch from here if we stopped going in circles?"

Ethan glanced up sharply then gave him a slow, guilty smile. "About twenty minutes."

"We've been going in circles? Why?" Ellie asked in exasperation.

"To make me think they're farther from town then they actually are. That way I'm less likely to leave abruptly. Isn't that right, Ethan?"

"Yep."

He shook his head. "I thought you were on my side."

"I thought you weren't in a hurry to get where we're going, anyway. It seemed to fit everyone's purposes."

Lawson pulled off his hat to let the breeze cool his face. "We might as well stop for a few minutes and stretch."

"Amen," Ellie muttered as she dismounted and they did the same.

Ethan frowned at her. "I thought you rode horses all the time."

"I do, but not for two hours straight after riding to town and then traveling by train."

Lawson took a swig from his canteen then slowly lowered it. His gaze scanned the woods for movement. His ears strained to listen. He put the canteen away while his right hand strayed to his holster. "Ethan, do you have neighbors close by?"

"No. Why?"

"We have company." He pulled his Colt from his holster. "Come here, Ellie."

Suddenly, four horsemen burst from the woods to surround them. Ethan's horse reared in protest as Ellie let out a startled scream. One of the men dismounted and edged toward her. "Saints above, aren't you a pretty sight? Do you belong to one of these never-do-wells?"

Lawson's protective instincts kicked in. He stepped closer to her saying a firm "yes" just as she squeaked out a "no." Her gaze collided with his in hope. "Yes?"

He eyed the men and Ethan for a moment. Realizing that everyone else looked particularly unconcerned about the situation, he slipped his gun back into its resting place. Another man dismounted. "Well, which is it?"

"Actually, I think that about sums it up." Ethan smirked. "What do y'all mean by rushing in here like that? You could have gotten yourselves shot. As it was, you scared the lady pretty good."

The first man pulled off his hat. "Sorry, miss. I guess we got a little overexcited."

Lawson snorted. "You think?"

Ethan smiled and gestured to the men. "Lawson, meet your father's ranch hands. Boys, this is Ellie. You aren't to bother her."

They grumbled for a minute, then offered to escort them the rest of the way. Lawson stepped forward to give Ellie a boost before anyone else could offer. As he passed her he mumbled, "Knowing my father, they're probably all a bunch of outlaws, anyway."

Her eyes lit with excitement. "Do you think so?"

"No." He ignored her laughter but it drew the attention of the other men. He frowned at them all. This was not good.

The churning of his stomach increased substantially when the ranch house came into sight. It was a large two-story, whitewashed with dark blue shutters that reminded him of bruises. The bright red barn and weathered gray outbuildings stood out on the green countryside. The property looked well maintained—almost picturesque, and a far cry from the bleak shantytown shack he remembered from his early childhood.

Clive was nowhere in sight as their caravan of sorts approached the house. Would Clive not come out to greet them? Perhaps he was busy in another area of the ranch. Lawson brought his horse to a stop near the steps of the house's porch. He unclenched his white-knuckled grip on the reins and warily surveyed his surroundings once more before dismounting.

That delay nearly cost him the prerogative of helping Ellie off her horse. She was obviously a skilled rider who needed no assistance, but the other men didn't seem to take that into account as they stepped toward her, then stopped in disappointment. Ellie gave him her thanks along with a curious look. He heard the door open behind him. Ellie stilled as her gaze trailed from that sound back to him.

Steeling himself, Lawson turned to face Clive. Tension filled the air as the man walked slowly along the porch. His footsteps sounded loudly on the hollow porch steps before being muffled by the grass at their base.

Lawson found himself widening his stance, pulling back his shoulders and meeting the man's gaze straight on. Clive eyed him carefully.

Lawson narrowed his eyes. It almost felt as if he'd been called out and Clive was waiting for him to make the first move so he could shoot him down fair and square. Lawson was wearing his gun belt, as was Clive, he noted. He didn't know how to gauge this man—this almost stranger with a violent past. Surely, this wouldn't turn into a fight.

Lawson's hand moved backward slightly—closer to his gun. Instead of the cold metal of his Colt, Ellie's warm fingers slid into his. She'd thought he'd been reaching for her. Maybe he had been. His hand tightened around hers. He let out a pent-up breath and managed a respectful nod. "Hello, Clive."

"I wasn't sure you'd come."

"Neither was I." He saw Clive notice their linked hands so he gestured to Ellie but didn't release her hand. He wasn't sure he could have if he'd wanted to, and he *didn't* want to. "You remember Ellie O'Brien."

Clive nodded. "Certainly. It's a pleasure to see you again."

"Thank you, sir."

Ethan stepped forward. "Ellie is here to help Lawson with the horses. I told her Ruth would look after her."

"Ruth will be glad of some female company. I know she's tired of mine." He turned to his men, ordering, "See that the horses are stabled. Ethan, let Ruth know of Miss O'Brien's arrival while I show our guests to their rooms."

Everyone hurried to do as they'd been told. Lawson pulled in a deep breath. He was here. He'd walk into the house and he'd stay for the required length of time but that didn't mean he'd be as submissive as everyone else in Clive's life seemed to be. Clive may not know it yet but they were going to do things Lawson's way, in Lawson's time. He'd start by getting at least half of Nathan's money up front so Clive wouldn't be able to play any games with it.

Lawson was distracted from his thoughts when Ethan gave him a supportive clasp on the shoulder as he passed. Clive stood by the door waiting for them to enter. Let him wait. Lawson glanced down at Ellie to see if she was ready. She smiled encouragingly. He nodded. *All right, then. Let's do this.*

Chapter Fifteen

Ellie couldn't believe she was on a real, live cattle ranch just like she'd read about in her dime novels. No one was looking so she stretched her arms wide and pulled in a deep breath. They were a little too close to the barn for that to be entirely pleasant. She smiled, anyway. This trip was exactly what she'd needed. At home, she couldn't seem to get out from under the cloud of guilt she'd been feeling since the night she'd remembered the truth about her parents' deaths. Even if the busyness of the day momentarily pushed it away, the ranch still carried so many reminders of her parents that it wasn't long before it returned.

A change of scenery might be just what she needed. Unfortunately, this wasn't likely to be a joyful trip for Lawson. He walked ahead of her with his father and Ethan. The distance between Lawson and Clive and the tension that filled it was nearly palpable.

Lawson's face had turned inscrutable when his father stepped out of the house. Yet, even in that difficult moment, he'd had enough strength and courage to turn around to greet the man respectfully. She'd taken a risk in slipping her hand into his when he'd reached for the comfort of his Colt. She knew he wasn't going to draw, but doing so allowed her to show she was standing with him. His hand had tightened to hold hers right back. He hadn't released it, either—not until they had to go their separate ways in the house. That meant something, didn't it?

Ethan noticed she'd fallen behind the group and dropped back to walk with her. "What do you think of the ranch?"

"It's wonderful. How many head of cattle are there?"

"About a thousand."

"Is that a lot? It sounds like a lot."

"It's more than a little."

They shared a smile at his silly response before Ellie lifted her chin toward the men in front of them. "How is it going with them?"

"No fisticuffs yet," he said blithely.

She sent him a censoring frown. "I don't think that's something to joke about."

"I wasn't joking."

"You don't really think it might come to that, do you?" she asked, walking sideways so she could see his face.

"I hope not. They still have some serious issues to work through but I'm not sure either of them is prepared to do that yet." He shrugged. "I guess it's something to pray about."

She threw him a curious glance. "I don't think I've ever heard you mention prayer before."

He ducked his head. "I've been doing it more lately—mainly because Lawson seems to put such stock in it."

"He's a good man." She sent him a smile. "So are you."

"Thanks. I might not have known Lawson long, but it's obvious that my cousin doesn't make it easy for anyone to get close to him." Ethan met her gaze seriously. "If you want him, you'll need to fight for him. Lawson told me the story of Uncle Clive and Aunt Gloria abandoning him. He remembers that feeling well, though he was only nine when it happened. He isn't going to pin his hope on anyone who can't convince him that it'll last."

She bit her lip. She didn't want to make anything worse between her and Lawson, but what else could she do to make it better? She watched Lawson stop at a nearby paddock as his father gestured to the large dark horse inside. His arms were crossed and his expression closed off. "I'm trying. I don't know how well it's working."

"He has feelings for you. Of that you can be sure. The rest is up to you."

She tilted her head as though that might help her discern the emotions to which Ethan seemed privy. Lawson caught her watching him and sent her a quizzical smile that quickly disappeared when he turned back to Clive. "Thanks, Ethan."

"You're welcome. Let's rejoin them. Lawson is starting to look nervous."

"What a beautiful horse," Ellie exclaimed at the sight of the large black stallion. The horse seemed agitated to be the subject of their examination.

Clive acknowledged her compliment with a nod but didn't bother to look her way. "This is Diablo. He's as mean as they come. There's never been a man that could stay seated on him."

Lawson eyed the horse skeptically. "This is the horse you want me to train? And you want me to do it in a week? That seems unrealistic."

"Diablo has the potential to be a great horse. He just needs to be gentled."

"I'll do my best but once the week is up I trust you'll stay true to your word and the contract by giving me the other half of the payment regardless of my results with Diablo."

"It's a deal." Clive put out his hand. After a moment of hesitation, Lawson shook it firmly. Clive cleared his throat. "We'll leave you two to decide how you'll go about this. Come along, Ethan."

Ethan obeyed but not before giving Ellie a significant look. She chuckled softly. It seemed she couldn't get away from matchmakers no matter where she went. Her laughter drew Lawson's attention so she wrinkled her nose. "Diablo is an awful name for a horse. Of course he'd act mean if everyone called him that. First things first, he needs a new name."

An amused smile tipped his lips slightly. "Like what?"

"Let's see." She crossed her arms on the paddock fence and surveyed the horse thoughtfully. "He looks like a Midnight to me."

He copied her posture, leaning onto the paddock fence, as well. "I guess so since you named your horse Starlight."

"They are kind of similar."

He sighed. "This is a ruse, you know."

"What is?"

"This whole thing." He turned to face her. "That stipulation for the horses to be delivered, this horse that has never been ridden—he's been using it all to get me here and keep me here."

"I figured." She paused then quietly continued, "But, you did choose to come."

"I know."

She touched his arm in concern. "How are you holding up so far?"

"Fine...I think. I know what's coming, though. I knew it when I came. I'll have to listen to him try to explain away leaving me behind. That's all right, though, because I have a few questions I'd like some answers to and I aim to get them."

She wondered if he caught the glimmer of admiration in her eyes before he turned his attention back to the horse. She certainly felt it. He was so brave not only to acknowledge his past but to travel all these miles to face it, as well. He didn't seem afraid—just determined. It was too bad she lacked the courage she saw in him. Not that there was anything left for her to face. Her parents were gone and there was nothing she could do to rectify that mistake.

Her situation with Lawson was different. She'd made her mistakes with him but perhaps that didn't have to be the end of the story. She didn't want it to be. *Lord, I know I said I'd try to follow Your lead. For the first time in a long time, I think maybe I will. I think I still have a chance. If I do...well, Lord, I intend to take it.*

The next few days passed without the altercation Lawson expected. He dedicated himself to Diablo—or Midnight, as Ellie renamed him. His interactions with

Clive remained polite and distant, if slightly cold. That sufficed since Lawson rarely saw the man except for at mealtimes or when Clive would wander over to Midnight's stall to check on their progress—like now. Lawson tried not to let the man's presence distract him from his task. "Do you have the saddle blanket ready, Ellie?"

Her affirmative reply came softly so as not to frighten the horse that flinched but otherwise didn't protest when Lawson stroked his mane. Ellie stood a few feet away outside the fence but close enough to be at his side at a moment's notice. That pretty much summed up her behavior during their visit so far.

He was grateful—incredibly grateful for her presence during all of this. She'd been supportive of him while managing to charm everyone from the ranch hands to the housekeeper to Midnight. Even Clive seemed to enjoy talking to her, though Ellie adhered to Lawson's plea that she keep her distance. Midnight stepped toward her to examine the blanket as she calmly approached the stallion. "He's doing well, isn't he, Lawson?"

"Better than I'd hoped," he admitted as his hands traveled across Midnight's back. "It helps that he's fallen in love with you along with everyone else at this ranch."

"Well, I wouldn't say *everyone.*" The look in her green eyes betrayed a subtle hope that he might contradict her statement.

He wasn't sure how to respond to that and a quick glance over his shoulder at Clive told him this was not the time to try to figure it out. He forced his focus back on the horse. His fingers brushed over something hard. Frowning, he stepped closer to examine the horse and found a patchwork of scars across its back. He instinctively flashed accusatory eyes at Clive. "This horse has been abused."

Hurt swept across Clive's face before he managed to mask it. "Not by me. The previous owner thought beating the fight out of Diablo would tame him. That's why I convinced the man to sell the horse to me."

Ellie's fingers examined the black scars that were nearly indiscernible from the horse's black coat. "The scars are old, Lawson."

He knew that but it hadn't changed his first thought. He glanced back at Clive wondering if he should apologize. He didn't. He wouldn't have meant it. Clive seemed to sense that.

"I understand why you might assume..." the man began then cleared his throat. "I'm not that person anymore."

Ellie mumbled something about getting sugar cubes for the horse, then left them alone. He watched her go, feeling his jaw tighten. So this was it—the moment he'd been planning for and dreading in equal measure. He released Midnight from the long lead rope. The horse wandered away as Lawson turned to face the man who was supposed to be his father. "Your name's Clive Hardy, isn't it?"

"You know it is."

"Then you're still the man who abandoned me."

Clive gave an accepting nod. "I guess to you I always will be."

He began coiling the rope in his hand with a bit more force than necessary. "Tell me. What kind of thoughts go through a man's head when he abandons his only son with nothing more than a dollar bill and a note no one else is literate enough to read?"

"Are you sure you want me to tell that story?"

"No, but it belongs to me as much as it belongs to you so I reckon I've a right to know."

Clive braced his boot on the last rung on the fence. "It will be no surprise to you to know I'd had a few drinks. Not enough that I couldn't function but just enough to make my judgment shady. I thought I needed the courage for the job I had to do."

"Which was?"

"Robbery." He pulled a pipe from his pocket and tapped it on the wooden fence. "It wasn't my first but it was my last. The whole thing was a disaster from start to finish. I got shot. I knew worse would happen if the sheriff or my boss caught up to me."

The story matched what Lawson remembered. "So you ran out on me. You thought I'd slow you down and you couldn't take the risk."

Clive didn't deny that. Instead, he continued, "It was the worst decision I ever made. Your mother never forgave me for putting her in that situation."

Lawson glanced past Clive toward the open land and shook his head. "She had a choice, same as you. Whatever happened, you were both equally guilty— equally wrong."

"After a couple of weeks, we came back to look for you." He tried to strike a match to light his pipe but gave up and tucked it away. "There was no trace of you."

He nodded. "I was young but I wasn't dumb. I knew you intended to leave me for good. The rent was due in the morning so I wasn't going to stick around just to get kicked out. I'm sure I was long gone by the time you two moseyed back."

"Well, your ma sort of snapped when we couldn't

find you. She threw all the whiskey out of the house and told me if I ever came home drunk I'd sleep outside. A few rainy nights sobered me up enough to realize what a miserable cur I was. I thought that would make things better between me and your ma, but I'd done too much damage. One day she up and left. No note. No anything."

Lawson crossed his arms. If Clive was looking for sympathy on that point, he wouldn't get any. He didn't seem to notice because he was staring off into the distance as if seeing the whole thing play out before him. "I think now she might have been in the family way and didn't trust me to be a better father than I'd been before."

"So I might have a sibling out there somewhere suffering from the same ill fortune of birth that I am."

Clive winced. "I don't know. Maybe. Once your ma left I went searching for both of y'all. I didn't find either of you. Instead, I found the only other male child in that area of Texas answering to the name of Lawson."

"Ethan."

Clive nodded. "I took him in and did for him what I should have done for you. One day I heard about a Ranger named Lawson Williams. I thought maybe it might be you at last. I had to find you. So I did."

"So you did and here I am…. I guess I'm supposed to feel better about all of this because you looked for me." Lawson eyed the man before him and shook his head. "I'm not sure how this makes up for what you did but if it feels good to see me here, to talk to me, to tell me your story—then I guess for you it was worth it." He ran his fingers through his hair. "To me, it isn't worth much. It doesn't change what I went through. It doesn't change who I am, or what you put me through. It wasn't just a matter of you abandoning me. As long as I carried your name, I got followed by your trouble. People who otherwise might have helped me didn't want anything to do with me when they learned I was your son."

He paused and let that sink in for a moment. "For better or worse, I'm still the one who gets left behind. The one that can't get the folks who matter—really matter—to stay, or to let *me* stay." He should shut his mouth but he couldn't seem to stop. "The O'Briens and the Williamses—they're the only ones who seemed to care enough to want to keep me. I wonder what they see that others don't. Or maybe it's just that they're blind to the thing that drives everyone else away." He glanced up at his father. "The thing that drove you away…from a nine-year-old boy who didn't even have sense enough to ask to go along. You wouldn't have let me, if I had. Would you?"

He didn't need to wait for an answer. He slipped through the corral fence and let the rope he held fall to the ground. He wasn't sure where to go. He just kept walking until he found a solitary place where he could sit under a shade tree. He was a grown man. This shouldn't bother him, but it did. It always had. He'd seen that abandonment repeated in his life time and time again—maybe even when it wasn't there…like with Ellie. He'd just come to expect it to happen eventually in each relationship. Even with God, he'd been afraid to get too close.

He shook his head. He couldn't remember the last time he'd thought about God. He couldn't remember the last time he'd prayed without prompting from others. He tilted his head back against the rough bark of the tree to stare at the patches of sky that peeked through the auburn canopy. "Are You still there or did You walk away, too?"

He could almost hear Nathan's words from that long-ago night when he'd first met the Lord. *You're part of God's family now. He'll never leave you or forsake you.* He swallowed. "That's a big promise. I hope You're living up to it."

A strange feeling filled his chest. It wasn't peace exactly, just a powerful feeling that he wasn't alone in this. God might not be able to reach out and hold his hand like Ellie but He hadn't left. How else would Lawson have survived in those rough Western towns or found the O'Briens or settled with the Williamses?

If that was so—if God had been with him his entire life—then why had he been brought to this moment? What was the purpose? It hurt worse than many of the others. It was if all the pain he'd stuffed inside for so long finally popped like a loose button on one of those old raggedy shirts he used to wear.

A faint prickling sensation danced around his eyes. He fought it back. He hadn't cried when his parents left him and he wouldn't start now. He was stronger than that. He'd make it through. He always did. He'd leave this place soon, anyway. Maybe he'd never see Clive again. Maybe this was the last time he'd have to relive any of this. Maybe he'd finally be able to put his family shadows behind him once and for all. As soon as he left this ranch, he'd start looking toward the future. Whatever it was, it had to be better than his past. It just had to be.

Chapter Sixteen

Ellie was in the kitchen when Clive breezed through on the way to his study. He paused as if to say something, then shook his head and continued on. She followed him. "What happened?"

"Let's talk in my study."

She ignored the frown Ethan sent her from the sitting room when she shut the door part of the way behind her. Clive had never taken her into his confidence before and she didn't want to be interrupted. It was obvious that Clive and Lawson had finally gotten around to the talk that had been hanging over everyone's heads since the beginning of the trip. "How is he?"

"I don't know." He sank into a nearby chair with a sigh. "You can go after him if you wish but he might need some time to himself."

Ellie thought about this for a moment, then settled into the chair across from him. "I'll give him a few minutes."

"What was he like, Ellie, when you first met him?"

"He was a lot like Mid—Diablo. He was sort of wary about accepting any kindness. He had a lot of fight in him but was never violent. I got the impression he knew too much for his age—although I don't think we could ever figure out what age he was for sure."

Clive stood to riffle through some papers at his desk. "And now?"

"I think that tattered little boy is still a part of him but he's grown up since then. He has a dry sense of humor that is just sly enough to catch you off guard. He's very protective of women in general but especially the ones in my family and his adoptive mother. He's intelligent, hardworking, caring, gentle, yet he's always been a bit of a mystery to everyone. Even himself."

Clive finally took a piece of paper out of his desk, then settled back in the chair. "Does he know you love him?"

Her breath stilled in her throat. What was he talking about? *She* didn't even know she loved him.

All right, that wasn't entirely true. She was falling in love with him. She knew that. But how did a girl know when she was *completely* in love? Was there a sort of jarring sensation or did she just decide that she was? She glanced at Lawson's father. Or did someone have to tell her? She cleared her throat. "Honestly, Mr. Hardy, I'm not sure it would matter to him."

He seemed to understand what she meant for he nodded. "That's my fault as well as Gloria's. You're right. He is like Midnight. Isn't that what you call him? He's strong but with scars that run deep. I may not have inflicted them on the horse but I wielded that whip on my own son. That's a thousand times worse."

The man before her seemed to deflate. "You don't know how a mistake like that can eat at a man. Day in and day out to know that you were responsible for bringing harm to someone that close to you."

"Yes, I do," she said before she could stop herself. She reached out to touch his hand. "I know that feeling exactly. I did something that had horrible implications for people I loved. It was a mistake but that didn't change the outcome."

He patted her hand. "My dear, if there's one thing I've learned it's that you can't change what happened. You have to accept that you made the mistake, examine it closely to learn from it, then move on. Don't let it define your life as I have let my mistakes define mine. Seek to make peace if you can. If you can't, let it go. I hope you'll let me know how it's resolved."

"*If* it's resolved." She didn't hold out much hope and she wasn't sure what good it would do to go poking around in the matter.

He handed her the paper in his hand. "I want you to have this. I'd give it to Lawson but I'm not sure he'd take anything from me. It's his birth certificate."

She glanced at the document. "His middle name is Clive. I don't think he knows that."

"I don't think he'd want to know."

"His birthday is this month—next week, in fact. Perhaps we can throw him a party at home. He'd like that."

Clive nodded, then looked past her to the window. "I think I see Lawson under that far tree. You should go to him."

"I will." She folded the worn birth certificate into her pocket as she muttered a quick goodbye and breezed past a concerned-looking Ethan to walk down the porch steps.

Lawson stood from his spot at the base of the tree

when she neared. She stopped a few feet away and they just looked at each other. She wasn't sure what to say or do. He was obviously torn up inside over the conversation with his father. If she'd ask how he was he'd probably give her the same answer she'd gotten all week. "Fine...I think." That didn't say much. "You talked to Clive."

His eyes seemed slightly reddened. That broke her heart since she'd never seen him anywhere close to tears before. He glanced away, shoving his hands in his pockets. "It went about as I expected. The facts didn't change. I guess I'm just angry."

"At Clive?" She eased closer.

He nodded staunchly as if the words he said didn't really affect him. She knew better. "And Gloria, and the hand I've been dealt, and pretty much everything else."

"That's understandable."

Something in her voice must have caught his attention because he looked at her and caught her blinking away tears. He frowned. "Are you crying—for me?"

The incredulous tone in his voice made a tear slip free. "So what if I am?"

"That is not necessary." He pulled her toward him.

"Yes, it is." She resisted slightly so that she could look up at him. "Don't you dare comfort me at a time like this, Lawson Williams."

A smile played at the corner of his lips. "What's wrong with a time like this?"

"Nothing, except that *I* should be comforting *you!*"

He actually chuckled as he pulled her into his arms. She rested her cheek on his chest. He didn't bother to respond, which was just fine with her. She closed her eyes and prayed he wouldn't let go...ever.

His low voice rumbled against her ear. "You know something, Ellie?"

"What?" she whispered.

"You're getting to be like a bad penny," he murmured. Her eyes flew open. She pushed against his chest but he didn't let her go. "Now, hold on. I didn't mean that the way you took it."

"Oh?" she asked, tilting her head to stare at him in hurt disbelief. "How exactly did you mean it?"

"I meant it as a thank-you."

Her eyes dropped to the top button of his shirt. "You did?"

"Yes."

"Then you're welcome," she said, trying to ignore the fact that it hadn't sounded like much of a thanks. Surely he didn't think she was only throwing herself at him again. She wasn't. She was just concerned about him and a little bit in love with him. That was all.

"Hey," he protested as he lifted her chin to make her look at him. "That's what I really meant. I promise. To be honest, I don't mind you staying close. It's kind of nice."

Her eyebrows lifted incredulously. "Really?"

He nodded. "It's been the best part of this trip. That's for sure."

"Well, now," she drawled, allowing a slow smile to blossom on her lips. "That isn't really saying much, is it?"

"I guess not." She watched his gaze trail down her lips before he stepped away. "I don't know about you but I'm ready to go home."

What was she going to do when she got home? Would the guilt be as strong as it had been before? Her relationship with Lawson had taken a turn for the better. That should ease the burden, shouldn't it? She nodded. "So am I."

Maybe it won't be that bad. I can't stay away from home forever. I wouldn't want to, anyway. I can be brave like Lawson. Lord willing, I can go home and face this, then try to move past it.

The rhythm of the train wheels flying over the track slowed considerably when it reached the outskirts of town. Ellie tapped Ruth to awaken the woman who had succumbed to the lulling beat nearly an hour ago. The housekeeper was kind enough to accompany them all the way to Peppin, though the two-hour train ride hardly required it. Lawson was too busy peering out the window for his first sight of town to notice their chaperone's critical eye. Apparently, they passed inspection because the woman smiled and settled in for the last few minutes of their journey.

Their goodbyes at the ranch had been short and to the point. Lawson didn't have much to say to Clive but he made sure that Ethan knew what to do to keep Midnight progressing. The greetings at the Peppin train station promised to be something else entirely. A small crowd of their friends and family milled about. Lawson led the way as they filed out of the train with the other passengers. He paused and pointed to a droopy banner visible through the last window of the rail car. "Why does that say *congratulations?*"

"Maybe it's for someone else." That was all she managed to say because as soon as he helped her down from the train, their families rushed to greet them. Once she finished hugging everyone, Nathan pulled her forward so that she stood before the droopy-banner group. "Ellie, these folks won't believe me. Will you tell them once and for all that you did not elope with Lawson?"

Before she could answer, Maddie stepped forward. "It's been all over town since you left. Of course, we knew you wouldn't have told your families."

She knew that with her answer, she could easily trap Lawson into an engagement and maybe even into a wedding, but she didn't want him that way. "We didn't elope. We aren't engaged. We don't need to be because we had a chaperone the entire trip. Her name is Ruth Gordon and she's standing right there by Lawson. Did that cover everything?"

"Goodness," Sophia Johansen exclaimed. "I don't understand. Don't you like Lawson?"

"Of course I do."

Rhett frowned at her but kept sneaking looks at Amy, who didn't appear to notice. "Doesn't he like you?"

Ellie would have glanced over her shoulder for Lawson's response but her attention snagged on a rather familiar figure leaning against the wall near the ticket booth. Donovan Turner observed the unfolding scene intently. When he saw her watching, he didn't smile. He just kept chewing at the piece of hay in his mouth. Suddenly uncomfortable, she pulled her gaze back to Maddie, who took over the line of questioning again. "Then why are y'all fighting this matchmaking so hard? Don't you know this town is just trying to help?"

"I appreciate that, but some things a man and a woman just have to figure out on their own." She held up a hand to stall their comments. "I know that's ironic coming from me after all the matchmaking I've tried to do over the years, but it's true."

Jeff slipped an arm around Maddie. "Well, I think if Lawson had a lick of sense he'd propose to Ellie right here and now."

Ellie exchanged an exasperated look with her family. "I give up."

"Now, hold on folks," Lawson said in an authoritative voice as he stepped up beside her. "I'm not sure you're taking Ellie seriously here. She's right. While we appreciate and originally encouraged the thought behind the matchmaking, we've had enough. Jeff, you went so far on the matchmaking scheme that you put Ellie on that train out of town. That was uncalled for. Something bad could have happened to her. The rest of you have been spreading rumors and listening to gossip. That isn't right, either. I'm saying it's got to stop. I proposed to Ellie once in jest and she turned me down flat. If I ever proposed to her again, it wouldn't be at the town's command. Now, I think it would be best if we all minded our own business."

The crowd dispersed rather reluctantly. Some of them looked offended. Others looked smugly satisfied. After all, Lawson hadn't said that he would never propose again—just that if he did it would be on his terms not the town's. It left room for hope.

Ellie smiled. Yes, it certainly did.

Crisp autumn wind swept across Lawson's skin as the buggy meandered down a country road toward town. It was good to be back in Peppin. It had been just over a week since their return from his father's ranch and with each day, he gained more distance from the dark past and painful memories he'd visited there. They were still a part of him. He suspected they always would be. But at least now the pain he'd felt so deeply had lessened to the old familiar throb.

Somehow he'd expected to feel some sort of peace or relief at finally facing his memories and his father. It never came. That just didn't seem fair. The experience had been unpleasant at best but now—thankfully—it was over, so where was he supposed to go from here? Forward, maybe? Where would that lead?

His gaze slid to the woman sitting next to him. Ellie had been edging deeper and deeper into his heart since he'd left the Rangers and moved back to Peppin. After the trip to his father's ranch, his attempts to stop her had become dangerously close to halfhearted. She'd stayed by his side despite his at times prickly behavior. She'd always been faithful in her friendship even when he rejected her, and it was obvious that she was open to something more.

It was foolish of him to even consider a relationship with her. Somehow that didn't stop him from thinking about it. The O'Briens, along with his adoptive parents, had always been the family of his heart. He knew for certain they loved him even if no one else did. That meant that Ellie, as one of them, might be the one woman who could possibly see past his faults to truly love him for a lifetime.

She was reading, so she didn't seem to notice that he slowed down to extend their trip into town. He glanced at the book, wondering what was interesting enough about it to keep her from talking to him. It took him a minute to realize it was upside down and probably had been the entire time. A slow grin spread across his face. "Ellie O'Brien, what are you up to?"

"What makes you think I'm up to something?" she asked innocently, not looking up from her book.

"What was the last sentence you read?"

She stilled. The book snapped shut and she tucked it away. "It's a beautiful day, isn't it?"

He shook his head in amusement but agreed. "It certainly is."

She played with the strings of her reticule for a moment. She was nervous, he realized, nervous to be alone with him on the short trip to town. He dared to shift slightly closer. "You look especially nice today."

"Do I?"

He nodded. Her hair had been swept into a loose chignon instead of simply being pulled back with a ribbon like usual. She was wearing a light green dress instead of the usual blouse and riding skirt, which made her eyes look even greener while the cool wind painted her cheeks with a bright hue of pink. "Is today a special occasion or something?"

Her eyes widened in what seemed to be alarm before he realized it was just confusion. "Why? Do I only look nice on special occasions? It's hard to work with the horses in a dress."

"No." He laughed. "I guess I was wondering if you might have done it on my account."

She watched him blankly for a moment, then turned toward him with interest. "You mean you're wondering if I stand by my declaration of intent."

He nodded as they reached the outskirts of town. "Pretty much."

"I stand by it."

"You're not going to give up?" He turned onto his parents' street.

"No! And if you think you can wait me out you have another think coming."

He hopped from the buggy to help her down. "How long are you planning to visit my mother?"

"All afternoon if I can," she said as they walked toward the door. "Doc will take me home. Don't forget that we're having dinner with Sean and Lorelei."

"I won't."

Ellie didn't bother to knock. She just opened the door and hallooed the house. Lettie told her to come in. He would have gone in as well but Ellie turned to face him, effectively blocking his entry. "I want to talk to your mother privately."

"Why?"

"It's just woman talk. You wouldn't be interested."

"Something tells me I would be." He shifted to the right to try to get around her, but she wouldn't let him pass.

"I think you'd be more interested in hearing what I have to say to you." She waited for him to look her in the eye before she continued. "Lawson, I'm not going to force my attentions on you if you don't want them. If you can look me in the eye and tell me *honestly* that there isn't even the tiniest sliver of hope for us then I won't keep bothering you. Otherwise, I'm going to keep right on doing what I've been doing."

"Good."

A slow smile blossomed on Ellie's lips. "You mean it?"

"I mean it."

Love was the last thing his mother had spoken of before she'd abandoned him. Love didn't still a bottle of whiskey on trek to an eager mouth. It didn't still a hand before a painful slap. To him, that word hadn't meant much for a number of years. Yet, he was beginning to realize that to Ellie, that word meant something else entirely. She came from a family where love meant everything. Taking that into consideration, perhaps Ellie's love was something that truly would last—and that was more than worth capturing. He just needed to figure out some way to do it.

Chapter Seventeen

Ellie waited patiently for Lettie to turn away and check the icing recipe before she stole another taste of the chocolate fluff. It was delicious but she managed to school her ecstasy into an innocent expression before the woman turned around. When Lettie looked at her she was dutifully stirring the cake batter. "Are you sure Lawson doesn't suspect anything?"

Ellie shrugged. "Even if he realizes something is going on, he can't possibly know it's his birthday."

By this point he was probably the only person in town who didn't know. She'd invited half the town to his party tonight. She'd urged them all to be especially nice to him if they saw him in town but not to let the secret slip, no matter what. She prayed everyone would hold their tongue until then.

"He still thinks the two of you are the only ones invited to dinner at Sean and Lorelei's, then?"

"Yes, ma'am."

"Perfect." Lettie deftly handed her a napkin. "Everything is going according to plan."

Ellie lifted the napkin questioningly. "What is this for?"

Lettie tapped her own lips to indicate the chocolate clinging to Ellie's. She ignored Ellie's guilty grimace to continue. "Maddie insisted on bringing enough fried chicken for everyone. Lorelei and her mother are working on side dishes. We have the desserts and Kate is at home trying not to look suspicious."

"She cooked his favorite foods for breakfast and lunch. He noticed but she pretended it was just a co-incidence." Ellie carefully poured the batter into the baking pans. "Do you think the cake, pies and cookies will be enough?"

"Amelia said she'd bring apple turnovers so we'll have plenty. I don't think Peppin has ever seen a party like the one we're throwing. I hope he likes it."

"I'm sure he will." She slid the cake into the oven then froze. "*Amelia* is bringing turnovers? You don't mean Amelia Greene, do you?"

"Certainly."

Ellie closed the oven and turned to face Lettie. "I did *not* invite her."

"We invited the whole town," Lettie said absently as she measured out more cocoa.

"*Not* Mrs. Greene."

She glanced up to frown. "But she already said she was coming."

The last thing Ellie wanted was to spend what was supposed to be an enjoyable evening dodging disapproving looks from Mrs. Greene. Hardness entered into her voice as she insisted, "I don't want her there."

"Why, Ellie," Lettie said after a startled pause. "I don't think I've ever heard that tone from you before.

Has something happened between you and Amelia? Other than the usual annoyances, I mean."

Ellie didn't want to lie but she didn't want to tell the truth, either, so she just remained silent.

Lettie narrowed her eyes. "The only time you are ever that quiet is when something is really bothering you. Why don't you tell me what it is?"

"I can't." Emotion nearly choked her voice.

"Sure you can. Keeping it a secret won't make it any easier to deal with."

The tears she'd been holding in for weeks suddenly tumbled down her cheeks. Lettie embraced her but allowed her to cry it out before handing her the napkin to dry her tears. She finally gathered her courage enough to reveal what was bothering her. "Mrs. Greene told me the truth about what I did—and how it led to my parents' deaths. Oh, she didn't tell me it was my fault in so many words but she told me about the rumor I spread, and that triggered the memory of my parents leaving that day because of me, because they had to go apologize to Mrs. Greene. It's my fault they braved the storm that took their lives."

Lettie's eyes began to flash. "Amelia had no business telling you that."

"Why not? It's true. I know it is."

"It's *not* true that you're in any way responsible for your parents' deaths. They did come to town to apologize to Amelia but they didn't have the accident on the way into town. They had it when they left."

"What difference does it make?"

Lettie sighed and brushed the hair away from Ellie's brow. "I was the last one to see them alive. Did you know that?"

"No." Ellie frowned. "I thought it must have been Mrs. Greene."

She shook her head. "Your parents stopped by my house on the way out of town. They told me how they'd apologized to Mrs. Greene for what happened and how she refused to accept the apology. They spoke to me of you, Ellie."

Ellie pulled in a deep breath. "They were disappointed in me, weren't they?"

"No! They knew you'd made a mistake but that in no way changed their opinion of you or their love for you. No one is perfect all the time, Ellie. They never expected that from you."

She allowed that knowledge to settle within her for a moment before the guilt returned with a vengeance. "But it's still my fault they died. They wouldn't have been out there in the first place if it wasn't for me."

"I've thought the same thing about myself over the years." She shook her head sadly. "If only I'd paid more attention to the storm, I might have noticed it was getting worse in time to warn them to stay in town. Then perhaps you wouldn't have lost your parents and I wouldn't have lost my best friend. 'If only' can't change what happened. Your parents made their own decisions and that is no reflection on you or me. Neither of us controls the weather, or has any say in God's plan. I'll never stop missing them, but it's not anyone's fault that they're gone."

"I don't know, Ms. Lettie. I've felt that shame and guilt for so long—even before I remembered what I'd done to make me feel that way. Hearing you say these things doesn't make it disappear." She hugged her arms about herself. "Why, I don't know what I'd do if Sean or Kate found out about this."

"Your siblings knew."

Ellie's eyes widened in a mixture of surprise, horror and confusion. "They did? But they never told me. They never even acted as though they knew. I thought for sure they'd blame me even if they tried to hide it."

"Perhaps you should talk to them about it. However, I don't think they ever blamed you. That may be why they never made an issue of it."

Ellie shook her head in disbelief. "Mrs. Greene led me to believe she was the only one who knew about it. I've spent the last few weeks doing my best to keep this quiet."

"Amelia Greene needs to learn a few lessons about forgiveness. She's carried that anger in her heart until it turned her into a bitter woman. You just leave her to me."

"This is my battle."

"You are my best friend's daughter. If I can't fight for you against the likes of Amelia then who can? It's time she dealt with someone of her own age and standing. I mean to see that she does. Don't worry about her one more minute."

Ellie smiled at her. "Thank you for telling me all of this. I feel better—not exactly exonerated but better than before."

"I'm glad, dear." She paused thoughtfully before continuing, "I think in this situation, the only sin you might be guilty of is that you spread gossip when you were eight. I don't think you've indulged in that since then but you can ask God to forgive you of that and He will.

However, if you really want to get rid of the guilt you feel, you need to forgive yourself."

"I know you're right." Ellie bit her lip.

"Yes, but knowing it and doing it are two separate things, aren't they? You have to make the decision for yourself. Think it over. I'll be praying for you."

"Thank you. I'm sure I'll need it."

Lawson followed Ellie up the porch steps of Sean and Lorelei's house, inspecting the hat in his hands thoughtfully. "Ellie, do you like this hat?"

"What?" she asked distractedly. "Yes."

"That's what I said when Mr. Johansen asked me at his mercantile. He said he wouldn't be able to sell that hat to anyone else and outright asked me to take it off his hands for practically nothing. Don't you think that's odd? This is a perfectly good hat and I feel kind of like I stole it."

Ellie stopped to survey him laughingly. "Maybe he meant it as a gift."

"Why would he give me a gift?" He reached out to stop her when she continued walking toward the door. "Come to think of it, that happened a lot today. Maddie wouldn't let me pay for the pie and coffee I had at her café."

"Uh-huh." She tugged him onward.

"Maybe the town is trying to make up for the matchmaking fiasco—"

"I don't think so." She knocked on the door.

"Well, it's downright peculiar."

Lorelei's voice called from inside, "Come in. The door is open."

"People have been really nice—almost overly so.

There has to be an explanation." Ellie stared at him with an amused smile but she was listening intently, so he kept going. "Nathan took me aside to tell me what a good job I've been doing. At first I thought he was going to fire me or... Aren't you going to open the door?"

She stepped aside. "Be my guest."

He frowned but complied. She went in ahead of him so he pulled the door closed behind them. He realized the house was full of people only an instant before they all yelled, "Surprise!"

He glanced around at the familiar faces in confusion before settling on Ellie's. The party must be for her. He echoed "surprise" to pretend that he'd known all along. Why hadn't anyone told him this was a surprise party for Ellie? He hadn't gotten her a present or anything. *Wait a minute. Ellie's birthday already passed.*

"What is going on?"

"It's your birthday," Ellie explained. "Everyone is here to celebrate you."

He pulled her closer as if that would give them some modicum of privacy. "Ellie, you know I don't celebrate my birthday because I don't know when it is."

"It's today. Your birth certificate says so." She handed him a folded piece of paper.

"My birth certificate?" He stared at the paper. *Lawson Clive Hardy.* His gaze stumbled over his middle name and he frowned before he moved on. *Born...* His head shot up. "It's my birthday!"

Cheers echoed through the room. Suddenly, he was receiving hugs from everyone, which was no small feat since it looked as though half the town had shown up. Everyone had a quick word or good wish for him. It was overwhelming. He was glad when his parents finally made it through the fray for their chance to hug him. "Y'all didn't have to do this."

Lettie smiled knowingly. "*We* didn't. Ellie was the main one who planned and carried this out."

Doc nodded. "A few others chipped in but it was her idea."

"Why would she go through the trouble of doing all this?" He frowned as he spotted her talking with Amy, Sophia and Lorelei.

Doc placed a hand on his shoulder. "Son, I think it's pretty obvious to everyone how that girl feels about you. Don't you think it's about time you figured out what you're going to do about it?"

A wry smile touched his lips. "I'm working on it."

"Well, praise the Lord for that," Lettie said with such obvious relief that he laughed.

Lawson was surprised to discover that an entire meal had been planned in his honor. Sean and Lorelei's dining room was too small to accommodate a sit-down dinner inside, so pretty soon everyone headed outside to a small clearing behind the house. It seemed this was where the real party was going to take place. Several long tables filled the clearing, including one that functioned as a buffet. Lanterns hung from the trees in preparation for nightfall. Guests wasted little time in filling their plates and settled in for a night filled with friends and laughter.

Lawson found himself seated at a table with his parents, the Rutledges and the O'Briens. They automatically saved the seat beside him for Ellie, who, after bustling about to make sure that all was well, finally made her way to the table. He waited until they were nearly finished eating to say, "I can't believe you did all of this for me."

She blushed in the fading light of sunset. "It was fun. Honestly, it sort of took on a life of its own once the town caught wind of it. I hadn't planned on this many people coming. Apparently, this town is very fond of you."

"I never would have imagined this many people really cared about me."

He didn't realize how pitiful that statement must have sounded until Ellie's eyes filled with compassion. "Of course they do. You grew up here. It's your hometown. You belong here."

"I didn't stumble into Peppin until I was fourteen," he corrected doubtfully.

She lifted her chin. "I don't see how that changes anything I just said."

He grinned slowly and shook his head. "That's because you're stubborn."

"This town is blessed to have you and we know it. You're blessed to have us, too, so it's equal all the way around." She hesitated a moment before shifting closer. "You know what I've realized since we came back from the ranch?"

He found himself leaning toward her. "What?"

"If your parents hadn't abandoned you, your life would be completely different and not necessarily for the better."

He stiffened slightly but decided to hear her out. "What are you getting at?"

"You would have stayed with them. Your father told me that coming to terms with leaving you behind was what made him turn his life around. If you were with them, your parents would have continued with the drinking, the fighting, the stealing. You would have been subjected to the lifestyle they led and the environment they lived in. You wouldn't have had the same opportunities. You probably never would have come to this town, which means you wouldn't have met Nathan. He's the one who led you to the Lord, so you may not even have become a Christian. Doc and Ms. Lettie wouldn't have adopted you. You would never have known what a normal family is supposed to be like. You might have followed in your father's footsteps and become an outlaw. Should I go on?"

"No," he said quietly as he leaned back in his chair to take it all in. He'd known all along that he was blessed to live in a town like Peppin, to have met Ellie's family and have been adopted into one of his own. However, he hadn't been willing to connect his parents' abandonment to the life he led now. Was this what the Bible meant about God taking the bad and working it out for something good? Was that what grace was— being able to live in the "good" that wasn't a sensible outcome of life's events?

He remembered Pastor Brightly's sermon on the subject not so long ago. He'd focused on the Scripture about the sins of the fathers not being visited on the sons, but if he remembered correctly, there was another key component to living in grace—forgiveness. Suddenly, he thought about his father. He swallowed hard. Surely he didn't have to forgive his parents for what they'd done to him. It wasn't fair of God to ask such a thing of him.

What would I get in return for that, Lord? Would the pain go away? How about whatever stigma I might have that keeps people from loving me? Something inside of him seemed to check that thought and make him take stock of all the people who had gathered to celebrate him. It was then he realized the truth. People *did* care about him. They *did* love him. He was the one who kept holding back out of fear they would abandon him.

Would it take forgiving his parents to break free of that fear? His jaw clenched. He hoped not because he wasn't even sure if doing that was possible.

"Lawson, did I say something wrong?"

He glanced up to meet her concern and covered her hand with his. "No. You said something right. I am a very blessed man. I appreciate the life God has given me. The problem is that the past is just always...there."

"I know it is but so is God." She glanced at their hands and turned hers to allow her fingers to thread through his. She met his gaze. "And so am I."

He stared at the incredible woman before him in awe. Physically she was so beautiful that she could make his heart forget to beat with just a look. But more important, she was everything he'd never allowed himself to hope for on the inside. She was warm, genuine, *committed*—and to him, no less. She saw past his protective barriers to the man he truly was. Yet, her time, her attention, even the look in her eyes, telegraphed that he mattered—not only to her but to the world in general.

He knew right then and there that she was the only woman he'd be willing to risk his heart for. He also knew that to do so would take courage on his part. Not just when he asked her to marry him, which he surely would, but every day for the rest of his life. It would take courage to believe that he was enough to make her stay. He couldn't—not yet...but one day. One day soon.

A throat cleared a few feet away. He suddenly realized how close he was to Ellie and how they must appear to everyone with their heads together and hands clasped. He released her hand to direct his attention to Lettie, who stood at his side. Her smile barely hid her excitement at the scene before her. "I hate to interrupt but I can't find the candles and it's nearly time to cut the cake."

"I think I left them in the kitchen." Ellie pushed back from the table. "I'll get them."

Both Ellie and Lettie walked away, leaving Lawson to take a swig of his forgotten glass of cider. He'd also forgotten that Ellie's brother had been sitting on the other side of her until Sean took the opportunity of her absence to turn toward him. "So when are you going to propose to my little sister?"

After a momentary pause in which he decided against playing dumb, Lawson set his cup aside and shrugged. "I'm not sure. I didn't even know I was going to marry her until about a minute ago."

Sean nodded. "Yep, I saw that poleaxed look from all the way over here."

"When the time comes will I be asking your permission or Nathan's or both?"

"Why don't the three of us talk about it on my day off next week?"

Lawson nodded soberly. No doubt they would have a few deep questions to ask, most likely spiritual in nature. Lawson would be ready for them. At least, he hoped he would be.

Chapter Eighteen

Ellie breathed a prayer of thanks for Lettie's timely interruption. She'd never seen Lawson's gaze quite as intense as it had been a few minutes ago and had certainly never been the subject of it. It had done funny things to her…chiefly, it had stopped her ability to think and hampered her ability to breathe. The connection between them had been so real—nearly tangible. What did it mean?

She brushed her cool hand across her warm cheek and tucked a wisp of hair behind her ear as she forced herself to focus on the task at hand. She entered the house to find a few stragglers remained. Her eyes narrowed at the sight of Mrs. Greene conversing with Donovan Turner in the sitting room. *I definitely did* not *invite him, either.*

"I guess some people think they can just show up anywhere whether invited or not," she muttered to herself as she snatched the candles from the counter, then searched for matches. She let a drawer close with a bit too much force. The bang was enough to draw the attention of the two people she was glaring at. Caught, she quickly turned her grimace into a detached smile, though she felt more like sticking out her tongue.

Mrs. Greene glanced away almost guiltily. No doubt she'd been gossiping about Ellie and Lawson. Donovan didn't have the sense to look away. He even offered Ellie a smile, which she pretended not to see before she breezed out the door. She *wouldn't* let either of them ruin her evening. She'd promised to leave Mrs. Greene to Lettie. She'd also promised Nathan and Lawson to avoid Donovan. She planned to do both of those things starting now.

She pulled in a deep breath of cool autumn air as she followed the lighted path back to the clearing. The combination of perfect weather and clear skies prepared the way for the dusky descent of twilight. It would be easy to enjoy the rest of the evening. If her resolve to do so was ever in danger, she knew she'd only have to take one look at Lawson's joyful if slightly stunned face to remember the true purpose of the evening.

She finally reached the clearing. As she glanced around for Lettie, a shadow separated from the trail behind her to step into the light. She swallowed her alarm. Donovan. He had probably been only a few feet behind her the entire time and she'd never even noticed. She tried to calm her nerves. There was no reason to be frightened. Perhaps he just happened to be walking the same direction at the same time.

Right, she thought sarcastically. Still, there was no real cause for her to be jumpy. It was just Nathan's overprotective warnings that had her on edge. He stepped toward her as if her frown was an invitation to speak. "I got my pig farm back."

Oh, thank goodness. He had some reason for seeking her out after all. "Did the judge help you?"

"No." His chest expanded with pride. "The man I sold it to gave me my deed back."

She tilted her head in confusion. "He *gave* it to you—just like that?"

His smile seemed to take on an almost sinister gleam in the dim light. "Well, I might have used a little persuasion."

She blinked and his smiled seemed normal again. She backed up a step. "I should probably go."

"What's the rush?"

"Ellie, there you are," Ms. Lettie said, unintentionally coming to her rescue. She didn't seem to notice that Ellie was speaking with someone else. Perhaps because Donovan remained in the shadows. "Let's put the candles on the cake. I think people are getting restless."

Grateful for the interruption, she gave a little wave to Donovan, then helped Lettie place the candles on the cake. After a few minutes, she was able to put the unsettling episode out of mind—or at least save it to examine later. They were about to light the candles when Lawson stopped them. "Before we cut the cake, I'd like to say a few words."

It took a moment for everyone to gather around. Ellie stepped closer to Lettie when Mrs. Greene appeared at her husband's side. Lettie whispered, "I haven't talked to her yet but I will."

Ellie nodded, then focused on Lawson. He cleared his throat, looking endearingly unused to being the center of attention. "I just want to thank everyone for coming. It means the world to me to have you all here. I can tell you right now that it's the best birthday I've ever had."

Laughter filled the air. Lawson grinned, seeming more at ease. "I've never had an opportunity like this where practically the whole town is listening to my every word. It probably won't happen again so I figure I'd better make the most of it by saying a few words to some very special people. Doc and Lettie, you raised me to be the man I am today. I don't think I tell you enough what that meant to me or how much *you* mean to me."

Doc stepped up to put his arm around his wife. "It's been an honor."

"It surely has," Lettie echoed.

Lawson nodded, took a moment to wrangle his emotions to a more manageable state and continued. "I'm also grateful to Nathan and Kate Rutledge. If you hadn't taken me in all those years ago, I don't want to imagine where I'd be or who I would be now."

Nathan grinned. "That was definitely one of our better decisions. Wouldn't you agree, Mrs. Rutledge?"

"It was." Kate nodded then teased, "He didn't stay with us for more than a few months back then but we have him now, don't we?"

Lawson laughed as did everyone else. "Aside from thanking you for hosting this shindig, Sean and Lorelei, what can I say? Y'all are just about the best friends a man could ask for."

Sean nodded his appreciation and Lorelei smiled but they refrained from commenting. Then Lawson looked at Ellie. Was it her imagination or did anticipation float through on a breeze? Suddenly, everyone was at attention. Her friends even leaned forward slightly. She barely refrained from rolling her eyes. What did they think was going to happen? A proposal? Not likely.

She tilted her head thoughtfully. *What is he going*

to say, though? I wonder if he'll try to be romantic or if he'll just focus on our friendship. No doubt everyone will pick whatever statement he makes apart in an effort to discern his feelings for me... He is taking an awfully long time to come up with something.

"Ellie," he began, "I think what I said to you earlier today made it pretty clear how much I've come to—" he cast about for an appropriate word before settling on "—*appreciate* your...ah...friendship."

It took her a moment to realize he was referring to their conversation in the buggy. "Oh. Yes, of course."

I will not blush. That would give away too much to all of the folks staring at me right now. For once her cheeks obeyed. A smile tilted her lips and she nodded at him in deference. *Very clever. You told me something yet managed not to tell them anything at all. Won't that leave everyone just itching to know what you said earlier today?*

He seemed to understand what she was thinking for he grinned. "I hear you are also the one to thank for co-ordinating this celebration. You did a great job. Now... how about that cake?"

"Yeah, Ellie, how about that cake?" Sean asked, obviously not referring to the cake and with no other purpose than to tease her.

He wasn't the only one wondering, because the conversations that should have continued now that Lawson was done with his announcement, didn't. She just smiled secretively as she lit the candles. "Wouldn't you like to know? It's too bad I'm not telling."

Sean winked at her as if he already knew. She wrinkled her nose at him then stepped aside so Lawson could make his wish and blow out the candles. It only took one breath from him to make those tiny fires go out but the one in her heart blazed all the brighter. She would just focus on that, not on the ache that filled her chest from her conversation with Lettie earlier today. Her gaze met Lawson's and somehow that made it easier to smile.

A nod from Nathan was enough to make Lawson push back from the table after their midday meal a few days later. Sean did the same. Lorelei looked at them in confusion. "Where are you men going in such a hurry?"

"We're just going to have a talk," Nathan answered. "Make sure we aren't disturbed, will you, Kate?"

"Since when do men talk?"

"Very funny." Nathan pressed a kiss on Kate's forehead before leaving the room.

"We promised the children we'd play with them," Lorelei reminded Sean.

He kissed her cheek. "We will when I come back."

Lawson looked at Ellie. She watched Sean leave the room then met his gaze with a cheeky smile. "I think I'm supposed to protest."

"And I'm supposed to kiss you." He glanced at the other women. "Or is that only for married folks?"

Kate shook her head and swept a hand in Ellie's direction. "Go right ahead."

Lorelei nodded. "Just keep it respectable."

He leaned over, lifted Ellie's chin and placed a kiss on the tip of her nose. "How was that?"

"Well done," Kate said.

As soon as he left the room he heard Lorelei ask, "What *did* he say to you on his birthday?"

He met the other men outside. Nathan told them to follow him, then led them into the barn and up the ladder to the hayloft. Lawson let out a low whistle once he saw a huge fort made out of hay. "That's impressive."

Nathan nodded. "The children started it. I told them to take it down but as we moved things around, it turned into this instead."

Sean shook his head in awe. "Lawson, why didn't we think of doing this when we were children?"

"I don't know." He frowned. "Are we really going to have this discussion in a hay fort? What's wrong with the parlor?"

"The sound carries."

"I always forget that."

"Everyone does unless they're in the kitchen…except for me. Sometimes that's the only way I know what's going on in my own house." Nathan clasped him on the shoulder. "Now, stop being nervous and enjoy the moment. Let's go inside."

Lawson's first impression of the fort was right. It was impressive. It had four outer walls of hay. Each wall had a window and the front one had a door they had to crawl to get through. The inside was partitioned into three rooms. They found their hay chairs in the last one. Nathan was the first to start things off. "Sean tells me there is a question you want to ask me."

"I'd like to marry Ellie."

"I figured that." Nathan nodded, then leaned forward, bracing his elbows on his knees. "You know you're like a brother to Sean and me, so this discussion isn't so much about whether you're suitable or not. I told you a long time ago that I couldn't imagine a better man for our Ellie. However, we're still going to ask you some questions to make sure you know you're doing the right thing for the both of you."

"Fair enough."

"Why do you want to marry Ellie?"

"I love her."

"What does God say about it?"

The question threw him for a moment. He cleared his throat. "I can't say that I've heard a direct command from Him to marry her. It's just more of a knowing inside me."

That seemed to satisfy Nathan. Lawson turned to Sean expecting him to speak up now. He wasn't disappointed. "How has your father's sudden reappearance affected your relationship with Ellie?"

"I think it's made my feelings for her stronger. She stood by me during my trip to his ranch. That meant a lot to me."

Sean played with a loose piece of hay as he considered that. "Have you forgiven your father, Lawson?"

"I thought we were talking about Ellie," he said tensely.

"We'll get back to her." Sean tossed the hay on the floor. "This is important, too."

Lawson looked to Nathan, hoping the man might be able to get their discussion back on track. He was disappointed when his boss shrugged. "I'm concerned about that, too. For your sake, I hope you have, but I can tell you probably haven't. There is a lot of anger stored up inside of you, Lawson. You hide it well but it's been there as long as I've known you."

"Anger isn't always a bad thing," he countered.

"You're right. The Bible says there is such a thing as righteous anger. But I have a feeling that holding on to that anger has let a lot of other things slip in, as well."

"Like what, exactly?"

"Fear…self-doubt…maybe a little bitterness. Am I hitting anywhere close to home?" At Lawson's hesitant nod, he gave a grim nod. "I thought so."

"It isn't worth it, Lawson," Sean advised. "It isn't worth holding on to that anger if you have to forfeit so much to keep it. You're a good man but I don't think you realize that. You seem to still see yourself as that child who was abandoned. That hasn't been you for a very long time."

"I know." He sighed. "I've been thinking the same thing myself lately. I'm not sure how to forgive Clive, though."

Nathan shrugged and leaned back onto the hay wall. "I think you just have to let it go. Make the decision to forgive him even if you don't feel it, then let God work out the rest."

Sean nodded. "It may not happen immediately but it will in time."

"What about the anger?"

Nathan smiled wryly. "I've found that if I'm angry at someone it helps to pray for them. It's probably the last thing I want to do at the moment but it's effective eventually."

"I'll try that."

Sean nodded. "I asked you about your father because I see how your inability to forgive him—as wrong as he was—could transfer to others you care about, including Ellie. I love my sister but she isn't perfect, which means she's going to mess up. So what happens if she disappoints you in some way? Are you going to turn away from her? Or will you love her anyway and seek her out to show her that? That's the kind of love I want for both of you."

Lawson stared at the hay-laden floor thoughtfully. Had he ever loved in that way before? No, he hadn't. But that was the kind of love he'd always wanted for himself. If he hadn't given it then why did he expect to receive it?

He gritted his teeth. *I really have let my anger and unforgiveness bind me to my past. Nathan and Sean are right. I have to let it go. It's the only way to have the life that I want.*

"All right, Lord," he prayed, hardly realizing he spoke aloud until Sean and Nathan bowed their heads. "I'm letting go of my anger and I choose to forgive my father." He paused, realizing that was the first time he'd ever called Clive that. Just like that, anger welled up inside of him. He shook his head. "You know I don't feel it but I guess I'll have to trust You to fix that. Help me to love Ellie the way You love her. In Jesus' name, Amen."

He eyed the men he'd hoped to call his brothers-in-law. "I guess this means I don't have your permission to marry Ellie."

Nathan and Sean exchanged a look before Sean said, "Are you crazy? Of course you can marry Ellie."

"You mean it?" he asked, even as relief settled over him in a thick wave.

Nathan nodded. "Everybody is working on something in their faith. If they aren't, then they should be. That isn't enough to disqualify you. Just be mindful of what we said. That prayer was proof you're already working on it."

"How soon are you going to propose?"

"I don't know. I'd like to be a bit surer of her feelings for me before I ask."

Sean grinned. "The only way to know for sure is to ask."

"I guess you're right." To be honest, the thought of doing so slightly terrified him. If she said no, he'd just keep loving her and hope eventually that love would turn back into just plain friendship. Wasn't that the right answer? He hoped so because it was the only one he had.

Chapter Nineteen

Ellie placed her chin on her fist as she stared thoughtfully out of the sitting room window toward the barn. "What do you think they're doing out there?"

Lorelei spilled a handful of jacks on the low table as she tried to beat her niece's record score. "They're probably playing Cowboys and Indians in that fort Timothy was telling us about."

Everyone giggled at that. Ellie sat back in her chair. "Oh, I haven't played that game in such a long time. I wish they would have invited me."

Lorelei glanced up with a grin. "I keep forgetting you were a tomboy growing up."

"I'll never forget." Kate groaned. "I thought I'd never see the end of those knee-patched bloomers you always wore."

"They were comfortable. I'll tell you that much." She glanced out the window. "Here they come. Oh, no!"

"Did someone get shot with an arrow?" Kate asked.

Dread filled her stomach as the men greeted their new visitor. "Worse. Mrs. Greene is here. What on earth could she want?"

A thousand awful scenarios played out in her mind as they all came inside. When Mrs. Greene announced her desire to speak to Ellie alone, curious looks were exchanged but everyone left them alone in the parlor. Ellie closed the door firmly behind them. She smoothed her skirt, then turned around to face her foe. "How can I help you, Mrs. Greene?"

Mrs. Greene took a seat on the settee, though Ellie hadn't offered her one. "Please sit down. I'd like to say what I came here to say without you hovering."

Ellie took her sweet time in taking the chair next to the settee. "Go right ahead."

The woman pulled in a deep breath. "I did wrong by you and I'm sorry for it. You came to me that day hoping for reconciliation. Instead, I offered you your worst nightmare served on a silver platter."

"Ms. Lettie talked to you."

"She did. My conscience had been bothering me, anyway."

Ellie surveyed her for a moment. "I hope you know how hard it is for me to believe you're sincere right now."

"I don't know how I'd be able to prove it to you." She grimaced and took her handkerchief out of her reticule to twist it nervously. "I realized how upset your parents would be if they knew I'd let you take the full blame for their deaths. We didn't part on good terms, and as disappointed as they were in you for spreading the secret, I think they were equally disappointed in me for refusing to forgive a child's mistake. They told me if I so much as mentioned that episode in your presence I'd have them to deal with and not you. I guess all of that anger in me built and built until even your apology wasn't enough. I wanted to hurt you and I suppose I did. I don't expect you to forgive me, but I am sorry."

"I understand why you felt the need to tell me." Ellie sighed. "For some reason, forgiving you isn't that hard. It's me I can't forgive." She shook away her thoughts and stood. "Thank you for coming, Mrs. Greene. I hope this means we can call a truce. We've done enough damage to each other already, haven't we?"

"I reckon we have." Mrs. Greene reached out to squeeze her hand. "I truly am sorry. Goodbye, dear."

Having Mrs. Greene call her "dear" somehow took the last of Ellie's strength out of her. She managed to wait until the woman left before collapsing onto the chair. She covered her face with her hands and tried to ignore the tears that stole down her cheek. It made no sense to cry now. Mrs. Greene had apologized. That was one load off her shoulders.

Perhaps it was just the reminder of her hand in her parents' deaths that did it. She'd been so good at avoiding that fact since she'd gotten back from the ranch. She'd stopped thinking about it every hour and now only thought about it every day or so. She tried to put Clive's words into action. *Don't let one mistake define your life.* That had only worked to an extent. Maybe it was time to try Lettie's advice about forgiving herself.

Suddenly she was aware that she was not alone. She glanced up to find her entire family and Lawson filing into the room. A small cry of dismay filtered through her lips as she realized they had probably all gone to the kitchen, which meant they'd heard every word of her exchange with Mrs. Greene. She wiped the tears from her cheeks and grimaced. "All of you heard. Well, it's true.

All of it's true. It's my fault our parents died. I didn't want to tell you, but Ms. Lettie said you already knew."

Kate nodded slowly. "I knew why they went into town that day but I had no idea you thought it was your fault. Oh, my dear little sister."

Suddenly she was enveloped in her sister's arms. Tears fell freely down Ellie's face. "You don't have to pretend that you don't blame me. Please, don't. I couldn't stand it."

"No one has to pretend, Ellie. We don't blame you," Sean said fiercely as he wrapped his arms around them both. "You were a child. You couldn't have known what you said, let alone that Ma and Pa would rush out into a threatening storm the moment they found out."

Kate stepped back to look at her face. "Tell me you believe us."

Ellie searched their faces. She wasn't sure yet if she agreed with them, but she could see that they meant what they'd said. She nodded. Sean handed her a freshly pressed handkerchief from his pocket. As she wiped away her tears he said, "As for you not forgiving yourself…"

"Yes?"

His tone gentled. "I don't see the point of it. You aren't going to bring Ma and Pa back by doing that. You're only going to make us sad and yourself miserable."

"He's right, Ellie."

"I suppose." She sounded about as unconvinced as she felt. It seemed after that everyone else wanted a chance to hug her—even her nieces and nephew. Lawson hugged her last. Once she stepped from his embrace she turned to everyone else and offered a trembling smile. "So what's this I hear about a fort?"

The first fire of the season blazed in the farmhouse's fireplace the next evening. The snap of cooler weather seemed to make everyone huddle a little closer to each other for the Rutledge family's Bible reading. At least that was the excuse Lawson gave himself for his close proximity to Ellie. She sat beside him on the settee with her feet tucked under her and a shawl draped around her shoulders. Kate sat in the rocker with Grace on her lap. Hope and Timothy sat at their father's feet as he read. Baby Matthew was already asleep.

Everything around Lawson seemed peaceful, homey and warm. He was beginning to think this sort of life might be possible for him.... His gaze slid to Ellie. For them. He was going to ask her soon. He just needed to figure out what to do about getting a ring.

Nathan seemed to give special emphasis to the last few passages, which conveniently focused on forgiveness, before closing the Bible. Kate and Nathan ushered their children off to bed, leaving him alone with Ellie. Kate paused at the door on her way out. "Lawson, I finished mending that sweater of yours. Be sure to get it from me before you leave."

He agreed to find her as Ellie yawned and stretched like a drowsy cat. He smiled at her. "Don't tell me you were sleeping. I'm pretty sure Nathan read that selection specifically for us."

"I wasn't sleeping." She groaned as she pushed the wisps of hair away from her face. She'd taken to wearing it up more often but by the end of the day it always seemed to anticipate its escape from the orderly style. "I barely slept last night. I just lay awake thinking."

"About your parents?" At her nod, he frowned. "I had no idea you were going through that. I wish I could have helped you in some way since you've been so supportive of me."

"I was ashamed. I didn't want anyone to know. I thought it would be easier that way."

"Was it?"

"No." Her smile signaled she was ready to change the subject. "I know Nathan read those passages to try to help me forgive myself. Why do you think he was directing them at you?"

He smiled wryly. "I decided to forgive my father."

"Really?" She leaned forward with interest. "How is that working for you?"

"Better than I thought it would, actually." He rose to bank the fire. "It seems like you just have to decide that's what you're going to do and stick with it."

Her silence made him glance over his shoulder at her. She watched him thoughtfully for a moment then joined him in front of the fireplace. "I don't think I'm quite as brave as you are."

"I'm not brave. I just got tired of feeling so many negative emotions all the time." He shoveled ashes over the fire logs then paused, realizing this was as good a time as any to try to get one last reading on her feelings for him. Setting the shovel aside, he captured her gaze. "I thought maybe I'd try a few more positive ones for a change."

Her fingers stilled for an instant before they continued on their route to tuck an escaping piece of golden hair behind her ear. Curiosity tinged her green eyes with gold, or perhaps that was just from the remnants of the fire. "Like what, for instance?"

He hid a grin, thankful that somehow she'd asked exactly the right question. He stood to his feet. Should he tell her he loved her right here and now? He couldn't seem to form the words. Despite her talk of his bravery, he didn't have the courage to declare his independence from his personal history. Surely that's what those three little words would mean—that he believed the abandonment of the past would stop here and now because he loved her and she loved him. Or did she?

He might not be able to ask that question with words but he needed to know how she felt. She must have recognized his intent, for her eyes widened as he erased the distance between them. She didn't step away. He lowered his head. Her lashes drifted down to rest on her cheek, so she didn't see the hopeful smile that passed across his lips in the moment before he kissed her.

She leaned into him. One hand came to rest on his chest and the other behind his neck. His arms encircled her waist before he broke away to press a kiss against her temple.

Well, that settles it, he thought as he held her close. *There is no way she'd kiss me like that if she didn't love me.*

Footsteps sounded in the hall. He released her just before Nathan walked in. His friend took one look at them and raised his eyebrows. "Don't mind me. I just needed one of these lamps."

Ellie blushed then said good-night to both of them before slipping out of the room. Lawson ignored the knowing look on Nathan's face to ask, "Is Kate around?"

"In the kitchen, I think."

Lawson found Kate folding his sweater. "Thanks for doing this."

"You're welcome. Before you go… Nathan can't keep a secret from me to save his life so I wanted to give you this." She opened a small leather pouch and pulled out a ring. "This has passed down through the women in my family for generations. My grandmother gave it to my father before he asked Ma to marry him. Now, I'm giving it to you."

"Didn't you want it?"

She smiled. "Nathan gave me a ring of his own. I didn't want to refuse it. Lorelei ended up using her family's ring since she was an only child. I hoped to catch you before you made any arrangements and that you'd want to give it to Ellie."

"Of course I do." He accepted the gold ring from her to examine it carefully. Two hands embraced a heart-shaped emerald that rested under a crown. "I've never seen anything like this."

"It's a traditional Irish token of undying love called a Claddagh ring."

"I think I'd better keep it in that pouch until it's time for me to use it." He carefully slid the ring inside then tucked it into his shirt pocket. "I was thinking tomorrow might be a good time."

"You move fast."

He nodded. "I've made up my mind so I see no use in stalling. Do you think you could prepare a picnic basket for us? She'd probably enjoy another visit to the creek before it gets too cold."

Kate's blue eyes began to dance. "I'd be honored."

He nodded his thanks. He was finally going to put his past behind him. He was ready and he was pretty sure Ellie was, too.

Ellie spread out the picnic blanket on the grassy bank of the creek, making sure to stay far enough from the water to keep from getting muddy. She set aside the picnic basket Kate had given her and lay in a warm patch of sunlight to read her book as she waited for Lawson to arrive. It was awfully sweet of him to invite her on this picnic. She smiled, thinking of last night's kiss. His attentions had certainly been marked as of late. Perhaps he would ask to court her again soon. Then maybe she would have rectified at least one mistake. Not that doing so was the only reason she hoped he'd ask. After all, she was pretty sure this was what love must feel like.

Had it only been a few months since she'd resolved to find a husband and petitioned God to help her? She'd had no idea what a mess she was going to get herself into. Thankfully, that mess seemed to straighten out after she'd asked God to lead her in her relationship with Lawson. She was thankful for that so why did she still feel as if she was holding back? Why could she only say she was "pretty sure" this was what love was like?

She lowered her book to frown at it thoughtfully. *I guess I'm still expecting my problems to vanish because Lawson cares for me. Kate told me that wouldn't happen. Why am I still longing for someone to ride in on a white horse and save me—rescue me from the stains of my past?*

Suddenly, the words of a hymn she'd learned as a child sprang to her lips. "What can wash away my sins? Nothing but the blood of Jesus."

She sat up abruptly. How on earth could she have forgotten something as basic as that? Romance didn't have the power to heal her hurts or make her feel clean. Only God could do that. Even He could only do that if she let Him. Lawson could and had been a tool God used to accomplish that but ultimately the hero she longed for was God. Could that be right?

It was. She could feel it all the way down to her soul. "Oh, what a fool I've been! Lord, I'm so sorry! Forgive me for seeking a man when I should have been seeking You. Wash me clean. I let go of my past and place it in Your hands."

Relief spread through her and blossomed into a burgeoning sense of peace. She'd loved her parents with all of her heart. She never would have done anything to hurt them intentionally. She'd made a mistake but that hadn't changed their love for her. It hadn't changed God's love for her. They would never have wanted her to live a life filled with guilt. God certainly didn't. So… though a tear slipped down her cheek, she finally let them go. She finally let their memory rest in peace.

She smiled and allowed herself to fall back onto the blanket. What a long journey it had taken to get to this point, but she was here and that's what mattered. She shook her head ruefully. *Poor Lawson. All this time I've been putting unreal expectations on his love. Given his past, I wonder how he could even care for me at all.*

It would be different now. She was different now, changed by love—God's love—the way she'd wanted to be. She was so lost in her thoughts that she didn't hear the sound of Lawson's approach until his boots landed in her peripheral vision. She sat up to greet him with a smile that stalled on her lips.

It wasn't Lawson.

Alarm filled her as she met the too intense gaze of the man before her. *Donovan.*

Ellie quickly stood to her feet, clenching her book in her hands nervously as she faced the man who watched her with what appeared to be a desperate hunger. "Donovan, what are you doing here?"

His hands slipped into his coat pockets as he seemed overcome with a sudden shyness. "I've wanted to talk to you for days but you were never alone."

She crossed her arms. "Have you been watching me all that time?"

"I wanted to talk to you," he repeated, avoiding her gaze.

She took that as a yes. Her gaze swept the woods around her as she suddenly became aware of their seclusion. No one would hear her if she screamed for help. Then again, she might not need help. She met Donovan's gaze once more. Maybe he really did just want to talk to her. *Alone...after he's been watching me for days...I don't think so.*

Suddenly, relief surged through her as she remembered. "Lawson will be here soon. You should leave. Come to the house later today and we'll talk then."

His entire demeanor changed from shy to contemptuous. "You're meeting Lawson? Why? That spoils everything.... No, that makes it better...much better."

"Yes, it does," she agreed. No doubt Lawson would be able to handle him in no time. "You two can figure things out and I'll just stay out of it."

"You don't understand." He caught her arm, which was crossed at her chest and thus brought him uncomfortably close to her. "I love you. I won't stand for you being with him anymore."

Right. She stepped away from his touch. "I don't see how you have any say in that matter."

"Oh, I'll have a say, all right. As a matter of fact, you're going to do *exactly* what I say. Do you understand?"

"Certainly not. I—" Her words stopped abruptly when she saw the gun he eased from his coat pocket. She realized that for now it was probably best to stop talking and listen to what he had to say. "What do you want me to do?"

He grinned and rocked back onto his heels. "That's more like it. First things first. You're going to sit down right where I found you and act like nothing has happened when he rides up. Then you're going to break things off with him. I want to hear you do it so no mumbling or whispering or trying to warn him because if you do—" he waggled the gun in her face "—that's it for him."

She stared at him trying to understand the strange words he was speaking. He couldn't be serious. But he was. He definitely was. Fear muddled her thoughts. He seemed to realize that for he stepped forward with the gun pointed at her chest. "I know I'm scaring you, Ellie. I'm sorry for that but you have to do what I say. I promise not to hurt you, but one little slip and I'll kill him."

He took her arm and led her back to the blanket. "That's it. Sit down right there. Read your book. I'm going to hide. I'll be close enough to hear and see you jilt him. Don't make a mistake. Remember that now."

She closed her eyes. *Don't make a mistake. Don't make a mistake. Don't...*

You did a bad thing, Ellie. A very bad thing.

She pushed away the memories but her mother's disappointed words lingered in her head. *Maybe Lawson won't come. Oh, Lord, please don't let him come.*

Her eyes jerked open at the sound of approaching hoofbeats. Dread filled her stomach. She scanned the woods for some sign of Donovan. Nothing—but he was there. She could feel him watching her. Could he hear her accelerated breathing? Probably. It seemed to fill the air around her.

Lawson appeared, riding on Starlight's sire, Samson. A hero on a white horse, but that wasn't right. She couldn't let him save her. Instead, she had to save *him*.

Chapter Twenty

She watched Lawson dismount and approach her with a grin so full of joy that it nearly broke her heart. She glanced down at the lines of black text to get her bearings. *Regulate your breathing. Unclench the book. Good. Now, hold it casually. Pretend to read.*

He knelt on the blanket beside her. "Aren't you going to say hello to me?"

She glanced up to see him eyeing the book in her hands. She set it aside and folded her hands nervously in her lap. "Hello."

"Hello," he responded, then proceeded to kiss her. She melted into his arms just like she had last night until she remembered who was watching them. She placed a hand on his chest and forced herself away from him.

"Lawson," she chided.

He searched her face. "I was just making sure. After that greeting—"

"I need to talk to you."

"I need to talk to you, too." His fingers threaded through hers. She almost removed them but realized that their position probably made it impossible for Donovan to see that connection from wherever he hid, so she didn't pull away.

She lifted her chin. "I'm—"

"No. Let me go first."

She bit her lip and scanned the forest. He was insisting so she had to let him if she didn't want him to suspect anything was wrong. Would Donovan understand that? She glanced down at their hands. "All right. If you insist…"

"I do." He smiled at his statement for some reason, then raked his free hand through his hair. "I didn't think I'd be this nervous. I guess I'd better just come out and say it. I love you, Ellie O'Brien."

Ellie's head shot up. She stared at Lawson. She must not have heard him correctly. This could not be happening. Not now. "What did you say?"

He grinned. "I love you! I love everything about you. I love the small things like the way your hair is always slipping out of place and the way your eyes dance when you laugh. I love the big things like the way you stand by me no matter what."

"Oh, Lawson." Her words came out half ecstasy and half despair but he didn't seem to notice.

Sincerity filled his every word as he continued. "You know how hard it is for me to believe that anyone, especially someone as wonderful as you, could care for me, but I have to take this chance to ask you. Do you love me?"

This was the question she'd been asking herself for weeks. She hadn't been sure of the answer before but right at that moment, looking into his eyes, she knew without a doubt what the answer was. Yes, she loved him. It wasn't even a question anymore. He didn't have to change her life to make her love him. She loved him just the way he was—strong yet scarred, caring and gentle yet protective and fierce. He was a true friend, but one glance from him could make her head spin.

Her heart begged to shout those three words loudly enough to shake the heavens, but the jubilant sound would only turn into a death knell. She held his hand tighter as her gaze raked the woods. She knew what she had to say.

"Ellie?"

Her gaze caught his and held on for dear life. *Oh, what a silly fool I've been. I couldn't tell if I really loved him. Now I know I do. Yet, I'm going to break his heart and that will break mine just as surely.* She allowed her heart to show in her eyes. He saw that and relaxed. She swallowed. "No."

He froze. *"No?"*

"No. I don't. I think you'd better leave." The words sounded hollow to her ears but she prayed he'd obey them. She wondered if he noticed that despite her rejection she hadn't released his hand. *Please, know that means something. Know that as soon as I can get away from Donovan I'll run straight to you.*

He couldn't know that. He couldn't read her mind. He didn't even seem to notice that they held hands as his hazel eyes filled with hurt and confusion. "You're lying. You love me. I'm sure of it—even if you never said it directly. I'm going to stay right here until you tell me the truth."

"No!" she cried in alarm before she could catch herself. She had to make something up—anything to make him go away before Donovan got impatient and shot him. "I'm not going to explain anything. I said I don't love you and that's that. It's over between us. Leave me alone."

He glanced down at their hands then back at her face. "You don't mean that."

She was glad he realized that but it didn't make him safe. Ellie grew desperate. She threw one more glance toward the woods then pushed him away. "Will you *get out of here* already? Go away! *Please.*"

Lawson stared at her as if he'd never seen her before. She watched his hurt turn to anger. Finally, he stood to his feet, rushed to his mount and rode back down the trail he'd come. Tension seeped from her body in relief. Donovan surfaced from behind a nearby bush. "You were brilliant. That performance would have made any actress proud."

"Why would you make me hurt him like that?"

"He was devastated, wasn't he? That, my love, was just an unexpected little treat. I had no intention of running into Lawson but I'm glad now that I did."

She glared at him. "You are insane. What is the point of all this?"

An angry muscle jerked in his jaw before he smiled. "I wish you wouldn't insult me like that. I've never insulted you, have I?"

She gritted her teeth and glanced toward the forest where no sign of Lawson remained before turning back to him. "What do you want?"

"You," he said calmly. "I want you. You're coming with me."

Lawson only made it a short distance before he had to get off his horse and lean against a tree to gather himself. Ellie had rejected him—outright rejected him without even providing a reason. He'd thought she was different. He'd thought if any woman in the world could love him, it was her. He shook his head. She didn't want him. She'd shooed him away like a pesky fly. So everything she'd said before and everything she'd done... did that mean nothing to her? Did *he* mean nothing to her? She said she didn't love him but he'd been so sure that she did. Her kiss had told him so last night. What could have changed between then and now?

"It's just so strange." He took the Claddagh ring out of his pocket and held it tightly. That was the right word for that episode—*strange*.

He'd ridden in and she hadn't seemed to care a whit that he was there. She just kept reading her book... upside down. He'd realized that, which was why he'd had the courage to kiss her. She'd responded almost desperately yet she'd pushed him away, and had seemed distracted. She kept looking off into the woods as if something out there was more important than his profession of love. Even when she'd rejected him, she'd done it while holding his hand the entire time.

He stared unseeingly into the woods. Something must have happened between last night and this morning. Perhaps it had something to do with her parents?

He took a step on the path back toward the creek then hesitated. She'd rejected him once already. Why should he risk that again? Maybe he just wasn't good enough. Maybe there really was something wrong with him—something that others could only sense when they got close to him. He shook his head. That didn't explain his relationship with his adoptive parents and the rest of Ellie's family.

He pulled in a deep breath. "Well, Lord, what is

it? Do I let her go and just assume something really is wrong with me? Or do I go after her and prove…what, exactly?"

That even though I've been abandoned I can still find the courage to seek out those I love. That my past doesn't determine my future. That Ellie loves me…and something must be wrong.

He stopped walking to peer down the path before him as the training he'd received as a Ranger kicked in along with his common sense. A woman alone in a secluded area, distracted enough not to notice her book is upside down, nervously watching the woods, behaving in completely uncharacteristic ways, clinging to his hand yet pleading with him to leave. Something really was wrong. Even if that wasn't the case, even if he was only seeing what he wanted to see, he wouldn't let Ellie go without a fight.

He rushed down the path back to the creek. The sound of the waterfall grew louder and he slowed his steps to a stealthy pace. He veered off the main path to shield himself in the trees. He spotted the blanket, the book and the picnic basket but Ellie was gone. Had she run off or had someone taken her? He studied the ground around the blanket and found her boot marks along with his…and another set—too large to be hers and slightly too small to be his.

He followed the prints away from the blanket into the woods, where they circled around to a large bush. A slight indention in the soft ground told him someone had recently been kneeling here. The prints then traveled back toward the blanket. They stopped about four feet away from it then veered off to the left. Ellie's soon joined them. Someone was with her. Lawson couldn't be far behind them if they were on foot. His relief came too soon for he discovered the distinctive marks left behind by horseshoes.

He could go back for help or he could continue on by himself and stand a chance of actually catching them. He was used to working alone as a Ranger so he let out a low whistle and Samson cantered toward him. He mounted the horse, then urged him on as they followed the tracks that would guide him to Ellie.

The smooth canter of Donovan's horse ate up the ground as the familiar hills around her family's farm faded into dense, unfamiliar woods. Dense except for the well-worn path they traveled on. A shortcut between their horse ranch and his pig farm, Donovan explained. It chilled her to realize how often he must have used it. It was unfortunate that no one had noticed it, but then her family tended to stay close to the farmhouse and barn. Interminable minutes passed by or at least it seemed that way since they were riding double and Donovan's arm stayed around her waist the entire time. She smelled the pig farm before she saw it.

They burst into a small clearing where a barn nestled close to a cabin. The pigs hardly seemed to notice their arrival. Donovan dismounted first then carefully helped her down. "I'm afraid I'll have to hold the gun on you while you stable the horse. I don't want to take any chance that you'll run off."

"What are you going to do with me?"

"I'll tell you once we get inside," he promised.

Minutes later she entered the cabin, taking stock of it while he barred the door behind them. It consisted of one room much like Lawson's, and it had probably been built around the same time. The first thing she noticed was that it was clean. Almost too clean. The bed stood against the back wall. The stove was in the corner while a table sat in the middle of the room. A warm bear rug covered much of the floor. Dozens of thin soft-cover books were stacked neatly next to the bed. Plays, she realized.

"Make yourself comfortable."

She glanced at her captor, then took the only chair at the table. She rubbed her arms against the slight chill that filled the room. He took that as his cue to warm a pot of coffee on the stove. Once done with that, he sat down on the bed and just looked at her with a contented smile on his face. *He really* is *unstable.* "Well, what do you want with me?"

"I want to marry you."

She sighed and crossed her legs and arms. "I guess it doesn't matter to you what I think about that."

"Of course it does," he chided. "I want you to be happy. I just know that you'll be happiest with me."

She bit her cheek to keep from laughing at that ridiculous statement. He really seemed to care for her in that strange, demented way of his. Other than poking a gun at her and threatening to shoot Lawson, he'd been very careful with her. She lifted her chin, daring to ask, "Are you going to hurt me?"

He shook his head and actually appeared offended. "I would never hurt you."

"I'm glad to hear that."

His jaw tightened. "Unless you try to leave, of course, but it would be for your own good."

"Of course," she said with a mirthless smile. "So how exactly do you plan to marry me? I have to give my consent to that, you know. Even if I did, someone else would probably object, like my brothers."

No doubt Lawson would, too, despite the way she'd been forced to treat him. However, she didn't think it would be wise to mention that to Donovan at the moment. He didn't look fazed by the prospect of anyone objecting.

"It won't matter if you want to or not. You'll have to do it." He rose to pour her a cup of coffee. "I'm going to keep you here all night. Come morning, your reputation will be ruined and we'll have to get married."

"Morning?" she asked skeptically. "As soon as my brothers figure out I'm missing, they'll start looking for me. What makes you think you'll have until morning?"

"They won't know where to look." He set the coffee in front of her, then produced a stale-looking cookie she recognized as being from Lawson's party a week ago.

She narrowed her eyes as she stared at the man. She hated to admit it but his idea was actually sort of clever…and sneaky, deplorable, heavy-handed and implausible. Her brothers would never force her into a marriage with Donovan. As long as he kept his promise not to hurt her, she would be fine. She just had to wait until someone found her. It was probably best to play along with Donovan and let him think she was cooperating, just to keep him happy.

She cleared her throat. "That's quite a plan, but if we're going to have to wait a while, I wish you would have let me bring my book so I'd have something to do."

"We can read one of these plays together." He smiled as he poured himself a cup of coffee, then placed it on the table to sort through his stack. "*Romeo and Juliet.*

I'll play Romeo. I know the lines by heart. You will be my Juliet."

She took a sip of the coffee to cover her incredulous smile. She shouldn't look at him as if he was crazy. It wouldn't help in the long run. Too many looks like that and he was bound to get insulted. That would make him angry, which wasn't good because he got even crazier when he was angry. "That's perfect."

He opened one of the thin booklets and flipped through the pages before handing it to her. He stood before her and placed a hand over his heart while he dramatically quoted the lines of the play in a strange sort of accent. She stared at him in confusion. All she caught was something about pilgrims, lips and a kiss. He stopped speaking and waited expectantly. She glanced down at the book. *Pilgrims...lips...kiss... Oh!*

"Good pilgrim, you do wrong your hand too much, which mannerly devotion shows in this..."

The rhythmic prose seemed to calm his nerves, which in turn made her less jittery. The satisfied look on Donovan's face told her that she was safe for now. *Please, Lord, send help and quickly.*

Chapter Twenty-One

Lawson could barely believe his ears as he listened to Ellie's lyrical Texas drawl launch into a Shakespearean verse in response to Donovan's cockeyed accent. He wanted to glance into the half-open window he crouched under, but resisted the action that would have given away his presence prematurely.

It sounded as if she was safe for the time being. That was a relief—as was the fact that her rejection hadn't been of her own hand but rather Donovan's. He could tell that much from the man's ridiculous plan to both ruin and save Ellie's reputation, thus binding her to him forever.

Yeah, that's not going to happen—not on my watch. He frowned when a giggle sounded through the window. What was going on in there? He didn't have to wait long to find out. Ellie's voice was filled with disbelief. "Did people really talk like this?"

Despite the danger of the situation, a smile curved Lawson's lips. She was outright adorable. That's all there was to it. Apparently, Donovan didn't agree because disapproval filled his voice. "I thought you knew Shakespeare and liked it."

"I knew *of* it." Her tone was more carefully modulated this time. Obviously, she remembered that it would not be wise to displease Donovan at a time like this. "I like it fine. I'm just not used to it."

"Keep going. Don't break character again."

"All right." She continued on with the play.

Lawson shook his head as he listened. This was a fine situation, wasn't it? He had to get Ellie out of that man's clutches. He just wasn't sure how. He could go in with both barrels blazing but Ellie could easily get caught in the cross fire of any violence in such a confined space. He needed to go for backup and he knew exactly where to find it.

He said a silent prayer for Ellie's safety, then crept away from his window to where he'd left reliable Samson. The stallion's ears perked up at Lawson's approach as if he was reporting for duty. Lawson mounted up and rode back along the path that had made it easy for him to track them down, until he reached the ranch. He rode into the barnyard just as Nathan exited the farmhouse with Kate. They must have been waiting for him to return with Ellie. His guess was right because when he dismounted, Nathan's first question was "Where's Ellie?"

"Did she say yes?" Kate asked.

"I didn't ask because she said she didn't love me, but I think Donovan forced her to."

Nathan narrowed his eyes. "Donovan?"

"He was hiding in the woods. I figured something was wrong after she rejected me so I went back to find out. He's taken her to his pig farm. He plans to keep her there until morning so she'll have to marry him to save her reputation."

"That isn't going to happen." Nathan's voice was laced with steel. "I reckon you already have a plan."

He nodded. "Donovan doesn't seem like he'll hurt Ellie unless she tries to run off or makes him angry. She's been smart and playing it safe by humoring him. I think that will give you enough time to ride into town and get Sean."

Nathan nodded. "That's probably the best thing to do since he's the sheriff."

"In the meantime, I'm going to ride back and keep an eye on things. There is a hedge of bushes near the smokehouse that will make a good lookout place. Y'all can meet me there."

"Sounds like a plan. Let's ride out."

How long have I been here? Ellie wondered. She wasn't sure but it was long enough for them to have lunch and make their way to the end of the play with her playing all the women's parts and Donovan playing the men's…by heart…using different voices. He'd skipped a few scenes here and there but seemed to relish being the Romeo to her Juliet. Thankfully, he'd been too caught up in hearing her speak the dialogue to try to act out stage directions. She didn't bother to read them out loud, either. No need to remind him that Juliet was supposed to kiss Romeo at certain points, like now. She just skipped to… "Thy lips are warm."

"Lead, boy: which way?" He perched on the edge of the bed in anticipation of the death scene.

She ignored the chills of foreboding that rose on her arms by lifting the fork from the ham she had barely touched. "Yea, noise? Then I'll be brief. O happy dagger!" She lifted the fork into the air. "This is thy sheath." She glanced down for her next line then plunged the fork toward her heart. "There rust and let me die."

The fork fell to the ground as she slumped against the chair and closed her eyes. She could feel him staring at her so rather than face that odd intensity, she kept them closed. Perhaps she could get away with this for the rest of the play. There didn't seem to be much left of it. What would they do after that? Perhaps they'd start another play. She wouldn't mind it as long as her own ending didn't turn out as tragic as Juliet's.

She started listening to Donovan again when his voice changed to reflect a different character. "The ground is bloody; search about the churchyard…"

Are You still there, Lord? You are, aren't You? I can feel You with me even though I'm scared. I'm trying hard not to be. You'll save me. Please, hurry. I'm waiting for You.

Suddenly she wondered if God might be waiting for her to act. After all, Lawson was safe. Donovan had tucked his gun into his holster, so it wasn't exactly an immediate threat anymore. Maybe she could hit him over the head with something.

She peeked one eye open to survey the clean room. Then she saw it. Right there on the stove was salvation in the form of a frying pan. It was cast iron and looked heavy enough to pack a wallop that would knock Donovan out long enough to ride for help on that mare she'd unsaddled for him. She just needed a distraction.

She had the entire rest of the play to think one up and as soon as they were finished, she reverently closed the play. "You read beautifully, Donovan. I'd love to hear you do another one."

He beamed. "Would you, really?"

"Oh, yes." She handed him the play. "I'll make us some more coffee while you find the next one."

"What shall I do?" He knelt beside the stack of plays as she walked to the stove and filled the coffeepot with water from the pitcher. *"Macbeth?"*

"No." She grasped the handle of the frying pan.

"Othello?" His back was to her.

"No." She took a deep breath. She had to do this right the first time because there wouldn't be a second chance. She needed to swing hard and swing true like she had when she'd played baseball with the boys at school. She trained her gaze on the back of his head.

"Taming of the Shrew?"

She swung and hit him right on the perfect spot to make him slump forward soundlessly. "That's the one."

She took his gun then put the pan on the table before unbolting the door. She stepped out into the sunlight and glanced around to get her bearings. The barn was in front of her. That was all she needed to know. She was only a few feet from the cabin when she heard a roar erupt from inside. Her eyes widened but she didn't look behind her. Her only hope was to get on his horse and gallop away. She took off running, begging the Lord for help.

Lawson tensed when the cabin door opened. Nathan and Sean hadn't arrived yet but if Donovan was planning to take Ellie somewhere else, Lawson would have to stop him here and now. He watched in amazement as Ellie walked out alone toward the barn with her arms swinging as if she didn't have a care in the world. Then he saw the gleam of black metal in her hand and realized she probably didn't.

He rose from his hiding place just as a roar sounded from inside the house. Ellie dashed toward the barn. He ran toward the house. Drawing his gun, he slid his back along the side of the house until he could peer inside the front door. Donovan was stumbling around inside, no doubt gathering weapons. Lawson cocked his gun. "Get your hands up where I can see them. Now!"

The man froze. Donovan turned slowly, then lifted fury-filled eyes to Lawson before he lifted his hand and threw a steak knife right at Lawson's chest. He dodged the worst of it as the blade whizzed past his shooting arm. Donovan used that distraction to rush past him. Lawson momentarily holstered his gun to tackle the man before he could escape more than a few yards.

They landed on the ground with a rolling thud. A blow landed across Lawson's jaw so hard that he tasted blood. His gun was wrenched from his holster but Lawson slammed his elbow into the man's arm, pinning it against the ground and sending the gun sliding in the dirt. Donovan threw his body toward it.

Lawson channeled the movement while shoving a hand down on the man's shoulder, then added his own strength until Donovan landed flat on his stomach. He knelt onto the man's back. Forcing his left arm behind his back, Lawson waited for the fight to drain from Donovan. A string of curses came out instead. Lawson jerked his arm a bit harder. "Watch your mouth. There's a lady present…I think."

He knew the moment the pain set in because Donovan stiffened. A moment later, he went limp. Lawson took that opportunity to scan his surroundings. Ellie was indeed present along with her two brothers. All of them had guns pointed toward Donovan. "Easy, folks. I'm down here, too, remember?"

Sean was the last to put his gun away. "I thought you needed help."

"It looks like I just need some handcuffs." He took the metal bracelets from Sean and clamped them on Donovan. "He's all yours, Sheriff."

Donovan somehow managed to turn his head enough to stare up at her with those desperate, chilling eyes of his. She wanted to turn away from his gaze but it held her still. She shook her head sadly. "The love you want so badly from me I can't give. However, there is Someone who can love you the way you deserve if you'll accept it."

He grunted as Sean hauled him to his feet again. "Who are you talking about?"

She gave a small smile and lifted her shoulders in a shrug. "God. No, don't look disappointed. His love is real and powerful. It doesn't hurt or try to control, like you did today. It gives life, it heals and it fulfills. It did that for me and it can do the same for you if you let it."

Donovan stared at her with his eyebrows drawn together, confusion in his eyes, and his mouth slightly agape. Had she been blabbering nonsensically? She realized the rest of the men were staring at her, too. Sean nodded at her as if in a silent *Amen.* A hint of pride touched Nathan's smile. Lawson? Well, he just stared at her with that unnervingly intense look he'd perfected at his birthday party.

Nathan cleared his throat. "Well said, Ellie. Now, I think we'd better get going."

Once Donovan was ready to be hauled to the town jail, Sean turned to Ellie and opened his arms. "Come here."

She stepped into his embrace as he gave her a fierce hug that nearly lifted her feet off the ground. He set her away from him to look her in the eye. "I love you."

"I love you, too."

"If you ever scare me like that again, I'll tan your hide."

She lifted her chin. "I'd like to see you try."

He gently cuffed her on the chin, then mounted his horse. Nathan was the next to hug her. "We'll travel with y'all as far as the farm, then Sean and I'll go on into town with Donovan. You'd better ride with Lawson."

It wasn't long before the faithful drum of the waterfall filled the air. Ellie caught sight of the abandoned picnic basket and stiffened in resolve. She slid closer to Lawson in the saddle. "Stop the horse!"

"What?" He glanced over his shoulder in alarm. "Why?"

"I want to get down."

He immediately reined in Samson, most likely realizing she was going to get off whether he stopped or not. She dismounted with his help then placed a hand on his knee to keep him from doing the same before waving her curious brothers on. She turned to stare up at Lawson. He stared right back. "Is something wrong, Ellie?"

She tucked a piece of hair behind her ear and lifted her chin. "We're doing it again."

"Doing what?"

"The whole thing," she whispered fiercely. "The

whole thing from the very beginning. I'll go sit on the picnic blanket and you ride in from over there just like last time."

Realization filled his eyes along with a hint of wariness. He rubbed his jaw and glanced toward the woods as though avoiding the sight of her and the place of her rejection. She held her breath. Surely he knew that she was asking for a chance to undo the mess Donovan had caused. *Please, let me fix this.*

He glanced down at her then gave one almost indiscernible nod before he urged Samson into a canter toward the woods. She rushed to the blanket and smoothed out the wrinkles wrought by the wind before she settled onto it with her book. It seemed like an eternity until she heard the plod of Samson's powerful hooves. She waited until Lawson dismounted before she glanced up with a greeting on her lips. The intense look in his eyes stole her breath and her words. "You aren't going to say hello this time, either?"

She stood to greet him. "Hello, Lawson."

"Hello, Ellie." He lifted her chin to place a kiss on her nose. "Suppose we skip all the rest and just get right down to it?"

"All right." She tossed her book aside. "In that case… I love you, too, Lawson Williams."

A startled look crossed his face. "You—you do?"

She giggled. "Of course I do, silly. Do you really think anything other than having a gun at your back would keep me from saying that? I love you and I'll say those words a thousand times a day if that's what it will take to convince you."

"I don't know. Just hearing it once had a pretty strong effect seeing as I love you, too."

"I know," she said solemnly. "Which is why I think you ought to marry me."

He made a coughing sound somewhere between a choked laugh and a gasp. "Are you proposing to me?"

"I reckon."

"Ellie." He let out a frustrated groan.

"What?"

He shook his head. Catching her left hand, he gave it a quick kiss before stepping back and kneeling at her feet. He pulled a ring from his pocket and presented it to her. "Will you marry me?"

She stared down at him as confusion gave way to realization. "You had that ring the whole time."

He nodded.

"Then the picnic was…"

He smiled.

She gasped. Her free hand covered her cheek as she stared into the woods where her brothers had disappeared with Donovan. "You were trying to propose, weren't you?"

He tilted his head as his eyes took on a familiar teasing gleam. "Actually, I'm still trying to propose but I'm not getting an answer."

She laughed. "Yes! Oh, yes!"

He began to slip the ring on her finger, then hesitated. "You're serious, aren't you?"

"Of course!" Her heart jumped to her throat. "Aren't you?"

He searched her face for a long moment. Finally, he stood to his feet and slid the ring into place. "I'm serious. I've never been more serious about anything or anyone in my life."

"Lawson Williams." She stared at him in awe. "Are you crying?"

He grimaced and scrubbed a stray of wetness from his cheek. "I don't know. I haven't done much of it before. I've never felt this much love before—from you, God, the town, our families. Maybe it was there all the time but I didn't trust that it was enough. Now that I do, I feel like my heart is going to burst, it's so full. I can hardly believe this is happening." His hand brushed reverently across her cheek, then strayed to her hair. "That somehow God loved me enough to let me end up with you."

"In that case, He must love me an awful lot, too." She smiled and swayed forward to kiss his damp cheek, then leaned against him when his arms encircled her waist. Resting her cheek against his firm chest, she sighed. "I can't explain it, but somehow I know that it was always supposed to end exactly like this."

"I think there's one thing we forgot." His voice rumbled in her ear.

She pulled away slightly to look at him. "What's that?"

Her confusion was short-lived, for his lips captured hers as completely as he'd captured her heart, leaving her breathless when he pulled away. "How's that for a finish?"

"I don't know. I think it also makes a pretty fine beginning."

Epilogue

The whole town showed for the wedding—or at least it seemed that way from the glimpses of the sanctuary Lawson managed to glean through the crack in the foyer door. Ellie was tucked out of sight in the storage/bride's room. He'd sent everyone else away in preparation for this moment. He swallowed and straightened his tie a moment before the door opened.

"Nathan said you wanted to see me."

Lawson braced himself before meeting Clive's gaze. The man seemed just as nervous as he felt. Lawson cleared his throat. "I guess you were surprised to receive my invitation to come here for the wedding."

Clive allowed a nod. "I was surprised and pleased. Ellie is a wonderful young woman. I'm sure you two will be very happy."

"Thank you. The real reason I asked you here was to tell you something important." He pulled in a deep breath. "I forgive you."

"You forgive me?"

"Yes." He ran his fingers through his hair. "I know

it may seem presumptuous for me to say that since you haven't said you wanted it but it's there all the same."

"I do want your forgiveness. I just didn't dare ask for it." Clive wiped his eyes, which had become suspiciously red. "What made you decide to forgive me?"

"First of all, I knew God wanted me to do it. Then I realized that despite how it may feel sometimes, I'm not that little boy you left behind anymore. I am a grown man who has been blessed enough to know the love of family, friends and a good woman. The past can't be rewritten. It is what it is. Now it's time for me to plan my future."

Clive stopped trying to hide his tears and scrubbed his face with a handkerchief. "I know it is too soon for this but I hope that one day that future might include me."

Lawson stared at the broken man before him. For the first time, he looked deep enough to see the regret, vulnerability and pain staring back. Gathering his courage, he held out his hand. "It isn't too soon, Clive."

Clive froze in stunned disbelief. Finally, he reached out and grasped Lawson's hand in a hearty shake. His voice was solemn. "Thank you."

Kate stepped out of the bride room and quietly interrupted the scene. "Ellie is almost ready, Lawson. I think you can go to the altar now."

With his past behind him and the future promising nothing but happiness, Lawson smiled. "I'm ready, too. Will you tell her I'm waiting for her?"

"I will." Kate smiled, then slipped her arms around him in a quick hug. "You've always been a part of our family but I'm so glad it's going to be official."

"So am I." He turned to Clive and grinned. "It's time to watch your son get married."

The ceremony was short and sweet. As the rest of the town migrated toward the hotel where the reception would take place, Ellie and Lawson slipped out the back of the church. Ellie wrapped her arms around Lawson's waist and kissed his cheek. "I am so proud of you."

He chuckled. "Why?"

"Kate told me that you and your father seem to be on better terms. That must have taken a lot of courage."

He shrugged, then nodded toward the graveyard before them. "So does this."

She followed his gaze to her parents' tombstones. She sank to her knees in front of them, heedless of the stains the grass might cause on her ivory dress, but aware of Lawson's supportive presence behind her. Pulling two roses free from her bouquet, she laid one on her mother's grave, then one on her father's. Her hand rubbed the names inscribed in cold stone. "I wish you could be here today. Sean walked me down the aisle and Kate helped me get ready. Y'all would have been so proud of them.

"Y'all would have been proud of me, too." She smiled and glanced back at Lawson when he stepped forward to place a comforting hand on her shoulder. "Y'all would have loved Lawson. Perhaps not as much as I do but that's how it should be, seeing as I'm his wife and all. I love you both. I'll see y'all one day and when I do I want the longest, fiercest hug any of us have ever experienced. Until then, I'll just appreciate everything God has given me."

She stood to meet Lawson's gaze and smiled. "He sure has given me a whole lot."

"And me."

She placed a stilling hand on his when he lowered his head toward hers. "Don't forget that the whole town is waiting for us at the hotel."

"Let them wait."

She allowed him one more kiss, then grabbed his hand and hurried him down the sidewalk into the hotel ballroom. The moment they stepped inside, the town burst into applause and the hotel band struck up a waltz. Lawson sent her a sideways glance. She shrugged. "I didn't do any of this. It was all the town's idea."

"Well, this explains why my mother insisted I brush up on my dancing." He held out his hand to her. She stepped into his arms and allowed him to lead her around the dance floor. Pretty soon Kate and Nathan joined in, then Sean and Lorelei. Finally, the dance floor crowded with people. As they whirled around the floor, Ellie pulled back slightly to look up at him. "About that Bachelor List..."

"What about it?"

She held up a folded piece of paper. "It's finished. Should we burn it?"

He chuckled. "I don't know but I think I'm entitled to look at the finished product first."

She tugged him away from the dance floor to a secluded spot near the door to the garden. "Can you believe I did this?"

"Yes," he said heartily. She sent him an unappreciative look, which only caused him to laugh. She handed him the list, then watched his eyebrows raise as his gaze darted back and forth from the list to the crowd. Finally, he let out a low whistle. "It would be an awful shame to destroy that valuable information."

She searched his face. "Do you really think that I was right—that this works?"

"Well, it worked for Jeff and Maddie." He slipped his arm around her waist. "It worked for us."

She wrinkled her nose. "I suppose it did in a way."

"Maybe you were right about all of them."

"That is highly improbable."

He smiled. "So what are you going to do?"

She eyed the list, then surveyed the room full of swirling dancers. Her gaze stopped on one slightly morose figure standing sentry behind the punch bowl. Ellie took the list from Lawson and squeezed his arm. "I think I know."

She wound her way to the punch bowl and stopped in front of Amy. The girl rushed around the table to give her a hug and exclaim about Ellie's wedding dress. Ellie thanked her then stepped slightly closer to lower her voice. "I want to give you something. What you do with it is up to you but do try to keep it safe and private."

Amy's brow furrowed. "What is it?"

"The Bachelor List." Ellie slipped the folded paper into Amy's hand.

Amy froze. She stared down at the paper, then immediately slipped it into her pocket as though sensing its secrecy. "Why did you choose me?"

"I can't say, exactly. It just seemed right."

Amy nodded gravely. "I'll keep it safe."

Ellie gave the girl a parting hug then returned to her groom, who waited for her away from the hustle of the reception, on a secluded nook of the hotel's garden porch. "Did she take the list?"

"She did." She pretended to dust off her hands. "I believe my work here is done."

"Either that, or you started something else entirely."

"That's what I meant." She gave him a saucy wink.

He grinned. "What am I going to do with you?"

"You'll figure something out." She stood on her tiptoes to place a quick kiss on his lips.

His arms caught her around the waist before she could step away. "I think I just did."

"Hmm." She lifted an eyebrow and glanced down at her left hand then back at Lawson. "I bet this means you're going to kiss me all the time now."

He caught her hand and kissed it. "What do you think?"

Her lips curved into a smile, issuing a standing invitation. "I think you'd better."

And so he did.

* * * * *

Dear Reader,

It is always hard to say goodbye to dear friends so please bear with my sentimentality as we say farewell to the O'Brien family. I hope you have enjoyed their journeys through the pages of *Unlawfully Wedded Bride*, *The Runaway Bride*, and *A Texas-Made Match* to this moment where they are all hopeful, healed and loved. When these characters first formed in my imagination I never dreamed that one of their stories would end up as a published book—let alone that all three would. I am so grateful to God for this moment and all the ones that brought me here.

Now, it's time for me to somewhat reluctantly move on to new characters and new stories. I won't have to go far for the little town of Peppin, Texas is ripe with romance. So while this may be an ending it is also, as Ellie said, "a mighty fine beginning."

Thank you for reading my books! I'd love to hear from you. Connect with me through my website at www.NoelleMarchand.com. You can also find me on Goodreads, Facebook and Twitter.

Blessings!

Noelle Marchand

Questions for Discussion

1. What do you think about the town's matchmaking efforts? How did Ellie feel about having the tables turned? Do you think Ellie and Lawson handled the matchmaking in the right way?

2. Why was Ellie in such a hurry to get married? Have you ever gotten tired of waiting for God to move in an area of your life? How did that impatience affect you, the situation, or others?

3. What was Lawson's past like? How did it shape his identity? How did his perception of himself change throughout the book?

4. What were Ellie's expectations about a romantic relationship? How did they change by the end of the book?

5. Compare and contrast Ellie's family and Lawson's birth family. How did those similarities or difference impact their relationship?

6. What were Mrs. Greene's reasons for disliking Ellie? Were they legitimate? In what ways could Mrs. Greene have handled the situation better?

7. What was Lawson's relationship like with his birth family versus his adoptive parents and the O'Briens? What do you think his relationship with Clive will be like in the future?

8. Ellie and Lawson both struggle with forgiving themselves or others. Have you ever struggled with that? How did you overcome it?

9. What do you think the future will hold for Ellie and Lawson?

10. It's your turn to be the matchmaker. Think about your favorite supporting characters in the book. Who would you match up with whom?

REQUEST YOUR FREE BOOKS!

2 FREE INSPIRATIONAL NOVELS
PLUS 2
FREE
MYSTERY GIFTS

Love Inspired
HISTORICAL
INSPIRATIONAL HISTORICAL ROMANCE

YES! Please send me 2 FREE Love Inspired® Historical novels and my 2 FREE mystery gifts (gifts are worth about $10). After receiving them, if I don't wish to receive any more books, I can return the shipping statement marked "cancel." If I don't cancel, I will receive 4 brand-new novels every month and be billed just $4.49 per book in the U.S. or $4.99 per book in Canada. That's a saving of at least 22% off the cover price. It's quite a bargain! Shipping and handling is just 50¢ per book in the U.S. and 75¢ per book in Canada.* I understand that accepting the 2 free books and gifts places me under no obligation to buy anything. I can always return a shipment and cancel at any time. Even if I never buy another book, the two free books and gifts are mine to keep forever.

102/302 IDN FVXK

Name	(PLEASE PRINT)	
Address		Apt. #
City	State/Prov.	Zip/Postal Code

Signature (if under 18, a parent or guardian must sign)

Mail to the Harlequin® Reader Service:
IN U.S.A.: P.O. Box 1867, Buffalo, NY 14240-1867
IN CANADA: P.O. Box 609, Fort Erie, Ontario L2A 5X3

**Want to try two free books from another series?
Call 1-800-873-8635 or visit www.ReaderService.com.**

* Terms and prices subject to change without notice. Prices do not include applicable taxes. Sales tax applicable in N.Y. Canadian residents will be charged applicable taxes. Offer not valid in Quebec. This offer is limited to one order per household. Not valid for current subscribers to Love Inspired Historical books. All orders subject to credit approval. Credit or debit balances in a customer's account(s) may be offset by any other outstanding balance owed by or to the customer. Please allow 4 to 6 weeks for delivery. Offer available while quantities last.

Your Privacy—The Harlequin® Reader Service is committed to protecting your privacy. Our Privacy Policy is available online at www.ReaderService.com or upon request from the Harlequin Reader Service.

We make a portion of our mailing list available to reputable third parties that offer products we believe may interest you. If you prefer that we not exchange your name with third parties, or if you wish to clarify or modify your communication preferences, please visit us at www.ReaderService.com/consumerschoice or write to us at Harlequin Reader Service Preference Service, P.O. Box 9062, Buffalo, NY 14269. Include your complete name and address.

LIH13

SPECIAL EXCERPT FROM

Love Inspired **HISTORICAL**

When a tragedy brings a group of orphans to a small Nebraska town, shy schoolteacher Holly Sanders is determined to find the children homes...and soften dour sheriff Mason Wright's heart, along the way! Read on for a sneak preview of

FAMILY LESSONS by Allie Pleiter, *the first in the ORPHAN TRAIN series.*

"You saved us," Holly said, as she moved toward Sheriff Wright.

He looked at her, his blue eyes brittle and hollow. She so rarely viewed those eyes—downcast as they often were or hidden in the shadow of his hat brim. "No."

"But it is true." Mason Wright was the kind of man who would take Arlington's loss as a personal failure, ignoring all the lives—including hers—he had just saved, and she hated that. Hated that she'd fail in this attempt just as she failed in *every* attempt to make him see his worth.

He held her gaze just then. "No," he repeated, but only a little softer. Then his attention spread out beyond her to take in the larger crisis at hand.

"Is she the other agent?" He nodded toward Rebecca Sterling and the upset children, now surrounded by the few other railcar passengers. "Liam mentioned a Miss…"

"Sterling, yes, that's her. Liam!" Holly suddenly remembered the brave orphan boy who'd run off to get help. "Is Liam all right?"

"Shaken, but fine. Clever boy."

"I was so worried, sending him off."

He looked at her again, this time with something she could almost fool herself into thinking was admiration. "It was quick and clever. If anyone saved the day here, it was you."

Holly blinked. From Mason Wright, that was akin to a complimentary gush. "It was the only thing I could think of to do."

A child's cry turned them both toward the bedlam surrounding Miss Sterling. The children were understandably out of control with fear and shock, and Miss Sterling didn't seem to be in any shape to take things in hand. Who would be in such a situation?

She would, that's who. Holly was an excellent teacher with a full bag of tricks at her disposal to wrangle unruly children. With one more deep breath, she strode off to save the day a second time.

Don't miss FAMILY LESSONS
by Allie Pleiter, available April 2013
from Love Inspired Historical.

Love Inspired HISTORICAL

In the fan-favorite miniseries
Amish Brides of Celery Fields

ANNA SCHMIDT

presents

Second Chance Proposal

*The sweetest homecoming.
He came home…for her.
A love rekindled.*

Lydia Goodloe hasn't forgotten a single thing about John Amman—including the way he broke her heart eight years ago. Since John left Celery Fields to make his fortune, Lydia has devoted herself to teaching. John risked becoming an outcast to give Lydia everything she deserved. He couldn't see that what she really wanted was a simple life—with him. Lydia is no longer the girl he knew. Now she's the woman who can help him reclaim their long-ago dream of home and family…if he can only win her trust once more.

Amish Brides
of
CELERY FIELDS

Love awaits these Amish women.

LIH82959

Love the Harlequin book
you just read?

Your opinion matters.

**Review this book on your favorite
book site, review site, blog or your own
social media properties and share
your opinion with other readers!**

Be sure to connect with us at:
Harlequin.com/Newsletters
Facebook.com/LoveInspiredBooks
Twitter.com/LoveInspiredBks